DOWN TOWN

DownTown

A FANTASY

VIIDO POLIKARPUS AND TAPPAN KING

by **VIIDO POLIKARPUS**
and **TAPPAN KING**

ARBOR
HOUSE
NEW YORK

Manufactured in the United States of America

10 9 8 7 6 5 4 3 2 1

This book is printed on acid free paper. The paper in this book meets the guidelines for permanence and durability of the Committee on Production Guidelines for Book Longevity of the Council on Library Resources.

Library of Congress Cataloging in Publication Data

Polikarpus, Viido.
  Down Town.

  I. King, Tappan. II. Title.
PS3566.046D6 1985   813'.54   85–1209
ISBN 0-87795-673-1 (alk. paper)

To Carolyn and Maarika, and
to Baby Vicky.

—*Viido Polikarpus*

To Beth.

—*Tappan King*

ONE

CARY NEWMAN WAS feeling down.

Chin sunk in palm, cheek pressed against the rain-spattered windowpane, Cary gazed through the grimy glass at the wet city street below.

It was the worst day of the worst summer in all of Cary's twelve years.

Everything about it was dismal and ugly and gray. Yellow taxis hissed past, and people with black umbrellas barged by, clutching their coats about them. The only hint of green was the lone, bedraggled tree across the street, whipped by the wind and rain.

Cary's eyes burned, and his vision blurred. There was a rush of wind in his ears, and for a moment the world disappeared in a haze of golden green. . . .

If Mom and Dad hadn't had that fight, he'd be in his own house near the woods or hanging out with his friends, instead of being trapped here in this depressing old city for the rest of his life. And this fall he'd be going back to school with the kids he'd known all his life, instead of being the new kid in some ratty old city school that was probably filled with killers and drug addicts.

Mom and Dad had had fights before. But they'd always end with Mom crying and Dad apologizing, and then they'd kiss and make up. But the fights got really bad after Grandmama got sick, and after she died, and all those extra bills started coming in, they got worse.

The last one was the worst of all. Dad had started it, as usual, by coming home late from the city for the umpteenth time, with another story about how "unexpected problems" had come up at the office. Big surprise. Mom blew her stack and started yelling about how he was "shirking his responsibilities to his family." That was old news, too. Cary figured that sooner or later they'd patch this one up, too, just like always.

But not this time. This time Mom kept on screaming, saying that he was wasting his time on one of his "famous lost causes," that other men could provide a decent living and still find time to see their wife and child occasionally. Dad told her not to start, that he wasn't in the mood. But then she said that Gram and Gramp were right: he was a failure as a husband and father and she never should have married him in the first place.

Dad didn't fight back. He just stood there getting madder and not saying anything. And of course that only made *Mom* madder. She told him she couldn't take it anymore, that this was the last straw, and if he wasn't going to shape up, he might just as well get out.

Smart move. Because this time Dad just stared at her for a long while with a cold, hard look on his face, picked up his briefcase, and turned and walked out the door.

The next thing Cary knew, the house was up for sale, his

great-grandmother's big, beautiful old house by the woods, where he'd lived all his life. And he and Mom were packing all their clothes and half the furniture, and moving into this run-down brownstone in the city, while Dad found himself some hole-in-the-wall hotel room somewhere downtown near his law office.

Mom tried to smooth things over, like parents always do, telling him that she and Dad were "just having problems," that they needed some time apart to "think things over." Fat chance. His friends told him parents always say that just before they call in the lawyers.

She'd said that it was probably all for the best, that living in the city would be a good experience for him, like it had been for her. Right. Go off to work and leave your kid all alone in a rat-infested old apartment with no place to go and nobody to talk to, just when he needed somebody to talk to most, and tell him it was a "good experience." Screw up your only kid's life and tell him it was "all for the best."

Cary would never admit it, but the city frightened him. He'd heard a lot of stories about how terrific the city was, not just from Mom but from Grandmama, too, who'd lived here with Grandpapa way back in the twenties. She had told him it was the most exciting place in the world, with something new happening every minute.

But it didn't seem that way to Cary. From the first moment he'd seen those endless rows of dreary apartment towers rearing up out of the smog, Cary could feel the weight of the city pressing down on him. It was so big, so loud and ugly. There were so many people with scowls on their faces all in a hurry with no place to go.

The street they were living on gave Cary the creeps. While a couple of the brownstones had been fixed up, half the buildings still had wood or tin over their windows, and there were always people sitting out on their stoops in their underwear, yelling to one another and playing loud music. Worst of all, there was no nature to speak of, except for a few scraggly trees and dinky little parks where you could probably get mugged or killed or worse —nothing like the woods and fields back home, at any rate. It had taken him weeks just to get up his nerve to go down to the corner delicatessen for milk.

Mostly he just stayed inside the brownstone, watching TV or reading. When he'd first seen the place, he'd hated it. The front steps were a mess, chipped and spray-painted. Pieces of the iron fencing were missing, and chunks of the brick courtyard were torn up. The bottom two floors were still a mess, with falling tinned ceilings and cracked plaster. What they were going to do with them, Cary didn't know. There was plenty of room for him and Mom on the top floor. Now, if Dad came back . . . but it was no use thinking like that.

The upstairs was a little better. His bedroom had a skylight, his own brass bed from home, and even a couple of Gramp's old model sailing ships that he'd got on the condition he'd never take them out from under the glass. There was lots of familiar old furniture from the house, and a good-sized study with all of their books (except Dad's law books, of course).

He spent a lot of time in that study, rereading some of his old books: schoolbooks and science fiction, even some of the beautiful old fairy-tale books with the colored pictures, the ones Grandmama used to read to him when he was very small. Then he'd turned to his Mom's collection of books on history and geography, trying to lose himself in other times and places for a while. But now he was beginning to feel trapped, filled with a sort of restless impatience.

The little tree outside the window shuddered under the pelting raindrops. Cary bit his lip hard to stop the tears that threatened to fall, pawing at his eyes with his knuckles. He was damned if he was going to start crying for no reason.

Mom had been real weird and touchy lately. She'd been on his case constantly about all kinds of things—a couple of phone calls he'd made to his friends upstate, helping out with the dishes and the housework. She kept asking him when he was going to grow up and start pulling his own weight. And she was getting just like Dad: more interested in her work than in her own family.

She'd promised him they'd go to Central Park today—the first free Saturday she'd had in weeks—and maybe visit the Museum of Natural History. But the rain had pretty much washed that out. Then her boss had called while they were having breakfast, asking her if she could have the big report she'd been working on finished and in his office by the end of the day. He wanted it ready for some dumb ceremony tomorrow evening. The Mayor and the Governor were going to be there, and Mom had already agreed to be the hostess for it while Cary was visiting his dad on Sunday.

Mom said as long as it was raining and they weren't going anywhere anyway, she ought to get to work on it. If it cleared up later, she said, they could still go out. Sure. The next thing Cary knew she was heading into the study to work on her damn computer.

Damn and triple goddamn damn! Why did it all have to turn out this way? Why did Grandmama have to die? Why did Mom and Dad have to break up and sell their beautiful old house? Why did good things *ever* have to end?

Cary wished he could somehow wish everything back the way it used to be, but that only happened in fairy tales. Before he could stop them, tears were coursing down Cary's cheeks like the raindrops on the sooty windowpane.

The world swirled away in a rushing roar and his eyes were filled with an eerie greengold glow. The leaves of the little tree seemed to beckon to him and a voice seemed to be calling his name, over and over, a high and wavery voice, sweet but filled with urgency. . . .

"*Cary?*"

Cary jumped, startled by his mother's voice. Pushing his hair from his eyes, he rubbed his wrist roughly across his eyes and nose, and turned to face her.

"Do you want to go shopping with me, Cary?" she asked. "I finished up my report sooner than I'd expected. It was strange —it all just sort of fell into place at once. I thought that as long as I have to go out in the rain anyway, I might as well pick up a few clothes at the same time."

She had her green canvas bag in one hand, and one of the microdisks from the computer in the other. The way the light gleamed off the disk dazzled Cary's eyes like a rainbow on the edge of a mirror, and he felt the dizziness beginning all over again.

Cary shook his head to clear it. What had happened to him? He'd been dreaming, drifting somewhere, and someone had been calling him, a voice that was at once strange and familiar.

"Listen, if you don't want to go with me, just say so," said his mother. "I can come back in time to take you down to meet your father. You're spending this weekend with him, in case you'd forgotten."

In case *he'd* forgotten! It was *Dad* who'd gotten so tied up with his job two weeks running that they hadn't gotten together. Not that Cary was looking forward to the weekend. Dinner at some dumb restaurant at the top of some skyscraper, and a dumb ball game. Dad hated ball games. And he'd only be thinking about his work all the time anyway.

"What do you say, Skipper? I know it's not the Park, but it's better than being cooped up here all day." She stopped when she saw his strange, faraway expression. "Are you okay, Cary?"

"I'm okay, Mom," said Cary. "I—I really do want to get out of the—this place for a while. It's kind of depressing, and it's getting on my nerves, you know?"

His mother nodded and touched his hair for a moment. "I know," she said softly. "It's not your fault you inherited my Irish temper. Tell you what. You put up with my shopping, and I'll buy you that jacket you've been asking for. How's that?"

"That would be great," said Cary. It wasn't really all that great. He didn't feel much like shopping. But something was building up inside of him that he didn't understand. All he knew was that suddenly he wanted more than anything to get out of the brownstone, into the open air.

"Let me get my keys and change my shirt," said Cary, "and let's get going."

"You're on, Skipper."

THE RAIN HAD let up, but it was still muggy and overcast, and Cary figured he'd better take an umbrella. He went ahead of his mother down the stairs and waited while she did all the locks. Although the air was still heavy, and a few fat drops of rain kept splashing down, the kids on the street had started a basketball game.

As Cary reached the street, a ball came bouncing over and bumped against his foot. One of the kids, a young girl about his age, shouted for him to throw it back. But as he was bending down to reach it, his mom gave him a sharp look, so he just nudged it back with his foot and followed her to the subway.

Cary braced himself for the descent down the stairs. He hated subways. They were darker and dirtier and smellier than the rest of the city, with people pushing and shoving and trains making so much noise you couldn't hear yourself think. When they came, that is. This time they had to wait nearly a half hour on the narrow, crowded platform before they could cram onto a train that was broiling hot and covered with graffiti.

When they finally reached Herald Square and escaped from the packed subway car, they still had to climb up two steep flights of steps in sweltering heat. The store was freezing, because the air conditioning was turned up way too high. By the time they reached the main floor, Cary was feeling kind of sick and feverish.

AFTER A COUPLE of hours of shopping, Cary was really feeling terrible.

First they'd gone to get the jacket that Cary had seen on sale in the newspaper. There was only one left in his size, and that one was full price. Mom had made a big scene about it, insisting on the sale price. Cary wanted to forget the whole thing, but she wouldn't hear of it. Then, when he put the jacket on because the store was so cold, she gave him a hard time, saying it "made him look like a hoodlum."

Then they'd gone up to Women's Clothing. Cary thought they'd set up the place just to give him a headache. Some of the sections were loud and jangly, with neon flashing and music booming from dozens of speakers. Then there were fancy rooms with dark-brown carpets where men in pink shirts and women wearing scarves looked at him like he was a dead fish.

Cary waited for what seemed like hours, sitting on dinky little chairs, while his mother tried on outfit after outfit. Nothing seemed to suit her. Everything cheap was badly made and anything that was any good cost twice as much as she felt like paying. And when she *did* find something she liked, nine times out of ten it was the wrong size—usually too small.

They ended up in a flashy little boutique filled with girls half Mom's age. She dumped her bag on the counter next to Cary's umbrella, and told him to keep an eye on it while she tried on a few things. Cary's headache was getting worse by the minute, but he amused himself by trying on some weird sunglasses he found on a counter rack. Then his mom turned up right behind him, startling him.

"Well, what do you think, Cary? Pretty spiffy, huh?" She was wearing a bright knit top and fancy jeans with a matching jacket. She looked like she was trying out for a TV commercial. She'd never dressed that way with Dad. What was she trying to prove? Well, he wasn't going to let her see it bothered him. If she wanted to dress like that, it was her business.

"Great, Mom. It looks great."

"There's no need to be sarcastic, Cary. If you don't like it, just say so."

"It's *fine,* Mom. I'm glad you finally found something you liked."

"What's that supposed to mean? And take off those *ridiculous* sunglasses."

"*Nothing,* Mom. It's just that waiting for three hours while you pick out clothes isn't my idea of a terrific time."

"It hasn't been three hours. But I'm sorry it's been such a trial for you. Next time I won't bother—" There was a huge crash. Somehow, in trying to put the sunglasses back, Cary had knocked over the whole display, taking his mother's bag with it.

"*Now* look what you've done," she said, loud enough for everyone to hear. "You really are a chip off the old block, aren't you? Oh, damn!" She stopped suddenly, looking at her watch. "Look at the time! We'd better get moving if we're going to meet your father on time. Well, don't just stand there gawking —straighten this up while I go pay for these clothes!" A sales-clerk came over to try to help, but Cary's mother waved her away. "My son made this mess; he can clean it up."

Cary bent down to pick up the plastic rack, his face hot with humiliation and anger. When he'd finally gotten the stand back on the counter and the glasses back on their racks, he began to pile the contents of his mother's purse back in her bag.

"Here, let me have that," said his mother, bending down to take the bag out of his hand. A short distance away lay the microdisk, gleaming on the dark carpet. As he grabbed it and straightened up again, the whole store went out of focus, and he reeled against the counter, knocking over a cosmetics display.

"That does it," she snapped. "If you're going to insist on

making a scene, this is the last time I'm taking you anywhere with
me. You're on your own."

"That's fine with me," said Cary.

"Don't take that tone with me, young man. I'm still your
mother, you know."

"Well, you're not doing a very good job of it!" said Cary.

He was standing only a couple of inches from her, and he
suddenly realized they were eye to eye, that Mom was hardly any
taller than he was. She looked strange, almost like she was afraid
of him or something. Then she flushed and turned away, saying,
"Well, if that's the way you feel about it, mister, maybe you'd be
happier with your father—"

"Maybe I would," Cary snapped back, heading toward the
escalator to the basement.

"Now wait just one minute, young man," his mother called
after him. "You and I aren't finished yet . . ."

But Cary wasn't listening. Angry and confused, he just wanted
to get out of this loud, confining place to somewhere quiet,
someplace he could just stop and think things over for a while.
He could see his mother trying to catch up with him, but he
didn't feel like slowing down for her. Shaken with chills, he
walked quickly down the escalator and pushed through the
swinging doors that exited from the store basement into the
subway.

The heat hit him like a linebacker, and he reeled, not sure of
where to go next. He couldn't make sense of the signs. He stood
still for a moment, then headed down a set of stairs with a sign
over it that read DOWN TOWN.

Before him was a metal fence separating him from a crowded
subway platform. The only entrance seemed to be a tall revolv-
ing turnstile and a closed exit door. Pulling the door open and
stepping through, he found himself on a subway platform just
as a train was pulling in.

He could hear the attendant calling after him and saw his
mother waving frantically at him as she stopped to pay his fare.

Then the doors of the train were opening, and hundreds of people were streaming past him.

Someone hit his shoulder, spinning him around. Before he could regain his balance, he was hit again from behind. The stream of people became a flood, whirling him around as they washed past. Cary's head began to spin along with his body, and there was a roaring sound in his ears as the train pulled out. Then everything became a blur, and Cary felt himself falling through darkness toward a faraway voice that called his name.

TWO

At last, Cary's head stopped spinning.

He'd closed his eyes and pulled his arms tight to his body, like a skater, when the crowd started to crush him. Now he opened them again.

He was all alone.

The subway platform was deserted. The lights had dimmed and the air had gone cold, and there was no sign of anyone else, even his mother. Cary fought down a wave of nausea and panic, steadying himself against the grimy tiled wall. Where *was* everybody?

He'd only closed his eyes for a couple of seconds, hadn't he? Maybe he'd gotten knocked out without knowing it and had just now come to, hours later. He felt his head for bumps. His head still throbbed, but there was no sign of a sore spot. Well, no sense staying here. He'd better try to find some way out.

He was way down at the end of the platform, where a little walkway led down a short flight of steps to the subway tracks and off into the darkness. There was an eerie, echoing silence about the place and a musty stillness in the air, as if it had been deserted for years, not hours. The only light was a wan square of gray that came from a grating high overhead. His umbrella lay a few feet away, looking slightly bent. Picking it up, he made his way up the platform toward the exit.

The huge old wooden turnstiles wouldn't turn. Ducking under one, Cary headed for the stairway beyond. A massive iron door barred his way, chained with a huge padlock that was covered with years of soot and dust—the same door he had just opened. On the wall beside it was a grimy mosaic made out of thousands of multicolored tiles. It read

DOWN TOWN
NO EXIT
MONDAY THRU SUNDAY
BETWEEN
6:00 A.M. AND 5:45 A.M.

Cary stared at the sign, shook his head, stared at it again. He read the sign twice more, but it still didn't make any sense. Placing his palms on the turnstiles, he vaulted back over them and looked up and down the platform. There didn't seem to be any other way out. He was trapped. Lost. Stuck down here for hours, maybe even days. *Maybe even forever.*

He slumped down against the wall, trying to think of a way out, trying not to give in to the hopelessness that was welling up inside of him. Mom was probably looking for him right now. *If she even cared.* Maybe they'd find him here when they came to open up in the morning. *If they ever did.* Maybe he should yell as loud as he could, so someone could hear him. *Maybe they'll find my rat-eaten old bones down here a hundred years from now.*

There was a scuffling noise. Something was moving at the far end of the platform. Something was coming toward him out of the shadows. Cary ducked into an alcove by a locked rest room, his heart pounding.

The platform seemed to grow even darker, and the walls seemed to close in. A huge, ragtag shape was lumbering toward him, muttering to itself as it came.

It was draped in baggy, shapeless skirts that dragged along the pavement. A scarf obscured its head. Each of its clawlike hands clutched an old, tattered paper shopping bag, stuffed with odds and ends, and it gave off a pungent smell as it passed. Cary pressed close to the wall, trying to make himself invisible.

The Bag Lady shuffled by without noticing him, and Cary started breathing again. She was probably trapped down here just like he was. Or maybe she knew the way out. She must; otherwise how had she gotten here? And where was she going?

The Bag Lady had stopped at the end of the platform and was running one withered hand up and down the tiles, dulled with decades of soot and smoke. Chattering to herself, she pushed first one and then another tile in a pattern that seemed to have some crazy meaning for her.

She gave what sounded like a chortle of triumph, and the wall gave way with a scraping noise, revealing a long tunnel stretching downward. Before Cary realized what was happening, the Bag Lady had waddled through the opening and the door was closing behind her.

Cary sprinted to the wall just as it closed behind the Bag Lady with a resounding thunk, leaving no trace of where the door had been.

Desperately, he slid his hands over the wall, touching each tile in turn, feeling for crevices. It was no use. At last he gave up, slumping against the wall in defeat, hands pushed into pockets.

One hand closed over something—the microdisk he'd picked

up in the store. He lifted it out, peering at it in the faint half-light.

It was a flat circle of metal not unlike stainless steel, a little larger than a silver dollar in size, sealed in hard, transparent plastic. As he held it up and tilted it to catch the light, he saw that it had hundreds of tiny circles etched on each side, like the rings of a tree, that gave off a rainbow shimmer as it moved.

At that moment, the hidden door swung inward, and Cary lost his balance, tumbling through. By the time he got to his feet, the door was already closing. He tried for a moment to stop it, then let it shut. Where else was there for him to go?

As soon as his eyes became accustomed to the light, Cary began to look around him. Behind him was the wall he'd just come through, smooth and solid to the touch. A tunnel, barely higher than his head, stretched downhill before him at a steep angle. The stone walls were set in a complicated pattern of long and short blocks that met in a curving arch above him. Here and there roots or branches pushed through the stone, with tiny leaves that seemed to give off a pale greenish glow at their tips.

That couldn't be right. Leaves didn't glow, did they? And as far as he knew, there weren't supposed to be secret passageways in the subways either, especially for Bag Ladies. Cary began to wonder if he hadn't gotten a knock on the head after all.

Cary could hear the scuffling and muttering of the Bag Lady echoing up the tunnel ahead of him, but she was out of sight. With a shrug, he started after her. After all, she was the only one around here who knew where she was going. He had to catch up with her. Cary ran for a while, then slowed to a walk, then ran again, but he was never able to reach her, although the echoing walls made it sound like she was right next to him.

The air grew cooler as he descended, and he could hear the sound of rushing water somewhere behind the walls. Occasionally, a corridor branched off to the side, but it was always clotted with cobwebs and reeking of old mold. Cary poked the tip of his umbrella into one, then withdrew it quickly when he heard a

scrabbling sound and saw gleaming points of light that might have been eyes looking back.

At last the tunnel began to level off. Cary saw a bright flash of light ahead. Then it was gone. As he drew closer, he could hear a humming sound, reedy and far away. There was another flash, and a third, which seemed to waver and flicker like the fireflies that glimmered on summer evenings back home. The thought made Cary homesick, and he blinked hard to stop his eyes from burning.

He began to make out a huge, dimly lit space at the end of the tunnel. A blue-white beam flashed across several times, piercing the dark like a lighthouse sweeping desolate waters. There were whispery echoes and a buzzing sound that grew louder as he came near.

He was standing at the entrance of an immense chamber. The walls of yellowed limestone rose in a soaring curve and met in a crisscross vault overhead, the ceiling dotted with tiny blue halos of light. Cary could barely make out gargoyle figures in the stone, leering down at him out of the shadows.

Pretty spooky down here. As a very little kid, Cary had been afraid of the dark. He'd even had a night-light in his room until his friends kidded him about it and he finally threw it out. This huge, dark room brought back all of those little-kid fears again. He felt as if something was waiting for him out in the middle of that room. He didn't know what it was, and he wasn't really eager to find out. But he had no choice but to keep moving.

Putting one hand against a damp wall, Cary made his way carefully about the edge of the chamber. He found himself brandishing his umbrella like a sword ahead of him, feeling a little foolish as he did so. That tuneless humming he'd heard before seemed to swell, and there were more of those on-again, off-again flashes of light. Then there was a rattling clank that Cary was sure he hadn't made, and a few of the blue lights on the ceiling detached themselves and began to move. Cary froze, squinting to see what was happening.

Something was scuttling across the stone.

Cary pulled his foot back as something brushed past. From all over the room—overhead, underfoot, across the walls—small shapes were converging on the distant wall. Rats? Bugs? It was hard to tell in the dark, but they were *something* creepy, that was certain.

Suddenly one was near his face. Fighting his squeamishness, Cary peered closer. It seemed to be about a foot long, with long, spidery legs and a shiny cylindrical body. Its front end had a little blue light on it that flashed white at erratic intervals.

This was crazy. He was alone in a room with a million walking flashlights! Now they were clustering on the far wall, and the humming grew louder. Then, one by one, the lights brightened. Cary could see that the wall was covered with dozens of the creatures, clambering over one another with the agility of insects. He could see that he'd made a mistake. *Well, that's a relief. They're not walking flashlights after all.*

They were walking paint cans.

Not the buckets with the wire handles, but big, oversized aerosol spray cans, complete with caps and labels, *and arms and legs* that looked like human limbs, only smaller. The caps were of every shade and hue, and each had a little light like a miner's lamp on it.

With little popping noises, a dozen of the caps lifted off to reveal little heads underneath. *Oh, terrific,* thought Cary. *Now I'm really going bonkers.*

There was no other explanation for it. He *had* gotten conked on the head in the subway, and all of this was some kind of dazed hallucination. He was probably lying on the ground somewhere delirious, or worse, roaming around who-knows-where in a fog, thinking people were little walking paint cans.

But if he *was* dreaming, then why did everything seem so vivid and real and *un*dreamlike? Cary had always thought of himself as a sensible person, who could tell real things from imaginary ones. But what did you do when things that couldn't be suddenly *were?* There didn't seem to be any rules to cover a situation like this.

I give up. If this was a dream, none of this was going to hurt him anyway. And if it *wasn't* a dream, then he'd better have his wits about him if he was ever going to get back up where he belonged. As he stared at the little creatures lit by one another's lamps, they began to make a kind of crazy sense to him.

They're wearing the cans like shells, just like hermit crabs, he told himself. *They must have suction cups or something on their hands and feet so they can walk up the walls like flies. But what are they all doing here? And why?*

His question was answered moments later. When they'd spread out across the far wall, washing it with the harsh light of their lamps, the buzzing began to rise to a crescendo.

Then, one by one, they pursed their lips, and sprayed paint out through curled tongues in bright slashes and splashes of color. As more and more turned on their lights, Cary could see that the whole wall was filled with their scrawls. Sometimes Cary thought he saw words or letters, faces or shapes. But then one of the creatures would climb over another, blotting out a corner or adding in a spot that obscured what Cary thought he'd seen.

His head ached just from looking at it. He'd always wondered how graffiti got written up in all those out-of-the-way places no human being could possibly reach. Well, now he knew, for all the good it did him.

Addled by the total weirdness of it all, Cary began to edge away. His foot struck something that clattered and clanked, sending cascades of echoes rebounding from the surrounding walls. All at once, the lights swiveled toward him, and the creatures started swarming across the ceiling to the corner where he was crouched.

Blinding him with blazing lights and deafening him with humming, they began to sputter and spatter him with droplets of paint as they drew near. As the drops turned into torrents, Cary popped open his umbrella in their faces, startling them and giving him room to run.

Sticking close to the wall, sliding on the wet paint, he sped round the rim of the room, looking for a way out. The wildly swinging lights cast baffling shadows under his feet, and the sluice of paint made the floor slick.

An archway opened to his right and he ducked inside. His feet faltered on a short flight of steps, then slipped out from under him altogether. His umbrella flew from his paint-spattered fingers, and he fell down into the darkness.

THREE

HE WAS SLIDING down an endless chute to nowhere at breakneck speed. Just when he thought he'd reached bottom, the slide took a turn, slamming him hard first against one wall, then the other, then dumping him face down in a heap of black dust.

Cary gasped and choked at the dry powder caught in his throat. He coughed and spat and shook himself free of the fine powder that filled his lungs and coated his body. In the dim light he saw that he was in the bottom of a great cast-iron bin, half filled with coal dust. Cary just sat where he was for a moment, afraid to move, feeling like he was still moving, knowing he had stopped. He was bruised and sore and more than a little shaken.

Finally, he pulled himself to his feet. Wedging his sneakers into the rough corners of the bin, he hauled himself up and out, dropping to the ground with a thud that jarred his ankles and sent a small cloud of coal dust flying.

He tried to brush himself off, but it wasn't much use. Both he and his new jacket were smeared with soot and peppered with paint. His umbrella was gone for good. If Mom could see him now, she'd probably throw a fit. At least he was still in one piece; that counted for something.

It was brighter here. Light was streaming in through high windows, making dust motes dance in the beams. Above the coal bin, which was pushed up against one wall, the chute he'd dropped from stuck out of the ceiling like a black bird's beak. At his feet was a floor of marble inlaid with patterns he could see when he scraped the dust away with his foot. Down the center of the room ran a shallow trench with two dull iron rails that disappeared into a dark archway. A pile of buckets and shovels and rags lay covered with cobwebs in one corner, and at the far end of the room was a pair of high bronze doors.

With a backward glance at the dark tunnel, Cary walked over to one of the doors and grasped one of the big bronze handles, pulling with all his might, hoping this might be the way out. To his surprise, it glided open easily. A long wood-paneled hallway stretched beyond it, lined with doors. Warm golden light was coming from an opening at the end, and he could faintly hear a murmur that sounded like voices.

It looked like this nightmare was finally ending, like he'd finally found the way out. Ignoring his aching side, Cary ran down the hall toward the light as fast as he could go.

A door on his left flew open, smacking him in his other side and sending him sprawling on his hands and knees.

"Hey!" he yelled, his eyes filling with angry tears. "Why don't you look—"

But he never finished. It was the Bag Lady again, hobbling heedlessly down the hallway. As Cary pushed himself to his feet, he stopped, staring in disbelief. Something weird was happening to her.

First her arms began to shudder and shake. Then buttons began to pop off her long, shapeless dress. Then Cary noticed that there were not two big shoes under it, but *dozens of little ones.* And dozens of tiny hands poked out of her sleeves. Then a tiny head popped out of her scarf, and another out of her pocket, and a third out from under the edge of her skirt. The rags collapsed in a heap on the ground, and a host of tiny elflike Bag Ladies scurried toward the light, each dragging an overstuffed, oversized bag.

Oh, great! groaned Cary, realizing this bad dream was far from over. *First walking spray cans, and now pint-sized Bag Ladies!* He rubbed his eyes and pinched himself hard for good measure, hoping this would all go away. But he just succeeded in giving himself another bruise, and the little Bag Ladies were still there, just like before. Shaking his head, he started after them.

As he drew near the source of the light, he heard a roar like the sound of the sea laced through with the strains of music, the reedy thread of a high-pitched pipe, the deep oompah of a tuba, the crash of a cymbal, the jangling of a steel drum. A thick and heady scent wafted toward him. There were enticing smells of freshly cooked food: roasting meats and chickens, bacon and bratwurst, chitlins and challah, falafel and fried rice. And there were other exotic scents as well: a hint of incense and a trace of hot tar, the musty funk of cigar smoke and the sweetness of roses, the tang of old leather, the sharpness of sweat, the pungence of kerosene.

Following his nose, Cary stepped out onto a narrow balcony with a sturdy brass rail overlooking an immense space that extended up and down a dozen times his height. It looked like an old train station, with great windows and tiers of balconies, sweeping staircases and sloping ramps, thick pillars and faded murals, arches and turnstiles, gates and booths. But it was a little like a cave, too, for it seemed to be carved out of solid rock. And far across on the other side, Cary thought he could see a patchwork quilt of green and golden fields stretching off into the distance.

The amber glow that lit this place came not from the sun, as Cary had hoped, but from a great clock that hung overhead from a massive chain that disappeared into clouds of mist, smoke, and steam. The milky, glowing disk of the clock had a face on it like one of those sun faces in old books. It was surrounded by squiggly rays like the ones on compasses at the corners of maps, and the hands of the clock made a sort of off-kilter moustache. All the time that Cary watched them, the hands never moved.

Below the clock stretched a faded banner that read

LAZY FAIR

A great stone floor strewn with dirt and sawdust was covered with a profusion of merchants, mendicants, musicians, and mountebanks, that reminded Cary of a circus or carnival or flea market. It was as crowded and noisy as anything he had seen in the city, but there was an odd charm about the place that drew Cary in spite of himself. Lured by the sights and scents and sounds, Cary followed his feet down the great staircase into the hurly-burly below.

There were hundreds of carts and kiosks, stalls and tables, and handmade stands, no two alike, each proudly and loudly hawking its wares in a wild babble of accents, dialects, and languages. There were fruit vendors and sausage sellers, chestnut carts and pastry wagons. There were piles of old shoes, hats, and wigs. There were broken toys and shiny trinkets, old and shopworn souvenirs. There were mirrors, clocks, shrunken heads, plums, and plumbing, parts of boats and Pullman cars, glass and brass, books and broadsides, geese and garnets, pencils and pens, and pythons.

There were puppeteers and sleight-of-hand artists, soapbox

orators, and demonstrators with flags of red, white, and black. There were dancers and divers, fiddlers and jugglers, actors and acrobats. There was one of every kind of thing that ever was, and two of every other, and all that Cary could do to make sense of it all was to let it wash over him and pick out one thing at a time to focus on.

The first thing he noticed was that what looked at first like chaos had a kind of underlying order to it. The crowded, cluttered aisles all made their way by twitches and turns to the broad open space at the center under the sun-clock. And, except for the food stalls, which were scattered everywhere, each area seemed to be grouped more or less by what was sold.

Here Cary saw mostly glass—flaking mirrors and cracked, frosted panes, delicate little vases and crystal chandeliers overlaid with dust. Against that wall were bookstalls and newsstands, giving off the unmistakable scent of old paper. And over there were the fishmongers with their crates piled high with ice and wood shavings and scads of shad, perch, pike, and mackerel, staring up at him with baleful glazed eyes.

Cary also noticed that the accents changed as he moved. Some of them he recognized: French, Spanish, German, Italian, the musical lilt of the islands. Others were bewildering and totally unfamiliar. And the speakers were dressed in the quaintest of costumes, as if they'd never heard of the latest fashions. Then Cary spotted something that made his mouth gape open with astonishment.

There were tiny people on the tables.

Not small people or children, but real Little People, each less than a foot high.

He'd missed them at first in the confusion. On almost every cart and stall was at least one tiny person, and sometimes half a dozen, dressed in clothes even quainter than those of the vendors.

There were some of the miniature Bag Ladies he'd seen earlier, each unloading a treasure at a stall. But by the fishmongers was a small fellow who looked more than a little like a fish himself, dressed in a striped shirt and sailor's pants, heaving halibut up onto the ice from a nearby cart. At a shoe-seller's stall, a little man in a leather apron stood in a slipper, sewing it up from the inside. And beyond, at a stand filled with masks and carvings, was a pot-bellied imp the color of mahogany, stretching skin over the head of a drum.

Now that he noticed it, even the regular-sized people weren't regular-sized after all. *Everyone* was small, at least compared to him. Not as small as the Little People, perhaps, but smaller than most grown-ups. In fact, as far as Cary could see, nobody was as tall as he was, and most were about a foot shorter. Their eyes were lively, their voices were loud, and their movements were broad, but they were all sort of compact models, and their carts and stalls were scaled down to match.

Terrific, thought Cary. *Munchkins.*

Some grown-up part of him knew that a place like this had no business existing. And even if it did, *he* certainly had no business being here. Things like this only happened in fairy tales. And he was too old for fairy tales, wasn't he? But some other part of him, a part he'd forgotten, told him it didn't matter much whether he believed in it or not; here it was.

He decided then that as long as he was down here he'd have to do his best to accept whatever happened. If he was ever going to get back from here to his own world, the first step was to find out just where *here* was.

Getting up his nerve, he crossed over to the edge of the market to a cart where a stout woman in a calico apron sold penny candy.

"Excuse me," he said hesitantly, leaning on the side of the cart. "Could you tell me—"

But before he could finish, the woman started shaking her finger at him and scolding him in a language he couldn't quite understand. As he lifted a hand in protest, she gave it a stinging swat.

"What's the matter with you?" said Cary. "I was just asking—" But the woman had stepped from behind her stall and was shaking her fist at him, so Cary began edging away. He had no idea what he'd done to make her so mad.

A nearby fruit stand caught his eye, with the most luscious-looking peaches he'd ever seen. He paused, picking over the ripe fruit like Mom always did, then chose the biggest one he could find, digging into his pocket for some change.

A tiny being that was wrestling a cantaloupe into place started chittering at him like an angry monkey. The dark-haired man behind the stand started yelling at him. He thought Cary was trying to steal the peach! Baffled and confused, Cary dropped the peach and ducked around the corner out of sight.

It was the same everywhere. Every time he got too near a stall, the vendors would make a fuss and start chasing him away. Finally, feeling tired and hungry, he came to a kindly-looking old man who was selling pretzels. For a moment, he just gazed at them hungrily.

"Help ya, sonny?"

"Um, yes," said Cary. "I'd like a pretzel."

The pretzel man seemed to be sizing him up. "You got any money?"

"Of course I do," said Cary indignantly. "How much are they?"

"A penny each."

That sounded like a bargain. "One, please," said Cary, fishing a nickel out of his pocket. The man handed over a soft, hot pretzel, studded with chunks of salt and wrapped in a piece of newspaper, and took the coin. As Cary waited for his change, the old man held up the nickel, squinted at it, and bit it with one lone tooth.

"None of your tricks, you thieving scamp!" he shouted. "None of your tin slugs and wooden nickels this time! Now gimme back that pretzel. I've a mind to call the 'Mashers on you!" Cary was so confused and so hungry that he left his change and ran away as fast as he could, chewing on the pretzel as he ran. Behind him the cry of "Stop! Thief!" had begun. What was the matter with everybody? What was wrong with his money? Why was everyone giving him such a hard time?

The pretzel helped fill the empty space inside him a bit, but the salt made him very thirsty. He eyed some freshly squeezed lemonade, but one sharp look from the proprietor told him he'd have no luck there.

Then, from an alcove some distance ahead, he heard the tooting of a steam organ, saw the bright glow of colored lights, and caught a scent that smelled like grape soda and cotton candy. Off to one side, Cary saw a sort of arcade, lined with popcorn machines and doughnut dispensers and hot-dog roasters, with ringing bells and bright paintings on their sides.

Cary's eyes were caught by a tall, shiny machine all made of brass and glass, with jets of fizzy purple liquid shooting up into the air inside a big glass dome. On its top was a grinning bust with a long beard that bobbed like a jack-in-the-box. A sign on the front read DR. KOKAMOKA'S EFFERVESCENT TONIC, and from somewhere came the sound of hollow laughter. Cary was thirsty enough to try anything. There was a slot and a button on one side, and another sign next to it that read FIVE CENTS. Fishing a dime from his pocket, Cary dropped it into the machine and pressed the red button.

Lights flashed and bells rang, but nothing else happened. Cary slammed the machine with the heel of his hand, and then, when that didn't do any good, gave it a swift kick in the side. The flashing and clanging began again and a fat waxed-paper cup dropped down into the slot and filled with fizzing soda. A moment later an Indian-head nickel dropped from the change slot. Cary downed the soda in one gulp. It burned a bit going down, but it did quench his thirst.

He gazed at the plump hot dogs going round and round in their glass case, and pulled a handful of change out of his jacket.

"Psst! Buddy!" whispered a voice at his elbow. "Wanna make some quick change?"

It was a ratty little man in a sweat-stained boater and striped shirt with arm garters, standing behind a folding card table, whirling brightly colored cups back and forth over a shiny black ball.

"Care to try your luck?" he said in a confidential tone. "I'm just looking after the game until my boss comes back. If we work quick, you could win a bundle."

"Uh, no thanks," said Cary, staring at the moving ball. It was hard to keep track of it as it flashed in and out of sight. "I really should be trying to find my way back home."

"And where might that be?" asked the little man, with an air of genuine concern.

"West Eighty-seventh Street," said Cary. "Do you know how I get there from here?"

The little man pondered for a moment. "I might be able to help you at that," he said. "As soon as my boss gets back, that is," he added. "But as long as we're waiting, you might as well play a game. It's not that hard, once you figure it out. Who knows? You might win big."

"I don't know," said Cary. His gaze followed the cups, which had been moving all the while. "I don't think—"

"Don't. Listen. First game's on me—it's been a slow day. What do you say, sport?"

"Okay," said Cary. One game couldn't hurt. And if this fellow could help him get home . . . The man's nimble fingers swirled the cups around, and then he asked, "All right, which cup is it under?"

"That one," said Cary, who'd been watching carefully. The man's hands moved with blinding speed as he lifted up the cup to reveal the ball.

"Right you are!" said the man with a look of astonishment, placing a shiny Indian-head nickel on top of the table. "You're a pretty sharp customer. Care to try again?"

"Why not?" said Cary. *This doesn't look so hard,* he told himself.

"All right," said the little man. "What's your wager?"

"Wait a minute. Can't I just bet my nickel?" asked Cary.

The man's face fell. "Oh, I'm afraid not. If it was up to me, I'd let you. But if my boss caught me, it'd be my job. Dime or better. What'll it be?"

Cary pulled a dime from his pocket and put it on the table. The cups began to whirl and Cary pointed again. Under his cup was a black ball.

"I don't believe it!" gasped the little man. "Hey fellas!" he called out to a couple of men who were loitering around the arcade. "Get a load of this. A double winner! Anybody want to make a side bet?"

A crowd began to gather close around Cary. And several of them plunked coins down on the little man's table. "Ready to go again?" asked the little man.

"Um, sure," said Cary. "How much this time?"

"How much have you got?" Cary dug into his pocket and came up with two pennies—and the golden microdisk. The little man's eyes bugged out when he saw it, and he glanced furtively about.

"That'll be fine!" he whispered under his breath.

"Oh, no!" said Cary, sticking the disk back in his pocket. "I can't bet that."

"What else have you got?" said the little man.

Reaching into his other pocket, he found only two quarters. That was strange, he was sure he'd had more change than that with him. "How's this?"

"That'll be fine," said the little man. "Here we go." Once again the cups spun, as the crowd began cheering him on. Squinting his eyes, Cary pointed.

This time he lost. The ball was nowhere to be seen.

The little man swept all the coins off the table, saying, "Tough luck, kid. Care to try it again? Dollar or better and you win it all back."

"Hey, wait a minute," said Cary, beginning to get suspicious. "I *saw* that ball go under the red cup. This game is rigged. I want my money back!"

"Pipe down!" said the little man. "You want to get us all in trouble? Now are you in or out? Put up, or shut up!"

I'll show him, thought Cary, reaching into his back pants pocket for a dollar bill.

His wallet was gone.

He spun around to see who might have taken it. But the crowd had vanished. He turned just in time to see the little man folding up his table and scurrying off, calling out, "So long, sucker!" over his shoulder. Cary was about to run after him when he felt a tug at his side. There was a hand caught in his pocket!

Cary grabbed the wrist hard and yanked, pulling the pickpocket off the ground. Clutched in his palm was the microdisk, gleaming golden in the bright lights.

Cary felt a sharp pain in his shin as the pickpocket kicked him. His grip broke and the disk went flying into the air. *"Gold!"* someone shouted. "He's got gold!" Suddenly the crowd of ruffians was back, and they were climbing all over him, clutching for the disk. Because Cary was a bit taller, his hand closed on it first. Then they were on top of him, screaming and pummeling and punching.

Cary shook them off with surprising ease. But then they were at him again, and he had to struggle just to keep on his feet.

There was the sharp shriek of a whistle. At once Cary's attackers scattered in all directions, as if terrified.

"Beat it!" one shouted. "It's the 'Mashers!"

A half-dozen men in black suits were striding in his direction. They all wore black gloves and black boots; wide wraparound dark glasses covered their eyes. Cary thought they looked sort of silly, like movie gangsters.

"There they are!" Cary shouted, pointing after the fleeing crooks. "Those are the ones who stole—"

Two of the men in black grabbed his arms.

"Wait a minute!" cried Cary. "It's not *me* you want, it's *them!*
He tried to pull free. Although they were shorter than he was,
they were as tenacious as bulldogs. Exploding with frustration,
Cary threw his shoulder into one of his captors, sending him
sprawling. It was obvious that they weren't used to resistance,
because they stopped for a moment, stunned. Cary took that
moment to try to break for freedom.

"Don't let him get away!" someone squealed. "He's got *gold!*"
At that, the men in black closed in again, pinning Cary against
a nearby wall.

"Stop!" whispered a soft but commanding voice. Everyone
froze where they stood.

Cary turned toward the voice as if pulled by a cord. A tall man
in gray was approaching. He wore a gray suit with gloves of soft
gray suede, and about his neck a strange star-shaped pendant
hung from a gleaming chain. He had neatly parted hair, a slim
moustache, and the sharp, predatory features of a hawk. Then
Cary was caught by his eyes.

They were deep, dark eyes, the frosty black of a winter sky. A
gray-gloved hand grasped his chin and tilted it up to meet that
awful gaze. The coldness of those eyes filled Cary's vision and
his heart, and he could not look away.

The gold, rasped a voice in Cary's head. *Give me the gold,* that
terrible, irresistible voice whispered. Cary found his hand in his
pocket, closing around the microdisk. The metal was warm,
almost burning. The warmth spread up his arm to his chest.
From far away, another voice was calling, warm and sweet,
drowning out that icy one. Cary felt his lungs filling with warm
air, and was suddenly shouting "No!" with all of his might.

Suddenly the spell was broken. Cary's vision cleared, and that
cruel face flinched in pain, curling in on itself, staggering as if
struck by a blow. Cary tore himself away from the men who held
him with a strength he didn't know he had, and began pumping
his legs as fast as he could to get away.

Stop! came that awful voice again. Cary's legs felt like lead. His face and sides hurt, and tears welled up in his eyes. But he kept on running. He could hear heavy footfalls behind him. They were gaining on him as he rounded the corner.

Then a hand reached out of the darkness and yanked him out of sight.

FOUR

"**D**ON'T MOVE!" hissed a voice in Cary's ear. An arm pressed tightly against his throat, choking him.

"Hey! What's th—" The arm choked tighter, and a hand clamped hard over his mouth.

"Shut up!" the voice whispered. "Don't even *breathe* till I give you permission. Got it?"

Cary struggled frantically, but he was held firm. A moment later, the arm relaxed a little, and the voice said, "Okay. They're gone," and pushed him deeper into the darkness. Suddenly he was spun around and slammed hard against a cold stone wall, and the voiced hissed again, "Now what in *hell* did you think you were doing out there?" It was hard to see who was talking, but it looked like a skinny, tough-looking street kid a year or two

older than Cary, in dirty patched denim overalls and cap. "Who
gave you permission to prance around out in the Fair like that?
Don't you realize you almost brought the bulls down on us
again? You *dimbulb,* you stupid little *punk.* Why, I oughta bash
in your lights for pulling a stupid stunt like that—"

"I am not a punk!" said Cary, struggling to get free. "Get your
grimy paws off of me, you—"

The kid's hand clamped back over his mouth, and a leg went
behind his heel, throwing him down to the rough stones. Cary's
head was twisted back by the hair, and the kid sat down hard on
his chest, whispering close to his face, "What the hell is wrong
with you? Are you deaf, dumb, or just plain dense? Can't you
understand, Brand and his 'Mashers are scouring everywhere
for us, and you, like an ass, are braying your head off. I oughta
let 'em have you. It would serve you right, you little twerp!"

"*I am not a twerp!* Now let me up or I'll call a cop on you, you
—you *mutt.*" The kid's hand came down again over Cary's
mouth, but this time he was ready and took a big bite.

"Yow!" the kid howled. "That did it. Say your prayers, kid. I
been goin' easy on you, but now I—"

"You'll *what?*" said Cary. Surprised at his own bravery, he
pushed the kid off of him, rolling him over and pinning him to
the ground. They wrestled and fought for a few minutes, and
Cary thought he was just beginning to get the better of the kid,
when he was suddenly yanked to his feet by a half-dozen hands
that hustled him back through a heavy cloth drape. Beyond, a
crackling cooking fire dazed his eyes and bathed him in heat.
When he could see again, he found he was in a long alleyway
ending in a high wall, cluttered with crates and boxes and other
rubbish, surrounded by a circle of gaunt, smudged faces, all his
age or younger, glaring angrily down at him.

"What's goin' on, Chief?" said one of the younger kids.
"Who's the troublemaker?"

"I dunno," said the kid who'd grabbed him. "But I'm sure
gonna find out. The 'Mashers are out there and this kid is mixed

up in it somehow. Terry! Robin! Run back to the entrance and check the front drape. And move the cans back in case the 'Mashers decide to make a move on us."

In the firelight, the streaks and bruises on the gang leader's face looked almost like war paint, striped in faint swirling patterns of black and blue. The old denim cap had fallen off in the scuffle, and Cary was shocked to see a shaggy, shoulder-length mane of ill-cut hair, decorated with an old blue ribbon and a white feather.

"Hey!" said Cary with a gulp. "You're a—a *girl!*"

"Any fool knows that, fool," she shot back. "Any *Scamp* does, anyway. Louie! Davey! Hold onto this little creep while I beat some answers out of him."

Two of the bigger kids held him tight while the leader pulled him close. "Just as I thought. You ain't one of us. I ain't never seen you before in my life. I should've known. No Scamp would be stupid enough to get suckered at that old shell game."

Her fingernail flicked at his face. "Look at that. Paint. Now what the hell do you mean by impersonating a Scamp?" she demanded in a menacing tone. "Who *are* you?"

Cary tried to speak, but he couldn't make his mouth work.

"Now, listen," she said in a voice so low the others could barely hear. "I'm only gonna ask you this once. Who the hell are you? Now *talk!*"

"Cary Newman," said Cary, drawing himself up to his full height. "Th-thirty-seven West Eighty-seventh Street, New York, New York, one-oh-oh-two-four. Area code two-one-two, five-three-seven, six-five-nine—*Urk!*"

"Don't get cute with me," said the leader, a hand against Cary's windpipe. "Just the name."

"I told you, *Cary,*" said Cary, when he could breathe again. "Cary Newman. Who the hell are *you?*"

The gang gasped in astonishment.

"You hear that? He wants to know who the hell am *I?*"

"Well, who the hell *are* you?" Cary answered. He wasn't going to let these monkeys think he was scared.

She grabbed him by the shoulder and pulled him close. "You don't get it, do you, kid?" she answered in a low voice. "*I'm* the one who asks the questions around here. I'm *Allie,* that's who, and don't you forget it. And this is my gang, the Scamps. Now listen up, Cary, if that *is* your name—"

"It *is.* It's *Cary.* Cary Newman like I told you before. What do I have to do to prove it to you? It's *Cary,* you hear me, CARY NEWMAN!"

"All right! All right. So you're Cary Newman. So big hairy deal. So what are you doing making trouble in the Fair and pretending to be a Scamp?"

"What are you *talking* about?" said Cary. "I'm not pretending to be anybody. I'm *me,* Cary—"

"Well then, what are you doing wearing our colors?"

"What do you mean, *your* colors?"

"You're wearing a blue shirt, you've got a black jacket on, and you've got the Scamp markings on your face, although whoever painted them on you didn't do a very good job. But I don't know you. I ain't seen you and I ain't sworn you in, so that means you must be a spy or something."

"He's a goddamn snitch for the 'Mashers, Allie," said one of the older kids. "I say we fix his clock for him!"

"Yeah!" said another. "I say we terminate him with extreme prejudice."

"Right!" said a third. "Let me at the sneaking spy, Allie. Let me bust in his face!"

"Okay, dummy," said Allie, "give me one good reason why I shouldn't turn you over to these apes?"

"Look," said Cary desperately, as the kids began to come closer, "none of this is my *fault.* You see my mom and I had this fight, and I ended up all alone on this subway platform, and I tried to get out but all I could find was this smelly old Bag Lady, and then I got attacked by these weirdo creatures in paint cans who tried to drown me in paint, and then I fell down here and

I got attacked and my wallet was stolen. . . . I know it sounds crazy and I don't understand any of it myself, but if somebody can just tell me how to get home to my mom on West Eighty-seventh Street, I'll just go away and not bother anybody. But instead, just because I'm wearing some dumb jacket and got some paint and coal dust on me, everybody starts jumping down my throat. So if you're going to kill me just get it over with because I don't believe any of this is really happening to me and I've probably gone crazy or insane or have a concussion or something anyway!"

And with that, Cary sank down to the street, putting his head between his hands. The weight of the day came down on him like a hammer, and he began to sob quietly, tears rolling down his cheeks.

"Hey!" said one of the Scamps. "Look at that! He's *cryin'*!"

Cary lifted his head. All of the kids were staring at him in disbelief.

"Well, that settles it," said Allie in disgust. "He sure ain't no Scamp, 'cause Scamps *never* cry, no matter what. And he probably ain't no spy either. Commander Brand would never send a sniveling little wimp like him to check up on us."

"Who's Commander Brand?" asked Cary. The Scamps looked surprised.

"I guess you're right, Allie," said one of them. "He never even heard of him."

"I *told* you I wasn't a spy," said Cary sadly. "I'm just lost, that's all. I just want to find my mo—" He stopped, but not before all of the Scamps had figured out what he was going to say.

"His *moth*-ther!" whooped one of the younger kids. "He wants his *mother*!" At once the rest of the Scamps picked up the chorus: "He wants his ma-ma!" "He's cryin' fer his mommy!" "Poor wittle bay-bee, wants his mum-mee! Haw-haw!" Suddenly the whole place was rolling with convulsive laughter.

Cary's ears started burning, and his face turned red. "What's so funny?" he demanded. "What's *wrong* with wanting to go home? What's so funny about wanting to find my mother?" That just made them laugh all the harder.

"Aw, jeez," said Allie. "Not *another* one! Knock it off, you guys. I gotta fill this twerp in on the facts of life."

Pulling Cary over against the wall, Allie said quietly, "Wise up, kid. There's no sense in bawling over somethin' you can't have. Believe me, I know what you're goin' through. Each and every one of the Scamps went through it themselves when they first got here—it's just so long ago they've all forgotten."

"What do you mean?" asked Cary, puzzled.

"Don't play dumb with me, Cary. You know what I'm talking about. Look at 'em," said Allie with a wave of her hand.

Cary noticed that of all the kids, Allie was the oldest, and tallest. The other kids were much younger than they'd looked at first, some hardly more than babies. It was their lean drawn faces and the look in their eyes that made them look much older. And most of them had old bruises and healed-over scars that spoke of a childhood so harsh he could hardly imagine it.

"You won't catch the *Scamps* crying for home anymore," said Allie. "All 'home' ever meant for most of them was boiling in summer or freezing in winter with a dozen other kids in some damn tenement somewhere if they were lucky, a street corner if they weren't. And all most of them remember of their mothers and fathers is the back of a hand.

"Everybody's got their reasons for being here, Cary. Look at Annie over there. That blue streak on her face covers a burn her stepmother put there with a hot iron. And Mickey's arm hangs like that because his father busted it when he got tanked up over losing his job. They came here because the pain got too bad, because there wasn't enough to go around, or sometimes because they were just forgotten.

"But you can bet your life they're all better off without homes and families that starve them and hurt them and don't give a damn about them. Here we ain't got much more, but we do have each other. I don't know what happened to you at home, but it must've been pretty bad, or you wouldn't have come here."

"That's not true!" said Cary. "*My* mom cares about me, she hasn't forgotten about me. We just got separated in the subway, that's all."

"Sure, kid," said Allie with a shake of the head. "More likely she dumped you so as not to have another mouth to feed."

"But that's *crazy*. She wouldn't do that. She's—she's my *mother*."

"That don't mean nothin'. Open your eyes. There's dozens of kids here whose parents didn't think twice about hurting them."

"But *my* mom wouldn't do that. She cares about me, she—she loves me."

"What about your father? Does *he* love you?"

"Sure he does. The only reason he's not living with us right now is because Mom and Dad had this fight—"

"So your old man beat up on your old lady and walked out on her, huh?"

"Not *that* kind of fight. Nobody got *hurt* or anything like that."

"Sounds like *somebody* got hurt," said Allie. "Look, you ain't no different from the rest of us. The sooner you wise up and stop cryin' for some lost home you'll never see again, the better off you'll be, believe me."

"But I *haven't* lost my home," Cary protested. "I'm—I'm just having trouble finding it, that's all."

"All right, then, tell me—just where *is* your precious home, Cary?"

Suddenly Cary realized he didn't know. It used to be a beautiful old house in the country. But Mom said they were planning to tear the place down to build a shopping center, if they hadn't already. The old brownstone didn't really feel like home either. And home certainly wasn't that tiny little shoebox Dad lived in. . . .

"If I knew that, I wouldn't be here now," said Cary sadly. Allie nodded.

"Well, that settles it," said Allie. "You just been made a

Scamp. On probation, you understand, till you prove we can trust you. You can stay here with us."

"But I don't *want* to be a Scamp. I keep telling you, I just want to go back where I belong."

"You never give up, do you? And just how do you plan to do that? Wander around all over the place, asking everybody the way home?"

"I guess so. What do you care? What difference does it make to you?"

"I'll tell you what difference it makes," said Allie. "You know too much. You know where our hideout is, how many of us there are. The 'Mashers would nab you in no time, and when they did, you'd probably spill your guts to them, the way you did—"

"I would not!"

"Look. This ain't a game, Cary. The 'Mashers mean business. They've already gotten hold of two of my Scamps, and I ain't heard nothin' from them since. And we've just barely escaped 'em a half-dozen times. I don't know what they do with the kids they get, but I've heard stories, and believe me, you wouldn't last ten seconds with them."

"Why don't you let me worry about that?"

"No offense, Cary, but I just can't take the chance. There's too much at stake here. All of these kids depend on me. They've been hurt enough, and I'd rather die than let them down. You got just two choices—become a Scamp or become ancient history."

"But there *has* to be some other way," said Cary. "I can't just forget about my mom and dad and live in some dirty old alleyway for the rest of my life. This is all some kind of accident, some kind of mistake. Look at me. Do I look like I belong here?"

Allie looked at him closely, as if sizing him up. "I don't know," she said at last. "There's somethin' funny going on here."

"What do you mean?" asked Cary. The intent expression on her face made him a little nervous.

"See, I knew you were in trouble, even before I saw you there.

It's always that way with the Scamps. I always know when one of them's in trouble."

"How?" asked Cary, puzzled.

"I just *do*, that's all," she said. "But still, there's somethin' about you that don't fit, somehow. For one thing, you're bigger than anybody else here. And you're the first new one to come along in I don't know how long. But there's somethin' else. Somethin' in your eyes I don't see in the Scamps'."

"What's that?"

"Feelings. Look at these kids. Do you see any fear in those eyes? These kids are tough as nails, hardened by all the pain they've seen so they don't even feel it anymore. They've seen it all, and they don't give a damn for anybody but each other now. Your eyes still have all kinds of feelings: fear, warmth, anger, hope—hope that things will get better, that you can still find your parents, get back home again. As long as you got that, I guess you're right. You *don't* belong in Scamps' Alley."

"But what can I do about it?"

For a moment, Allie was silent, as if having some sort of argument with herself. "There ain't nothing you can do about it," she said at last. "There is one thing *I* can do for you, though why I should risk my neck for a blubbering little wimp like you I can't say. There's somebody I know who might be able to help you. He's a misfit like you; doesn't quite seem to belong here either. He's a strange old coot, but maybe the smartest guy I know. If anybody can help you out, it's gonna be him."

"Who is he? Where can I find him?"

"Not so fast. He ain't all that easy to find. I'm gonna have to take you to him myself. And that means the Scamps are gonna have to get along without me for a while. I don't give my word to someone unless I mean it, Cary. So if I take you to him—and that's a big *if*, mind you—you've got to swear to me you won't try to run off—"

"I promise," said Cary.

"Wait," said Allie. "You've got to swear you'll stick by me and do what I tell you. And if we *do* get split up, you've got to swear you'll do whatever you have to to keep out of the 'Mashers' hands, to keep the Scamps from getting hurt. 'Cause if you ever cross us, I'd hate to be you after we catch up with you."

"I *will*," said Cary.

"It ain't that easy, Cary," said Allie. "This is a blood oath we're talkin' about, on your name, your life, and your honor as a—an honorary Scamp. It could get tough out there, Cary. Everybody's got their price, and everybody's got their breaking point. I don't expect you to be no saint. I just want you to swear you'll do everythin' you can to keep my Scamps from gettin' hurt."

Cary's hand closed involuntarily around the microdisk in his pocket. "I swear," he said solemnly.

"Not good enough," said Allie. "You've gotta *mean* it. Here," she said, "do like I do." Pulling her feather from her hair, she jabbed herself in the thumb. A small drop of blood welled up. Cary took the feather and did the same. She pressed their thumbs together. "Now swear," she said.

Cary took a deep breath, and his hand tightened around the disk. Allie was watching him closely. He thought hard about what she was asking of him, and then said, "I swear I won't try to escape. And I'll do everything I can to keep the Scamps from getting hurt."

Allie gave a sigh of relief. "That's more like it. Now let's go get somethin' to eat. I'm starved!"

THE SCAMPS HAD been waiting, watching them talk. As they returned, one of the littlest ones, a pigtailed girl with no front teeth, piped up, "Whath the thcoop, Allie? Ith he a thpy? Do we get to thmash hith head in?"

"Naw, he's just lost, Thuthie," she said, settling the little girl on her hip. "I'm gonna help him find his way home."

"Too bad," said Thuthie with a malicious gap-toothed grin.

"Josh, get Cary here some soup. Me, too. And anybody else that needs it. Jaime, better double up the guard duty at the entrance in case the 'Mashers come round."

"Gotcha, Allie."

The alleyway made a zigzag at the back, opening out into a wider space. A high wall rose at the back, dotted with bricked-up windows, and a small cooking fire blazed in front of it in an old coal scuttle set up on a brick ledge. There were a half-dozen hammocks slung across the narrow street, and little niches cut out in the walls on both sides, which Cary guessed must do as the Scamps' beds. There was an old galvanized washtub under a bronze spigot that dribbled water down the wall into a tarnished grating. And high up on the wall, in ancient, faded letters, were painted the words "scamps allie."

There must have been two or three dozen kids living in that big, dusty alleyway. The youngest were almost babes in arms, and the oldest of them couldn't have been more than about ten or twelve. As he walked back, he saw a frightfully thin little girl with her skirts hiked up, washing her feet in the water, and a bare-bottomed little boy, about six or so, peeing into a drain by the wall.

"Well, how d'ya like it?" asked Allie proudly. "Not bad, huh?"

"It's—it's very nice," said Cary hesitantly.

Allie cuffed him jovially on the back. "Maybe it wasn't such a bad idea makin' a Scamp out of you after all, Cary."

A scrawny olive-skinned boy with a ragged white cloth for an apron dipped a cast-iron ladle into a big iron pot over the cooking fire and handed Cary a cracked wooden bowl of steaming soup with a crust of bread half submerged in it. It smelled good, and Cary's stomach started churning.

"Could I have a spoon?" asked Cary. One look at the Scamps and he immediately realized his mistake.

"Hear that?" one of them said with a laugh. "He wants a *spoon*."

"Oh, ain't we dainty!" mocked another. "I'll have a doily if you please!"

"Button it!" said Allie, cutting off more harsh laughter. "It ain't *Cary's* fault he don't know how to eat with his hands. Here," she said, fishing a bent old spoon from the pocket of her overalls.

It didn't look too clean, but Cary was too hungry to argue, and he wolfed down the soup in a few gulps, polishing off the bread crust with dripping fingers. "Terrific soup," he said, wiping his face on his sleeve. "What's in it?"

"Who remembers?" said Josh. "It's been cooking like that as long as I've been here. Mostly we throw in whatever we can pinch in the market."

"Pinch?" asked Cary. "You mean steal?"

"Uh-huh," said Allie, working on a large bowl of her own. "With Brand's Badmashers on our tails, it's the only way we get by these days."

"That's why everyone was yelling at me," said Cary. "They thought I was a Scamp, trying to steal their food. But who are these Madbashers, anyway?"

"I dunno, exactly. They're a sort of a gang that came out of nowhere not too long ago, and already they got a lock on Lazy Fair. They shake the place down every couple of days. Anybody who wants to keep his stall has to cough up a piece of the action."

"Why doesn't anybody stand up to them?"

"They're too scared. Anybody who *does* stand up to them just disappears—poof! Like that!"

"And they pinch kids who've got nobody to vouch for 'em," said Josh.

"Like Thcotty," said Thuthie, with a hint of a sniffle.

"Hush!" said Allie sharply. "I told you. Scotty'll be back. You just wait."

"Who's Scotty?" asked Cary.

"None of your business!" she said, and then relented. "Scotty used to help me run the Scamps. I kept tellin' him he was takin' too many chances, but he wouldn't listen. Then, one day, he just didn't come back." She glanced at little Thuthie. "You figure it out."

"See, the 'Mashers can't stand the Scamps," she continued after finishing a second bowl of soup. "We make 'em look like a big joke. We do as we please, and we keep the runaways out of their hands. Brand's put out the word that anybody helping us out will get in big trouble with him. That's why we—"

Suddenly, there was a low whistle from the other end of the alley.

"Josh! Cover the fire!" whispered Allie. "The rest of you, clam up!"

The Scamps clustered against the far wall, sitting in a tight, huddled knot of silence. The loud tramp of oversized boots went by, stopped, came back, paused for endless minutes near the end of the alley. There was a low barking of orders and what sounded like an argument. Finally, after what seemed like hours, the lookout signaled all clear.

"That was a close one," said Allie. "They've never gotten that near this place before. I wonder what they were after?"

"I *tol'* you he wath a thpy!" said Thuthie.

"That does it," said Allie. "It ain't gonna get any easier to take Cary to the Poet than it is right now."

"But *Allie*," said Jaime, "what if they catch you like they did—"

"Decision's final. I gave my word. I can take care of myself, Jaime—as long as *this* turkey doesn't make any stupid moves."

"But—"

"You arguin' with me? I didn't think so. Now listen up. You and Katie are in charge till I get back. I want you all to lay low until you hear from me. Don't take no chances! Got it?"

"Got it, Allie," said Katie glumly.

"Good. C'mon, Cary. Let's get going, before the 'Mashers get back."

As they reached the drape that camouflaged the entrance to

the alley, Cary said, "Thanks for helping me out. I really appreciate it."

"I gave my word, didn't I?" said Allie gruffly. "Besides, I ain't doin' it all for you. I'm doin' it to take the heat off the Scamps. Now quit jawin' and let's get movin'."

FIVE

"**I** DON'T GET IT," said Allie, as she warily scanned the marketplace. "There's no sign of the 'Mashers. It ain't right. There's always a few of 'em skulking about. C'mon, Cary. Let's see if we can't find the Poet. But look sharp. Somethin' is spooky around here."

Allie waved him through the parted drape, securing it tightly to a cleat on the ground. It was painted in an imitation of the gray stone next to it good enough to fool the eye from only inches away.

"Help me move these cans back," said Allie, pushing an old-fashioned ash can in front of the cloth.

"Oof!" said Cary as he helped her wrestle it in place. "This thing feels like it's filled with rocks!"

"It is," said Allie nonchalantly. "They're good for throwin'. Now let's get goin'." At once she was off, working her way swiftly along one of the walls, ducking in and out of sight and moving so fast Cary could hardly keep up with her.

"Hey, Allie," gasped Cary. "Slow down, will you?"

"And risk the 'Mashers getting us?" she called back. "No way. The sooner I get you to the Poet, the better for all of us."

"Who is this Poet anyway?" asked Cary.

"Just about the smartest guy I know," said Allie, "that's who. And just about the only *grown-up* friend the Scamps have got. Now stop askin' questions and start walkin'."

They were squeezing through a narrow passageway between the high wall and the canvas backs of the market stalls. With practiced deftness, Allie reached around and handed him a plum.

"Take it," she said, popping one whole into her mouth. "It'll keep your strength up," she added, spitting out the pit. He took a bite. It was delicious. A moment later, her elbow smacked into his gut, knocking the wind—and the fruit—out of him.

"What's the big idea?" croaked Cary.

"Will you dummy up?" Allie whispered. "Somethin' is up."

Peeking around a stall, Allie watched for a moment, then turned him roughly around. "Move!" she hissed, and Cary started moving. A couple of minutes later, she grabbed his arm again to stop him. A large piece of board held in place by a ten-penny nail covered a stretch of the wall. Allie swung it aside, revealing a narrow corridor, its floor thick with dust. Cary hesitated, and Allie pushed him through and followed, swinging the board back behind them.

"What's the big idea?" said Cary. "How come you keep pushing me and shoving me around all the time?"

"We almost walked into a trap up there, Cary. You got a price on your head, kid."

"What are you talking about?"

"Listen to me when I'm talking. Brand's offering a *reward* to

anybody who turns you in. And anybody who's caught hidin'
you . . ." She drew her finger across her throat with a slicing
noise.

"What's that supposed to mean?" asked Cary.

"What do you *think* it means, dimbulb?"

"M-maybe you better just let me go on by myself," said Cary.

"Why you little . . . What kind of person do you think I am?
I *gave* my damn word and I'm goin' to keep it if it kills me, which
is looking more likely all the time. Now *move*," she said with a
rough shove.

"I told you, you don't have to *push* me," said Cary, brushing
her hand away. "I'm not stupid, you know. Just tell me where
we're going, and I'll go."

Allie's hand dropped. "You're right, kid. I'm just a bit jumpy,
is all."

"And don't call me *kid*," said Cary.

"Okay, okay. Down the corridor all the way, and then left."

THE CORRIDOR PASSED dozens of train tracks with hand-painted
signs that looked like roll-up window shades, and each with a
list of destinations Cary had never heard of. They looked deserted, as if they hadn't been used for decades. Beyond was an
enormous underground rail yard held up by massive pillars,
with hundreds of tracks crisscrossing in all directions. Allie
kept peering into each track as if looking for someone or
something.

At the end, the corridor turned left, ending in a broad staircase. Cary heard a melancholy melody. On the landing, halfway
up, someone sat, whistling.

He looked like some sort of seedy street Santa Claus out of
uniform. He wore a patched and baggy pair of striped pants,
held up by multicolored suspenders, and a blue T-shirt covered with clouds that seemed to move a bit when Cary wasn't
watching. Great splayed toes poked out of sandals cut from

black leather wing-tipped shoes.

At the back of his great pink head was a fringe of wild and wispy white hair that swept over his ears and down his chin into an even wilder and wispier beard. His brows were great white horns that tangled in the middle, his nose was big and red, and seemed screwed on a little crooked, and there was a faraway, dreamy smile on his craggy face.

Allie climbed up the steps, and he turned to face her, his sad blue eyes alight with life.

"Allie, my little mayfly!" he called out in a musical voice. "Still living on borrowed time, I see. Who's your young friend?"

"I'm Cary," said Cary. "Who are you?"

"I'm Nobody. Who are you?"

"Don't you have a name?"

"A name? Why, no. I had one once, I'm sure. But I never had much use for it. Didn't rhyme. Nowadays everyone just calls me the Poet:

> "Who will buy my pretty poems;
> Witty ditties, somber to-ems?
> Songs to make your spirits hearken,
> Sonnets Shakespearean and Petrarchan!
> Let me make a merry jingle,
> Jokes and japes to make you tingle,
> Lays spondaic and iambic,
> Anacreontic, dithyrhambic—"

"*You're* the Poet?" Cary blurted out. His heart sank and his face fell. This—this *bum* was the person Allie thought could help him?

"Not quite what you expected, eh?" said the Poet, seeing the disappointment in Cary's eyes. "Poets seldom are, I'm afraid. We spend so much time on our insides that we get a bit careless about our outsides. May I offer you a poem to console you, Cary? I'm afraid they're all I have of any worth:

"I've rhymes that never have been
    spoken,
Doggerel that's been housebroken,
Ancient truths in lines laconic,
Limerick or macaronic,
Odds and odes from bad to verse,
Take your pick, you've got your—

"—um, *cherce*!" he finished with a flourish.

"I didn't come here for a poem," said Cary. "I came for help, for advice."

The Poet nodded. "I'm not surprised. Hardly anybody comes for Poems these days. They're far too costly, you see. Why, they can cost you your Time, or your Head, or your Heart . . ." The Poet sighed. "Yes, most often your heart. . . ."

His eyes got a little misty, then he harrumphed and straightened up as Cary began to fidget. "Advice," he said, "is another matter. I always give advice for nothing. Because that's what it's worth. Nothing."

"Does he *always* talk like that?" said Cary to Allie, growing impatient.

"Uh-huh," said Allie. "But that's 'cause he's a poet," she said knowingly. "They *all* talk like that."

"What Advice do you need, Cary?"

"How to get home again."

"How's that?" asked the Poet with a quizzical twitch of his brows.

"It's kind of hard to explain. You see, I live on West Eighty-seventh Street, that is, I don't really live there, my mom and I are just staying there, because she and Dad had this fight. Only I guess I really do live there, because our old house upstate has probably been torn down by now. . . ."

Allie shook her head in disgust, but the Poet just nodded his head sympathetically.

"Anyway, it was raining and I was all cooped up in the house

—I mean the brownstone—and I was supposed to do the dishes, and Mom and I had this big fight. And—well, I guess I was crying a little, but all of a sudden everything went all green and blurry and there was this voice calling my name sort of high and sweet. And the next thing I know, Mom's finished her report and wants to go shopping. And we started fighting again, and I ran into the subway, and then—"

"Yes?" said the Poet.

"Well, this is the crazy part. I ended up on this deserted platform, and this Bag Lady came by and left by this secret passage. Only she wasn't really a Bag Lady at all, but a bunch of these tiny Little People all dressed up like one—see, I *told* you this was crazy.

"Anyway, I followed her," Cary continued, "and I came to this place where there were more of these Little People all in spray cans spraying the walls, and they sprayed me all over with paint, so that everybody in the market must have thought I belonged to Allie's gang. And then I got cheated in this crooked game, and then those Badbashers or whatever they're called came after me for some reason, I guess because they thought I had a gold piece or something—"

"Wait," said the Poet suddenly. "Did you say a *gold* piece?"

"Uh-huh. Only it wasn't gold at all, just this microdisk from Mom's computer. But everybody was beating up on me and trying to get it from me. And then Commander Brand came along and tried to use some kind of hypnotism or something on me but I got away from him—"

"You *did*? How curious!"

"Yeah, but then I rescued him," said Allie, "and made him a Scamp, and then I brought him here to you. Well, how 'bout it? Can you help the kid out?"

The Poet shook his head sadly. "I don't know, Allie." He'd been listening attentively, stroking his whiskers, and as he listened, all of the foolishness seemed to sort of drain out of him. "I'm afraid you have a Problem, Cary, one that I can't help you very much with."

"Why not?" asked Cary in distress.

"Because you're something that shouldn't be—an Uptowner who's come down to Down Town before his time."

"But I've been downtown before—to ride the ferry and see the World Trade Center and visit my dad—"

"I'm afraid you don't understand, Cary. *This* Down Town is a real town—a special town for everything that's past. And you belong to the present. By all the rules, you shouldn't be here."

"But I've never heard of any town called Down Town. It isn't on any map of the city *I* ever saw."

"Not every place a person can go is on a map, Cary," said the Poet. "Some are off the edges. Listen to me, Cary. Down Town is the place for all the people and things, real and imaginary, that the Uptown world no longer has any use for. The place where all the folks who can't, or won't, keep up end up. Whenever something's time is over Uptown, it ends up down here. Some are recent arrivals, like Allie here, and some have been here for centuries. Whole eras come down at once when their time has passed. That's why everyone is so much smaller down here."

"Huh?" said Cary.

"It's the Weight of History," said the Poet. "The longer you stay here, the smaller you get. If you stay here long enough, you become one of the Little People for good."

"Like those walking paint cans I saw, and the little Bag Ladies?" asked Cary.

"Not quite," the Poet answered. "Those are In-Betweeners, creatures that inhabit a sort of borderland between Uptown and Down Town. The painters are called Graffeets. They're cousins of the sprites that paint the leaves different colors in the fall, but somehow they got stuck in the tunnels and corridors of the city instead of in the trees where they belong. The little Bag Ladies are called Scroungers. They haunt the bargain basements and markdown sales, looking for things that have outlived their usefulness Uptown, and bring them down to Lazy Fair, here in Down Market."

"I thought the Little People only existed in fairy tales, in dreams," said Cary.

"And so they do," said the Poet, "in the Uptown world, where there's no other place for such nonsense. They've found a home here, where there are still people to believe in them—each of the Wee Folk of all of the hundreds of kinds of people in Down Town, from elves and boggles to jinns and devis."

"But those things aren't *real,*" said Cary.

"What is?" asked the Poet. "Your Uptown world is only a memory to you now. How real is that? In the same way, Down Town is made up of memories—memories of the past. Not as it *was,* mind you, but as we remember it to be—all the best and all the worst of it, and very little in between. You see, Cary, Down Town exists as long as there's someone who still remembers things the way they once were. If the past were ever forgotten, Down Town would just melt away to nothingness."

"But how did *you* get here?" asked Cary.

"We poets are travelers in time, in memory. We have a special license to come and go here, but only in our dreams. I came one day when—well, let's just say I found that those dreams were more precious to me than reality, that there was too much Reason and not enough Rhyme in the world to suit my fancy."

"But what am *I* doing here?" asked Cary. "I never *asked* to be here."

"Are you sure?"

"No," said Cary. "I mean, *yes*, that is—I'm not sure."

"But that's just my point!" said the Poet. "If you were, there would be no Problem. It's your *wanting* to get back Uptown that causes the troubles. If you had wished to be here, and were *happy* you came, then there would *be* no problem. For you to be here and *not* want to be here is where the Problem begins. You're neither Here nor There. Do you see what I mean?"

"I don't think so," said Cary. "Do *you* know what he's talking about, Allie?"

"I never know what he's talkin' about," Allie answered.

"That's how I know he's so smart."

"You mean you can't tell me how I can get back Uptown?" asked Cary in despair.

"I'm afraid not, Cary," said the Poet. "But I believe you'll find the answer in Time."

"Then Allie was wrong about you," said Cary bitterly. "You can't help me after all."

"I didn't say that, Cary."

"But—"

"I said you'd find your answer in Time. And the person in Down Town who knows the most about Time is the Watchman. If anyone can tell you how to get home, he can."

"Now we're gettin' somewhere!" said Allie. "See, I *told* you the Poet would be able to help you. Where do we find this Watchman anyway?"

"Why, in Time Square," said the Poet. "Where else?"

"Times Square?" said Cary. "But that's *Up*town."

"Not *Times* Square, Cary," the Poet replied. *"Time* Square. The highest point in Down Town, where the Future becomes the Past. The place where Uptown and Down Town come closest together."

"I know where that is," said Allie. "It's just up the Broad Way aways."

"Then what are we waiting for?" said Cary impatiently. "Let's get going."

"Just a moment, Cary. It may not be that simple."

"What do you mean?"

The Poet was silent for a moment, his face wearing a bemused expression. "I have an inkling," he said at last, "you are down here for a Purpose."

"What sort of purpose?"

"You'll have to find that out for yourself, Cary," said the Poet. "It seems to me that there's something out of balance. Perhaps your Purpose is to put it right. If there's an Uptowner who doesn't belong in Down Town, then perhaps there's a Down

Towner who doesn't belong Uptown. Of course, that's Logic,
not Poetry, so it probably isn't true. But *until* you find it, you
won't be able to get to where you're supposed to be."

"How am I supposed to find my purpose?"

"Not by *looking* for it, surely," said the Poet a bit sharply.
"That's like trying to look at the inside of a soap bubble. It can't
be done. Do you follow?"

"Not really," said Cary.

"It's quite simple, really," said the Poet. "A Purpose is almost
always something you already have but don't know you have—
something you already know, that you may not *know* you know.
It's my belief you came here to find something you already have
—something you brought with you."

"But the only thing I brought with me is *this*." Cary held out
the microdisk in the palm of his hand.

"That isn't quite what I meant, Cary," said the Poet, regarding the little gleaming circle, "but it might be a good place to
start. However, you won't find your Purpose by fretting over it.
Just put it out of your mind, and it's sure to turn up, just when
you need it most."

"If it's so important for me to find it, just how do you expect
me to stop fretting about it?" asked Cary.

"Ah!" said the Poet. "There I *do* have something that could
be of help. Of course, you'll have to pay for it."

"Pay for what?" asked Cary.

"Why, a poem, of course. What else do I have to sell?"

"I told you, they took all my money."

"Money? Oh, no. That wouldn't do at all. No, I'd need something useful—a quarterstaff, a dime novel, a penny whistle, a
farthingale—that sort of thing. What about a smile?"

"That doesn't seem like much of a payment," said Cary with
a sigh.

"There's where you're wrong, Cary. It's one of the most valuable things there is. Now let's get down to business," said the
Poet in a sober tone. "Is it a bargain? A poem for a smile?"

"Okay," said Cary, even though smiling was the last thing he felt like doing. He squinched up the corners of his mouth in a sort of a grin.

"Surely you can do better than *that*," said the Poet. "Here, watch." And with that, the Poet pointed to his whiskered mouth and gave the silliest grin that Cary had ever seen. It made Cary smile in spite of himself, if only for a moment.

The Poet bent forward, measuring the smile solemnly between thumb and forefinger, peering at it with one eye. "Hmph," said the Poet, shaking his head. "A *very* small smile. That requires a Very Small Poem. They're always the hardest. . . ."

"You mean the easiest, don't you?" said Cary.

"Oh, no," said the Poet. "With a big poem, all you have to do is get it started and get all rumbledy-tumbledy inside, and the rest of the poem follows naturally. Now with the *little* ones—"

"Uh, Mr. Poet?" said Allie. "Could you maybe get on with it?"

"Quite right, Allie. Hm. Let's see." He closed his eyes and placed his fingers on his temples, hopping from one foot to the other. Then his eyes popped open and he shouted, "Ahem! 'A Poem on Purpose':

"Breathely deep and gridely win,
Let the stealing hare eel in;
A sear's a sunny foe, and so,
You woe the nay, so get it low!

"There! I'd say that's fair value, wouldn't you?"

"I'm not sure," said Cary. "It sounds all jumbled. Are you sure you got it right?"

"Not at all!" exclaimed the Poet. "If you straighten it out, it won't be of any use to you. You might try reciting it a few times, so you won't forget it. Now run along, both of you. And, Cary, I'm sure you'll find what you're looking for in Time."

"Thanks," said Cary. "I sure hope so."

"I don't know, Allie," said Cary as they left the Poet whistling behind them. "Your friend the Poet seems like a nice man, but not much of what he said was very helpful after all. At least not as far as I could tell."

"Don't rub it in," said Allie sullenly. "Besides, we had to start somewhere. If you got any better ideas, let's hear 'em."

"No, Allie," said Cary sadly, "I don't."

"Okay, then," she answered curtly, "let's see if we can find this Watchman character."

THERE WERE STILL no Badmashers to be seen as they slipped back into the Fair. Allie seemed more skittish than ever, glancing about constantly. Finally, she waved him onward.

The passageway they'd left came out right at the end of the marketplace, by an enormous archway with a sign chiseled in ten-foot high letters reading HIGH STREET, and underneath it, THE BROAD WAY.

The open lane where they stood became a wide turning circle, where miniature carts pulled by short, stocky horses unloaded their wares onto pushcarts as dogs barked and mules brayed. A steady stream of wagons came up to the roundabout from the crowded thoroughfare beyond.

As he and Allie edged closer, he could see that they were up above an immense valley broken up into smaller vales. Above, a hint of rock could be seen through the constant mist. Below, the great road threaded itself over low hills and steep slopes, disappearing into dark tunnels, only to reappear farther on.

Little lanes fed the traffic that filled the highway—people, horses, carriages, no cars as far as Cary could see—and received the carts that returned empty or full from the market. Tiny villages dotted the hills and nestled against the rock walls that soared overhead. Cary couldn't tell how high up or how far down this crazy-quilt country reached, but it seemed to go on almost forever.

"When you're through gawkin' maybe we can get movin'," said Allie. "I ain't conducting no sight-seein' tour, ya know."

Dodging hooves and ducking under a sturdy wooden railing, Cary followed Allie as she strode out onto a narrow footpath running alongside the Broad Way. Suddenly she halted.

A large black structure blocked the road, a sort of makeshift turnstile or tollbooth. Traffic had backed up for hundreds of feet. Drivers were yelling and cursing at one another, and horses were shying and rearing in the air. A dark figure who was watching from the gatehouse pointed in their direction and blew a shrill whistle. Badmashers!

Cary and Allie turned as one, breaking into a run as a half-dozen 'Mashers started after them from the booth, elbowing startled Down Towners aside.

"Quick! Head for that wall!" shouted Allie. "I'll distract 'em!" Hesitating only a moment, Cary pumped toward the old stone wall lined with stalls. He heard an outraged shriek and a crash behind him, and a thudding sound like a herd of wild bowling balls, and he turned to look back.

Allie had managed to overturn a cart of melons just as the Badmashers drew near. An army of muskmelons and honeydews, cranshaws and cantaloupes, smashed into the 'Mashers, as the vendor ranted and wailed.

Cary put on a burst of speed, narrowing the distance between him and the wall. Then a whistle blew to his right. A pair of 'Mashers had emerged from a side tunnel. He glanced about wildly for Allie, but didn't see her, then changed course again, heading back toward the marketplace.

A line of 'Mashers blocked his way. He scooped up melons and started slinging them, knocking several of the 'Mashers off their feet. But for every one that went down, two more seemed to take their place. Then they were upon him, and Cary was surrounded by a circle of fists.

SIX

VIVIAN NEWMAN WAS worried.

Slumped down in her big leather office chair, she watched the sun set through the picture window on the lush greenery of Central Park, feeling tired and footsore and more than a little frightened.

It wasn't *like* Cary to run off like that, no matter *how* angry he was. Especially in the *subway.* He'd told her often enough ever since they'd arrived how much he hated it here.

That's what worried her. Cary wasn't used to city life, like she was. Even though he'd been born in the city while John was at Columbia Law and she was getting her history degree at Barnard, he'd spent most of his life in the comfortable security of suburbia. Of course, nobody could blame them for wanting their only son to grow up in a healthy, safe neighborhood, but sometimes Vivian thought that Cary had grown up *too* sheltered from the real world. He had almost no firsthand experience of how the "other half" lived; he didn't know how to behave.

She hadn't been too concerned when he'd made that scene in the store. She'd rather have him expressing his anger than bottling it up the way John always did. But when they'd gotten separated in the subway, she began to get worried. She wasn't sure Cary even remembered where John's apartment was, let alone which subway to take. He could easily get lost somewhere, and after dark who knew *what* might happen to him.

She couldn't understand what had gotten into Cary. Sure, it was rough on a boy his age having to deal with a separation, a move, and a death in the family, all in the space of a year. But these things happened. Life had its ups and downs, and the best thing was just to get on with it, to get involved in new things, the way she had.

Cary, however, had let it affect his whole outlook on life. He'd become sullen and withdrawn, and now he was getting downright hostile. It was partly her fault, of course, the famous O'-Reilly temper getting her into trouble again. Lord knows he didn't deserve it, even if he *had* been behaving impossibly.

She'd tried to reach John, to warn him that Cary might turn up at any moment, although she wasn't looking forward to telling him. When there was no answer at his apartment, she'd tried his office. Busy, as usual. But then, when had John ever been there when she really needed him?

She'd thought it best to head for her office. Cary knew she'd been planning to stop off there, and she thought he might head there after he'd had a chance to cool off. But the security guards downstairs hadn't seen him, and the receptionist said nobody had come by. Even Mr. Janos was out at a meeting somewhere.

Turning back to her desk, she checked her watch. Twenty of six. Maybe she could still catch John before he left. She picked up the phone, her fingers fumbling over the buttons as she punched in the number.

JOHN NEWMAN WAS at his wit's end.

The surface of the old, scarred worktable was covered with deeds and briefs, ledgers, law books, and legal pads, half-doughnuts and half-filled coffee cups. John had been burning the midnight oil ever since he and Vivian had split up, trying to find a loophole large enough to save the city's parks.

Nobody was quite sure how it had happened. Shortly after a new computerized auditing system was put in, a huge shortfall in park operating funds had been discovered. Unless the deficit could be made up, services and maintenance of the parks would have to be cut back drastically. The new Governor's solution was to create a private board of realtors, bankers, brokers, and businessmen, the Excelsior Corporation, which would provide the needed funds in exchange for control of the parks system.

Nobody was willing to take a public stand against the Governor's plan, although privately a lot of John's lawyer friends thought it set a bad precedent. But a group calling itself the Ad-hoc Partnership to Preserve the Public Lands (APPPL for short) had retained John's firm—Newman, Stone, Newman—as legal counsel in the fight against it.

APPPL denounced the board as "putting the fox in charge of the henhouse." They claimed that if a private corporation controlled the parks, there was nothing to stop it from granting concessions and encroachments on park property if it thought they were "in the interests of the city." It wasn't that city officials were all that much better, just that they were subject to pressure from the parks' main users—the people themselves.

John's father would have been appalled to see his firm taking on such a client. In his day, Newman, Stone had been one of the city's most prestigious partnerships, serving exclusively the wealthy and powerful. But since John took over, the firm had become almost entirely devoted to environmental law. They'd won a successful settlement the previous year against a large chemical firm for illegal dumping, but most of their "paying" clients these days were groups like APPPL—"lost causes," as Viv would call them.

But for John, it was the hopeless cases that were always the most challenging, even if they were the least profitable. Besides, they kept his mind off his personal problems. Nothing like burying yourself in your work to keep away the loneliness—he hadn't been getting all that much sleep anyway.

He hadn't had much luck so far. He'd managed to get a two-week stay in early June on a technicality. But now time was running out. At sundown Sunday, all of the parks and public lands inside the city limits would be turned over to Excelsior.

His latest lead was an old college chum who worked for an appellate court judge, who was supposed to call him back about an injunction. It was a long shot, but when the phone rang, John snapped his pencil in two.

"Hello. Bob? Any luck?"

"John, it's me."

"*Vivian?* Listen, I can't talk right now. I'm waiting for an important call and . . . Wait a minute. Tonight's my night to have Cary, isn't it? When am I supposed to meet you? . . . Oh, my God, six o'clock. That's *fifteen minutes* from now. How am I supposed to . . . Viv, where are you? Something's come up and it may take a while. Could we maybe put it off till later? I'd like to explain, but right now I've got to keep the phone free—"

"That's so typical, John! Your son has disappeared and all you can think about is keeping the damn *phone* free—"

"Get a hold of yourself, Vivian. What I'm working on right now is important. It's . . . Hold on. What do you mean *disappeared?* Where *is* Cary? Isn't he with you?"

"I—I was hoping he was with you, John."

"He's not here, Viv. At least not yet. What happened? When did you see him last?"

"In the subway. We—we had a fight and got separated. Oh, John I'm so worried!"

"In the *subway*? Oh, Viv, how could you . . . Never mind. Listen. Calm down. Relax. Let's take this one thing at a time. Where are you? What happened? When did you see him last? Have you called the police?"

"That's *four* things," Vivian answered. "If you'd just *listen* for a minute, I'll tell you everything!"

"All right. All right. Don't get hysterical—"

"I'm not getting *hysterical*. Listen, John," said Vivian, after a deep sigh, "Cary's been in a strange mood all day. While I was shopping at Macy's he seemed determined to make a nuisance of himself—"

"The way you shop, I'm not surprised—"

"What was that?"

"Nothing. So what happened?"

"I don't know. Before I knew it, he was stalking out of the store and into the subway."

"What did you say to him to set him off like that, Vivian?"

"What did *I*—that's not *important* right now, John. Anyway, by the time I spotted him, he was already on the downtown platform, and when the train pulled out, he was gone. I'm at my office right now."

"On a *Saturday*?"

"People *have* been known to work on weekends, John."

"Touché. But what if he heads back to the brownstone?"

"He *has* a key. And I've been calling ever since I arrived. It's *your* place I'm worried about. What happens if he comes to your apartment and can't get in? Assuming he can *find* it, that is."

"Cary's not a child, Vivian. I'm sure he knows how to take care of himself."

"Unlike his father—"

"What was that? Never mind. There's no problem. I'll call the super and have him call me if—*when* Cary shows up."

"You're not even going to leave the office, are you? I can't *believe* you!"

"All right, Vivian. I'm sorry. You're right. I don't know what I was thinking of. I'm just under a lot off pressure right now—"

"Join the club."

"Huh? Look. It's almost six. I'll get on the phone right now to the super, and I should be at my apartment in about . . . oh, twenty minutes at most. When are you going to be home?"

"I—I have some business to wrap up here, but I should be home by seven at the latest."

"All right. I'll call you then."

"Please do, John. Whether you've heard anything or not."

"I will. I promise. Oh, Viv?"

"Yes, John?"

"Look. Try not to worry. It'll be all right."

"I hope so, John. Good-bye."

"Bye."

John sat in silence for a moment, staring at the phone. Then, flipping open his address book, he punched in the super's number. After a dozen rings, he slammed down the receiver. With a last, guilty glance at the telephone, John picked up his briefcase, shrugged into his raincoat, and rode the elevator to the street, flagging a cab with his tightly furled umbrella.

As the cab battled its way through the traffic that clogged the concrete canyons, John asked himself for the thousandth time where he'd taken a wrong turn. How had the most important things in his life just slipped away from him when he wasn't looking? Ever since his grandmother's death, he'd drifted farther and farther away from his family. Vivian was right; he hadn't been much of a husband and father the past couple of years.

Of course, he had only his own father's example to go on. He'd barely spoken to John outside of mealtimes, spent ten hours a day or more at the office, sent him off to boarding school almost before he could walk. And now John was treating his own family just the way he'd been treated. First he'd lost Vivian.

Now, if his luck held, he might lose his son as well. *Nice work, John,* he told himself. *Nice work.*

VIVIAN DIALED THE apartment again, hung up after fifteen rings. She sat for a moment in silence, listening to the dial tone, watching the lights come on in the city as night fell. Then she heard a sound echoing down the corridor.

"Cary?"

It was coming from Mr. Janos's office. There was no one in the reception area, so she stepped quickly to the door of the inner office. Opening it slightly, she looked in.

Vivian found the opulence of Henry Janos's office overwhelming, with golden silk wallpaper, a splendid Persian carpet, several framed pen-and-ink drawings by fine artists, and what appeared to be lamps of Chinese porcelain. Oddly enough, none of the furnishings showed those subtle signs of wear that antiques usually had. Either Mr. Janos used the best restorers in the business, or they were copies at a level of craftsmanship she thought had been gone for over a century.

The room was empty, but as she looked in, a bell rang, a light glowed, and a small door at the back that she'd always assumed was a washroom slid sideways. Behind was a small elevator car, and in it, Mr. Janos.

"Ah, Vivian!" he said as he stepped from the car. "There you are at last."

Henry Janos was a slim, delicate man with thinning white hair and a close-trimmed goatee that set off a sharp nose and intense gray eyes. He wore an impeccably tailored suit of a conservative cut, carried a gold-handled cane, and walked with a slight limp. Glancing at his gold pocket watch, he spoke again, with just a trace of an accent. "You're a bit later than you promised. I trust you put your time to good use."

"Yes, sir," she said, "only—"

Mr. Janos's expression changed to concern.

"Why, what is it, Vivian? Something's troubling you, isn't it?"

"It's probably nothing, sir. I shouldn't bother you with it—"

"Nonsense. Come. Sit down. Tell me all about it."

She crossed the office, sank gratefully into the chair he offered her. "It's Cary, Mr. Janos."

He frowned for a moment, then brightened. "Ah, yes. Your charming young son. What's happened?"

"We—I lost track of him in the subway, just an hour or so ago. I don't know what's become of him. . . ."

When she'd finished explaining, he nodded in concern. "I understand," he said. "But I don't think you have anything to worry about. If he's anything like you, my dear, I'm sure he's an intelligent and capable young man. I'm certain he'll be all right."

"But he's only *twelve*."

"I wouldn't be too concerned if I were you. Boys are like that, you know. Once in a while they just have to let off a little steam. When I was a youngster I used to roam all over the city myself, uptown and down. He's most likely on his way to his father right now."

Mr. Janos sounded so sure of himself that Vivian found her fears beginning to ebb. That was one of the things she liked best about working for him. He was never at a loss. He always seemed to know what to do. If only John could be more like that. . . .

"You're probably right. I'm sorry I troubled you with it."

"No trouble at all," said Mr. Janos. "Now, let's clear up our own business, and then you can go home. You'll want to get your beauty sleep before the ceremonies tomorrow. You have the report?"

"Yes, sir." She put on her glasses and took the folder with the report out of her bag, glad to have something to take her mind off Cary for a moment. "Right here. I finally found everything we were looking for."

A business associate of Vivian's father, Mr. Janos was one of the city's most successful realtors. Last year he'd been named

Chairman of the Excelsior Corporation, a private consortium created to administer the city's financially troubled parks system. He'd sought Vivian out, just after her breakup with John, and asked for her help on a special project.

The work was part public relations and part research. The public relations part was to put together a blue-chip support group for the corporation. Mr. Janos admitted he was unashamedly making use of her social connections. With her father's political background and her mother's society friends, Vivian had at least a nodding acquaintance with most of the movers and shakers in town. She'd persuaded an impressive roster of VIPs to take part. They'd all be present for the signing ceremonies at the Plaza on the Park restaurant tomorrow evening.

But Mr. Janos seemed even more impressed with her background in urban history. He said that his project was "tailor-made" for her, and had told her more than once how lucky Excelsior was to have such a gifted scholar "on our side." She had to admit his confidence flattered her. Her assignment was to determine clear title to the city's parks and "common lands," the public areas that had been undeveloped since the city's beginnings.

The earliest deed for each parcel of land had to be located and recorded in Excelsior's computerized files before the agreement with the city could officially take effect. It had taken a lot of hard work to find the old records buried in obscure collections and forgotten archives, but she'd finally located the last of them the week before.

"I found the Van Addaam deed on Friday," Vivian announced proudly, glancing down at her report. "You'll never guess where it finally turned up."

"I'm sure I won't," Mr. Janos answered.

"Right here in our own files! There was no record of anyone signing it out from the city archives. It must have gotten misplaced."

"No doubt," said Mr. Janos. "But we have everything now?"

"Yes, sir," she said. "I ran it all through this morning. It's all in the report. There should be no problems with the transfer."

"Wonderful, Vivian. I knew I could count on you. I have some people to show this to," he said, holding up the report. "Did you have time to make copies?"

"Oh, no," she answered. "With—with everything that's been going on, I forgot."

"Quite understandable. Just give me the original, and I'll arrange to have them made." Vivian handed him the printouts, and he scanned them intently. "This is excellent work, Vivian. However did you get it done so quickly?"

Vivian smiled a small smile of pride. "I have to confess I took a shortcut, Mr. Janos. I made a copy of the master file onto a microdisk and worked on it on my personal computer at home."

Mr. Janos rose suddenly from his chair, steadying himself on his cane. "You *what*? But that information is confidential! No one has the access codes except—" He fell silent. "That was very resourceful of you, Vivian," he said at last, "but I'm afraid I'll have to ask you to turn that disk over to me. Just as a precaution, you understand." He held out his hand.

"Of course, Mr. Janos," she answered in surprise. She wondered what she'd said to upset him. She'd never seen him so agitated before. "It's right here," she said, fishing in her bag for the disk. She was certain she'd put it in the bag this morning. But now there was no sign of it.

"I don't understand it," said Vivian, dumping the contents of her purse on his desk without thinking. He recoiled from the clutter as if it were alive. Then she began to methodically transfer it all back. Lipstick, keys, compact, aspirin, nail file, building pass, pencil stub, tissues, matches, wallet, two pennies. But no disk. "It's gone!"

"What do you mean it's gone?" Janos demanded. "You must have left it at home."

Vivian shook her head. "No. I put it in my bag when I left

home this morning. Then I . . . *Cary!*"

"What on earth do you mean?"

"Cary has it! It fell out of my bag in the store. Cary picked it up!"

Mr. Janos turned pale. "How could you be so—" Then he stopped, took a deep breath, and smiled a thin, tight-lipped smile. "Well," he said at last, "it looks like we have more than one good reason to find your boy. You'd better go home now and see if you can reach your husband. I'd appreciate it if you could call me as soon as you locate him."

"Of course, Mr. Janos, but . . ." She couldn't understand why the disk was so important to him.

"Good. Now let me call you a car."

"Oh, but I couldn't, Mr. Janos."

"Nonsense. The sooner you've located your son, the better we'll all feel. And besides," he said with a strange smile, "I imagine you've had enough of subways for one day, eh, Vivian?"

As SHE RODE home in the back of a company limousine, Vivian felt a sudden pang of fear. Suppose Mr. Janos was wrong. Suppose something *had* happened to Cary. Then what would she do?

It was dark as the car pulled up at the steps of the brownstone. The driver held the door for her and offered to take her packages up, but she refused. There was a light on in the top-floor window, though Vivian thought she'd turned them all off. She hurried up the stairs, unlocking the locks as fast as her hands could manage, calling out, "Cary! I'm home!"

There was no answer.

SEVEN

"QUICK! THIS way!"

Through the tangle of Badmashers' boots all around him, Cary spotted Allie waving frantically at him from under a wooden table covered with a drab drape, heaped with faded remnants of fabric. Then, as the woman who ran the stand returned, Allie disappeared.

Lowering his head, Cary butted through the Badmashers, tumbling forward in a somersault that caused them to crack heads as they dove for him, and barreling under the drape into the cool darkness beneath the table.

"That was close!" said Cary. "What do we do now? We'll never get to Time Square at this rate. . . ."

"*Sh!*" Allie whispered. A pair of black boots neared the table and stopped within inches of them. "Get ready to run!"

"Have you by any chance seen a couple of Scamps?" The 'Masher's voice was low, quiet, without a trace of emotion.

"Scamps?" said the fabric seller. "Scamps? No, no I can't say as I have seen any Scamps, no. Can't say as I have. Of course, my eyesight isn't what it—"

There was a choking sound, then a silence. Cary saw the tiny feet of the old woman lift off the ground.

"Have you by any chance seen a couple of Scamps?" the 'Masher asked again in the same low voice. There was a thump as the old woman's heels hit the ground.

"All right! I'll tell you. They're—they're under the table!"

"Now!" said Allie, and was off on her hands and knees, scuttling like a crab under the tables. Cary followed as best he could, dodging the black boot tips that kicked and prodded under the drape.

He ached from a half-dozen new punches and bruises, and one knee was badly scraped. Every time it moved forward it dragged on the rough stone, causing him to wince, and he kept hitting his head on the bottoms of the tables. But he bit his lower lip and kept up with Allie as she scrambled from table to table, dodging between baskets, boxes, and jars in the open spaces.

At last, she stopped short, under a fishmonger's stall, which dripped chill, briny water. "I know it's around here someplace," she said over her shoulder. Then, moments later, she cried in triumph, "I knew it! Here we are!"

"Where?" asked Cary dubiously.

Without answering, Allie moved out of the way, and Cary could see a small semicircular iron door set in the wall. Fishing a jackknife out of her overalls, Allie pried up the rusted handle in the middle, wrapped three fingers around it, and yanked. It didn't budge. She tugged again. It still didn't move. Heavy footsteps were drawing near.

"Don't just gawk, help!" said Allie. Cary put his arm about her waist, and pulled back as she tugged. The door started to move.

He pulled again. The crack widened. A third yank and the door swung open. Absolute blackness yawned beyond, and a sultry breeze stirred Cary's hair.

"After you, kid," said Allie. "It's a kind of shortcut. The 'Mashers won't dare follow us down *there*." Cary wasn't sure he liked the sound of that.

"How do you *find* all these places, Allie?" he asked.

"I'm part rat, on my father's side. Now get *in*, willya? They're getting *closer*."

He could hear the 'Mashers' shrill whistles only yards away. Brushing away the cobwebs, he sat down at the edge of the opening, lowering himself down with his hands.

There was nothing under him.

Cary flailed about, then one foot felt a metal rung set into the wall. Swinging about, he wedged his other foot into it, and gripped another firmly with both his hands. A powerful updraft was coming from below, bringing a breath of hot air with it, but it was too dark to see how far down the shaft went. The sound of a table falling came from above, and a moment later the clang of the closing door. He nerved himself for the descent.

"Ow!" Cary yelled as Allie's shoe stepped onto his hand. "Why don't you watch where you're going?"

"Why don't *you* keep it moving?" Allie shouted back.

"Okay, okay! Don't rush me!" Cary had never really liked heights. At camp last summer he'd been the only one of the guys who'd chickened out when they dared him to walk along the edge of the old reservoir. A lucky thing, too. Two of his friends had lost their footing and nearly drowned. One of them ended up with a broken arm. For a moment he pictured his body twisted and broken. Then, gritting his teeth, Cary started down.

To his surprise, the air grew hotter as he descended, and his breath grew shorter. He could feel blisters beginning on his palms. His hands were slick with sweat, and he kept losing his grip. But the clank of Allie's tread kept shaking the ladder, so he lowered himself as fast as he could.

Then there was no rung under his feet. He panicked for a moment, then his heel hit ridged metal, and a moment later he was standing on solid ground. Well, not *solid*. A long iron catwalk stretched across the bottom of the shaft, with gaps between the slats almost wide enough for his foot to slip through. It ended in a steep metal staircase with steps that spiraled down and out of sight.

Cary felt a wave of vertigo as he peered hesitantly over the low railing, as if the stout cast-iron bars that held him were about to melt out from under him. But Allie was already plunging down the endless flight, so Cary hurried after her.

"UH, ALLIE, COULD we maybe stop for a while?"

It seemed like they'd been descending for hours. It was hot and dusty and dry, and in the shadows small shapes scuttled about. Every so often there were broad landings with great iron doors marked with cryptic legends and lit by flickering gaslights. Cary wondered where they led. But Allie just kept on going, down and turn, down and turn.

"What's the matter?" Allie panted. "You ain't gettin' *tired*, are you?"

All of a sudden it was all too much for Cary. "Tired? Why should I be tired? Just because I've gotten beaten up two—no, *three* times today, and walked and run a hundred times farther today than I have in my whole *life*, and haven't had anything to eat for hours and hours but a moldy old bowl of soup, you think I'm *tired*?" He sank suddenly to the step where he stood and sat down. "Yeah," he said quietly. "You're damn right I'm tired."

To his surprise, Allie sat down beside him. "So am I," she said, mopping her brow with her bandanna. "How 'bout some lunch?"

From the depths of her pockets, Allie pulled out a plum, a pear, a small loaf of dark bread, two dill pickles, and a large, grubby hunk of cheddar cheese. Cary's mouth watered.

"Well, dig in!" said Allie impatiently.

Cary didn't have to be told twice. After scarfing down some bread and cheese and quenching his thirst with the pear, Cary looked up to see that she'd finished off the rest.

"Thanks," said Cary. "But if you were just as tired and hungry as me, how come you didn't say anything before?"

"What? And let a creampuff like you think I was some kind of wilting lily? No way."

"Who are you calling a creampuff, you, you—"

"Easy, easy," said Allie. "I ain't *blamin'* you for bein' a creampuff. It's not your fault. You just ain't no street kid. You never had no hard knocks in life, that's all. I mean, even the Poet says you're from some fancy Uptown place."

"I am not a creampuff!" said Cary. "And besides, what do you call having your mom and dad split up and your favorite great-grandmother die out from under you and your house sold and being forced to live in a crummy old city with no friends and nothing to do? If that isn't hard knocks, I don't know what is!"

"What the hell are *you* complaining about?" snapped Allie. "You think you've got it so tough. At least you *had* a mother and a father and a home and a goddamn great-grandmother and all. There's kids in this world who never even *knew* their mothers, y'know. There's kids who grow up with never enough to eat and their brothers and sisters crying for more while their old man is out drinking up the weeks pay—"

"Like you, for instance?"

"Like me, for instance. You want to make something of it?"

"No," said Cary. "But there are also kids in the world whose moms scream at them one day for being a kid and the next day for being too grown-up, whose dads look right through them sometimes like they aren't even there, who walk out on them just because of some stupid fight—"

"Like *you* for instance?"

"Like me. I remember my dad forgot my birthday two years

in a row, and then the third time, when we'd made plans to have this big party, he didn't even come home that night—"

"I get it," said Allie. "Cheatin' on the old lady, huh?"

"Huh? Oh, no, it was his damn work. I remember my mom used to say that she sometimes wished it was another woman. That she could deal with."

"There was some nights I wished *my* old man wouldn't come home," said Allie. "Nights when he'd lost another day job and didn't have no money and was feeling so bad he'd hit us across the face if we said anything to him, would look at all those hungry mouths and curse the day we was born."

"What happened to your mother, Allie? Why couldn't she help?"

"I dunno. Sometimes I think I remember her, when I was real little, being held and sung to and all. But she died when I was just a baby, so it might've been my older sister. She took care of us for a while, but she got out as soon as she could, when the drinking and the beatings got too much for her."

"Well, how did you end up here?"

"I'm not sure, really. One night the old man comes home roarin' and ragin' and stinkin' of cheap booze, and before I says a word, he's knocked me halfway across the room. Next morning I woke up in Scamps' Allie. And one by one the little ones came to me, all kids that needed someone to look out for them, like I needed someone to look out for me."

"Sometimes I wish my dad *had* hauled off and hit me or something—"

"You don't know what you're talkin' about!"

"No, I mean *any* reaction would have been better than that blank stare of his. I did everything I could to make him notice me. I worked real hard in school, made the soccer team, got a lead in the school play, but he never came to any of it, never said a word.

"After a while I got to where I didn't care anymore. *Then* he noticed. I could tell he was mad at me, but he never did anything about it, like yelling or anything. No. Getting mad was my mom's department."

"Oh, I get it," said Allie. "Your *mom* was the one that gave you all them bruises, huh?"

"No, it wasn't like that. But when she was mad enough, she could figure out all kinds of things to say to twist you all up inside." Thinking about it brought all the hurt feelings back again, and Cary felt the tears welling up in his eyes again. He wiped them roughly away.

"Hey. Don't start *cryin'* on me now, for pete's sake," said Allie in a softer tone. "I guess what they did to you must have hurt pretty bad, in its own way."

Cary looked up in surprise. "Yeah. Yeah it did. Real bad. But not like being *hit* or anything."

"Oh, you get used to that after a while," said Allie. "You've got to. You can't let 'em ruin your whole life. Anyway, I take back what I said about you bein' a creampuff. You may not have had it as bad as me, but you got plenty of scars yourself—even if most of 'em are on the inside."

"I guess we all do," said Cary.

"Maybe so," said Allie. "Now let's get movin'. We got a long ways to cover."

"I thought you said this was a *short*cut," said Cary.

"It is. It's just a sort of a—a *long* shortcut is all."

And with that, she was up on her feet and starting down the stairs.

FEET PROPPED UP on the broad steel desk in his command center, Miles Brand drew deeply on his slim cigar and exhaled, watching its pale smoke drift slowly upward. For the first time since the Gnomes of Wall Street had chosen him to lead their takeover of Down Town, something had gone wrong. A little thing, perhaps, but then Brand had not gotten where he was through inattention to detail.

Someone had dared to resist him, to defy him openly—a mere street urchin. It was unheard of! After the incident, Brand had returned to headquarters, determined to find out just who this child was.

Now he turned his chrome-steel chair to face the full-length mirror behind his desk. Grasping the star-shaped pendant about his neck, he watched as the mirror clouded, then turned smoky gray. A moment later it began to darken, re-forming in the image of a great, glowing crimson eye that shimmered like an infernal furnace.

"Ah! Commander Brand. What can I do for you?" a deep voice rumbled from everywhere.

"I seek information on the identity and whereabouts of a certain boy, last seen in the South Sector of Lazy Fair, in the company of an unidentified Scamp."

"Is this a priority request?" the voice echoed.

"If necessary. I have reason to believe it may be important."

"As you wish."

There was a whirring noise, and then silence. Brand waited impatiently. When the Gnomes of Wall Street chose him to implement their plan to take over Down Town, they gave him access to all of their most advanced devices and discoveries, including Zenovac, the mechanical brain that ran their subterranean empire. Zenovac knew virtually everything that went on in Down Town. But it was also a stickler for protocol and detail, a trait that often tried Brand's patience.

"I have no record of any such individual in Down Town," Zenovac announced at last.

"Are you sure there's no such person?"

"I didn't say there was no such person." Zenovac corrected. *"Only that there is no record of such a person in Down Town. The individual in question is not a Down Towner at all. He's from Uptown."*

"But that's impossible," thundered Brand.

"No," answered Zenovac quietly. *"Just highly improbable."*

"Can you identify the boy?" asked Brand.

"Yes," said Zenovac.

Brand sighed. *"Will you identify the boy?"*

"Certainly." The mirror dimmed for a moment, then a still image of the boy appeared. *"The boy's name is Cary Newman. His companion is called Allie. She is a leader of a street gang known as the Scamps."*

Brand nodded. He'd had dealings with those guttersnipes before. "How did he get here?"

"Insufficient data," said Zenovac. *"A fluke. A fluctuation. A discontinuity. An inside job, perhaps."*

"How was he able to resist the power of the Telesm?"

The Telesm was the star-shaped control device the Gnomes had given him to help him carry out their plans. It had never failed Brand before; anyone he used it on obeyed him completely. Yet the boy had been able to throw off its effects almost without effort.

"He carries with him a metallic disk. According to my calculations, the disk has sufficient power not only to interfere with the operation of the Telesm, but to endanger the planned takeover of Down Town as well."

"What?" cried Brand. "But you assured me the odds of a disruption in the plan were a million to one."

"That is correct," said Zenovac. *"And Cary Newman is that one. Whoever possesses that disk holds Down Town's future in his hands. If you wish the plan to succeed, you must have that disk; otherwise, there is a small but distinct possibility it will be used against you."*

"Then I will need total surveillance," said Brand.

"That is a Priority One Order," Zenovac replied. *"A request of this magnitude will require personal authorization from Grand Kobold Van Damm."*

The Telesm allowed Brand's mirror to display whatever was seen by any reflective surface in Down Town—glass, metal, even polished stone. Only the Freeholds, those areas not yet under his control, and the Squares, those chaotic green areas devoid of any finished surfaces, were outside the range of the mirror.

But total surveillance required a considerable amount of

Zenovac's attention, causing other functions to be curtailed.
That meant Brand would have to make a request directly to the
Grand Kobold himself—a task he was not looking forward to.

"Very well," said Brand. "I'll get it. But for now, continue
monitoring on an emergency basis, on my authority."

"As you wish," said Zenovac. *"There is one more datum you should
know, Brand, even though you did not specifically request it."*

"What is it?"

*"There is a matter of Time involved here. Each hour that Cary Newman
and the disk are out of your hands, the odds of disruption to the plan grow
rapidly greater. You have perhaps twelve hours at most to find the boy
before the risk becomes too great to be controlled."* Then the burning
eyes vanished from the mirror, leaving only Brand's reflection.

Brand sat in brooding silence. He'd worked so long and
planned so carefully for this moment. And now one mere child
threatened to disrupt everything he'd accomplished. There was
no alternative. The boy must be neutralized, no matter what the
cost.

DOWN AND TURN, down and turn, down and turn. Cary had tried
to keep count of the steps for a while, or even the landings, but
he always seemed to lose track. Ahead of him Allie marched
along stolidly, never showing any sign of tiring. After they'd
been walking for so long that Cary had begun to fall into a sort
of trance, he noticed that it had gradually gotten a whole lot
warmer.

"Getting hot," Cary panted.

"Yup," said Allie. Then, relenting, she added, "We're nearly
there now. You'll see," as if that explained everything.

After a few more minutes, Cary was so warm that he had to
take off his jacket and knot it about his waist. His shirt was
soaked with sweat, and the hairs on the back of his neck were
plastered down. The air smelled like burnt sulfur, and shimmered as it rose off the hot metal.

At the bottom of the next flight of stairs was a large iron door painted fire-engine red. Grabbing the handle with her bandanna, Allie swung the door wide.

A breeze as steamy as a July day before a thunderstorm ruffled Cary's hair. Behind them, the door closed tightly in a high stone wall. Before them was a broad red-brick street so hot Cary could feel the heat of the stones through the soles of his sneakers. Above, where the sky should be, was a huge ceiling of red stone, supported by thick brick columns. Across the street was a high brick wall broken by a massive iron gate. Over the gate was a sign in giant metal letters that read HELL'S KITCHEN.

"Uh, say, Allie," said Cary hesitantly. "Are you *sure* this is where we want to be?"

"You mean *that*?" she answered, jerking her thumb at the sign. "Don't pay that no mind. They just call it that to scare people away. C'mon." And with that she was crossing the street, whistling slightly out of tune.

EIGHT

"**J**UST WHERE IN hell do you two think you're goin'?" said a voice at Cary's ear.

Leaning against the gate, arms folded over an oversized belly, was a red-haired young man in loose wool trousers and a sweat-stained sleeveless undershirt. A tweed cap was pulled down low over his eyes, and his nose looked like it had been broken more than once. Stuck in his belt was a stout cudgel of dark wood. As Allie drew near the gate, the youth stepped in front of her.

"Not so fast, m'girl," he said, dropping a hand on Allie's shoulder. "There's no one gets into Hell's Kitchen without my say-so. That's the Kingpin's orders."

"I ain't nobody's girl," said Allie, slapping his hand away, "and I don't need nobody's say-so, 'specially *yours,* pig-face."

Bad choice of words, thought Cary as he caught up with her. Although the sentry was barely her height, he outweighed Allie at least three to one.

A hand as big as a picnic ham grabbed Allie's arm. "Pig-face, is it?" he said with a malicious grin. "Is that any way to be talkin' to your own true sweetheart?" As Cary watched with horror, he pulled Allie close, pressing himself against her. "Now, be a good girl and give us a kiss," he said, closing his eyes and puckering up.

"Here's your kiss, lard-lips!" said Allie, belting him hard across the face. As the sentry howled and clutched his jaw, Allie drove her knee between his legs and her two fists hard into his gut, doubling him over and dropping him to his knees.

"What're you *doing*?" said Cary.

"Teaching porky here some manners!" said Allie. "C'mon, butter-buns. Stand up and fight like a man!"

"But he's six times your size, Allie!" said Cary. "Come on! Let's get out of here while we're still in one piece!"

*"Butter-*buns!" roared the sentry, struggling to his feet. There was a trickle of blood from his nose, and he sort of wobbled when he walked, but the look in his eyes was pure hellfire. "Why you little . . . PJ! Brian! On the double!" he shouted. From a side street came a half-dozen more toughs, some carrying broken bottles and broomsticks. Cary noticed with a shudder that the backs of their shirts were embroidered with the word "Hellions." A moment later, they were surrounded.

"What's goin' on, Jack?" said the oldest of the newcomers, a wiry fellow with just a hint of a moustache. "More of Brand's spies?"

"I caught these two sneakin' in, Brian," said the fat one. "When I tried to stop 'em, this one here starts beatin' up on me!"

"Her?" said Brian with a nasty laugh. *"That* skinny little bit o' business? Why she couldn't hurt no one, least of all a big fella like you!"

"Oh, yeah?" said Allie, stepping forward. "You're talkin' about a *Scamp*, ya know. We eat guys like you for *breakfast*—"

"Allie," began Cary, "I don't think this is such a good idea. . . ."

"Stay out of this, Cary," she said.

"A Scamp, huh?" said Jack. "Well, I hear yer all a bunch of weak-kneed wet-pants—"

"*That* did it!" said Allie, rolling up her sleeves. "Porkchops comin' up!"

"*Allieeeee!*" cried Cary, trying to hold her back. The next thing he knew, she'd thrown herself at fat Jack, butting him hard in the stomach with her head. He gasped, clutching his gut in agony, and the others were staring at each other in astonishment. Cary could see his tiny mind struggling with the situation. Then he was charging her like a wounded water buffalo.

Before he could stop himself, Cary had snatched a broomstick from the nearest of the toughs and swung it with a loud *crack* against Jack's dense skull. Cary stared down in shock at the stick in his hands. *What am I doing?* he thought. Jack stopped short, then swung around to Cary, his face turning purple.

"*Don't anybody move!*" Cary shouted in his deepest, most grown-up voice. To his surprise, everybody froze. *Now* what was he going to do?

Allie just stood there gaping at him. "Run!" Cary whispered. She hesitated just a moment, then tore off down the street. A couple of the gang members started after her.

"Hold it right there!" Cary barked. The stick had dropped from his hands, and he found himself digging deep into his pockets desperately for something, *anything*, that might be of use. His hand closed on the disk, and he held it high over his head. "*One more step and you're all dead!*" To Cary's astonishment it worked. The gang stepped back a pace. All eyes were on him. Sweat was pouring down his back and sides. Cary glanced about him. Allie was nowhere in sight.

"That's better," said Cary. "You know what this *is*, don't

you?" he asked, trying to sound and look like a crazed, wild-eyed maniac. Nobody moved. "Now if everybody stays *real* still, nobody'll get hurt. This thing's got a hair trigger, and there's no telling what will set it off."

Cary started edging away from them, moving the disk so it flashed in their faces. He began backing up, faster and faster. Brian and Jack started whispering to each other and shaking their heads. *So far, so good,* thought Cary, who was now running backward and trying not to trip.

"Hey! Wait a minute!" said Brian at last. Cary spun around and broke into a run. He could hear them close behind him. He pushed over a pile of boxes, hoping it would slow them down, but he didn't dare look back to find out.

At the far end of the lane was an open gate, painted with the words "Hell Mall." Cary dashed through, swinging around to push the heavy wooden bolt in place with all his might. The latch fell into place with a bone-jolting shock. Fists started pounding on the slats, but Cary soon left the sound far behind.

Cary caught up with Allie a few blocks ahead. She was seated on a wooden horse-watering trough, her hair damp and matted, her shoulders heaving as she struggled to catch her breath. When she saw him coming, she gave him a sullen look.

"What was the big idea of buttin' in on my fight?" she demanded. "You tryin' to be a hero or somethin'?"

"Get serious, Allie," said Cary. "That guy was *huge*. And there were a half-dozen more just like him. I thought he was going to *kill* you!"

"I've had worse odds," said Allie, in a tone that didn't sound very convincing. "Anyway, why didn't you run when you had the chance? You could've got away easy in all that ruckus."

"But I couldn't just leave you there to get *stomped*," Cary protested.

"Why not?" said Allie sharply.

"Because I . . . It just wouldn't be right, that's all," said Cary. He didn't understand what she was so sore about.

Allie shook her head. "I can't figure your angle," she said. "What's with you?"

"I just didn't want to see you get hurt, Allie. How come you rescued me from Brand and the 'Mashers?"

"That was different," said Allie. "I thought you was a Scamp. That's family."

"Well, what about the second time? With the melons?"

"I dunno. 'Cause you were outnumbered. You couldn't handle it yourself. Besides, I gave my word."

"Well, it's the same thing. You were—"

"Don't even think it. Now you listen here. I can handle myself. I don't need nobody to help me or look out for me or fight my fights for me, you hear?"

"Fine! Fine and dandy! Next time I'll just let some guy slobber all over you, let a dozen thugs pound you into the ground."

"Next time! What makes you think there's gonna *be* a next time? Or that you'll be any use if there is?"

Cary exploded. "Now *you* listen for a change! I don't much like getting into fights or anything. In fact, if there's a way I can get out of it, I will. But I thought I handled myself pretty well there. And considering the fix you were in, I think you ought to be grateful I figured out a way to get you out of it. I don't expect a *medal,* but a little thanks might be nice."

"Now wait just a minute—"

"No, *you* wait," said Cary. "I don't know what's eating you, Allie. Maybe you can't take the thought that somebody else besides you cares what happens to you. Well, if that's the way you feel about it, it's okay by me. I'll just find my way out of here by myself." And he started walking away slowly.

"Hold on! You ain't goin' nowhere without me," said Allie, pushing herself to her feet. Cary stopped, waiting. There was silence, then she frowned, and gave a funny little half smile.

"I gotta admit, you took care of yourself pretty good there," she said grudgingly. "I s'pose I *was* just a little outnumbered, and that stunt of yours was pretty quick thinkin'. Beginner's luck, probably." She clapped him roughly on the shoulder. "You're okay, kid. I guess you ain't a total loss after all." Cary shook his head. Coming from her, he guessed that was quite a compliment.

"Thanks, Allie," said Cary, a smile starting on his face.

"Don't go *thankin'* me all the time," said Allie. "We ain't got you home yet."

THE HEAT WAS relentless as Cary followed Allie through the cobbled streets. On every corner was a bright lamp that flared with a hissing roar, filling the air with a tangerine-colored glow like the last minutes of sunset.

Every so often, Allie glanced about her with a puzzled expression, like she was lost, but as soon as she saw Cary watching, she'd stride confidently on ahead. Finally, Cary asked, "Are you sure you know where we're going?"

"Sure, I'm sure," she answered breezily.

"Have you ever been here before?"

"Not exactly," she said, "but all these places are a snap once you get the hang of 'em." That didn't sound very reassuring.

There were row upon row of narrow lanes packed with narrow buildings of a dozen different styles that looked as if they'd been put together like a child's building blocks. Here was a once-elegant town house next to a ramshackle old shanty held together with tin and tar paper. There, a little chapel, barely wide enough for a bride and groom, was wedged in between a dilapidated saloon and a billiard parlor. Winding steps, bridges, and alleyways joined everything together, and in the courtyards between the buildings and on the rooftops above was a profusion of green, as if gardens had run riot.

Every stoop and stairstep, street corner and storefront, balcony and back porch, was filled with people, laughing and chattering, haggling and arguing, about a dozen different things. Almost everyone was thin, from the oldest to toddlers. Their clothes were old-fashioned, threadbare and patched, and their shoes (those who wore them at all) were scuffed and worn. And more than a usual number of people had scars and limps and other deformities. It was hard to keep from staring at them.

After a while, Cary noticed that people were staring back. Whenever they passed, people stopped what they were doing, and looked at them with hard, suspicious glances.

"Why's everybody looking at us like that, Allie?" he asked.

"You heard what that goon at the gate said about Brand's spies, didn't ya? They probably don't much trust outsiders these days. Can you blame 'em?"

A few blocks later, Allie suddenly stopped, nose in the air. On a nearby wall was a painted sign that read BAKER STREET, and, underneath it in smaller letters, THE STREET THAT LEADS TO THE PIE WOMAN.

"That's more like it," said Allie. "C'mon." As they followed the street, Allie inhaled deeply and said, "Taste that air! Smells like it's baked, don't it?" Seeing Cary's bewildered expression, she said, "Hell's Kitchen's known for two things: the toughest kids and the best eats. See what I mean?"

Ahead of them was a long residential street with dozens of identical brick row houses facing each other. There was a tantalizing scent in the air, and from the end of the street, Cary could hear the jingling of a bell. As the sound drew closer, Cary made out a young man in a white cap and apron wheeling a pushcart with a sign on it that read

SIMON'S PIES
All Homemade

THERE'S NOTHING SIMPLE ABOUT 'EM!

At each house the cart passed, a door or window would open and someone, usually a young woman in an apron, would emerge with a tray of hot pies. The man would look the pies

over, occasionally tasting a bit of blueberry or cherry that had
dripped over the edge, then hand the baker a few coins and a
stack of empty pie plates on a tray, and start off again to the
jingling of bells. The scent of the hot pies was heady, and Cary's
stomach twisted a bit in hunger.

"Look!" said Allie a moment later. "Now's our chance!" At
one of the houses, a pretty young girl came out, smiling and
blushing, her hands twisted behind her back. After a moment's
conversation, she invited the young pie man in, leaving his cart
unattended in the street. Cary took one look at Allie's face and
knew immediately what was on her mind.

"Allie, *no*!" he cried. But it was too late. She was heading for
the cart, full steam ahead. The cart was laden with luscious-
looking pies and tarts—cherry, apple, lemon meringue and
huckleberry, chocolate custard and coconut cream, mince,
quince, strawberry rhubarb, and banana. By the time Cary
reached her, her face was smeared with berries.

"Allie, you can't—" She shoved a slice in his face. Suddenly
his mouth was filled with hot pie. It was blueberry. It was delicious. He bit into it shamelessly, getting purple juice all over his
shirt. Then he heard a shriek. "Help! Help! Someone's stealing
my pies!"

"Let's get movin'!" said Allie. "Push, willya?"

She'd jumped up onto the front of the pie wagon and was
waving at him frantically. A rolling pin sailed past Cary's ear,
striking Allie on the side of the head. "Ow!" she yelped.
"C'mon, *push*!"

Wondering how one person could stir up so much trouble in
such a short time, he started pushing the cart up the slight grade
of the street. It was hard at first, but then the cart began to pick
up speed.

A nearby doorway flew open. An old man in a white cap
popped out, shaking his fist and shying pie plates at them with
deadly aim. Behind them, a chorus of voices was yelling, "Stop!
Pie thief! Stop!"

At the end of the street, Allie suddenly hopped down, grabbing the handle of the cart from Cary and swinging it around, starting it rolling toward the bakers. With screams and squeals, they scattered out of its path, and Allie and Cary ducked out of sight down a side street.

It was a dead end.

A group of baker women were approaching with mayhem in their eyes.

"Allie, quick!" shouted Cary, pointing at the metal ladder of a nearby fire escape that hung just out of reach. "Give me a hand!" After a couple of jumps and two pairs of hands pulling, the ladder swung down to the street. Cary scurried up, with Allie following after, pulling the ladder up behind them. Three flights later, they were on the rooftop and away.

They made rapid time as they dashed across the rooftops. By the time they'd reached the next street, the cries and whistles had died away in the distance. As Cary hung, panting, on the high wall about the roof, he looked over to see Allie doing the same. She looked a fright, covered with half a dozen different kinds of pies, and a drop of whipped cream on her nose.

She looked so ridiculous, Cary found himself shaking with laughter.

"What's so funny?" she demanded.

"You!" gasped Cary, barely able to speak.

"Well, you're a pretty picture yourself!" said Allie with a smile. A moment later they were both laughing hysterically, pointing at each other and pounding each other's backs. Cary's sides were starting to hurt. As he finally got his chuckling under control, he realized that it had been ages since he'd felt this alive, this—*happy.*

A short while later, they clambered down a little winding staircase from the rooftop to the street and found themselves at a treelined mall that led up to a steep hill.

Cary's eyes opened in wonder. A grass-covered knoll, rounded, like a beehive or a loaf of bread, rose up right in the middle of the brick-lined streets. From the mall where they stood, a narrow double path appeared to wind round and round it up to the top and back down again. A hanging sign near the gate in the low fence read SYLLIE HILL.

"See, I *told* you I knew where I was goin'," said Allie with a wave of her hand. "Start climbin', Cary. It's a long ways up to the top."

CARY'S LEGS WERE killing him as they neared the top of the hill, and he was feeling dizzy, too. It was partly from all the turnings, round and round the green hill. But the smell of the tall grasses and wildflowers that grew on the hill's side made him feel kind of dreamy and distant, like he wasn't quite all there. It didn't seem to have much effect on Allie though.

The path ended at the hill's flattened top in a wide courtyard. In its midst was a slender oak tree in full leaf. As Cary drew near, a hot breeze stirred his hair, and the leaves began to rustle. Again, in that soft sound, Cary thought he heard a voice calling his name, and the world began to spin slowly around him.

"Hey! Wake up!" said Allie. Cary rubbed his eyes and the dizziness disappeared.

Beyond was a great, rambling building built of rough-hewn stone overgrown with ivy and creepers and flowering vines. It had balconies and battlements and buttresses and towers and turrets and eaves, and windows of all shapes and sizes were stuck in odd places all over it. From its long, pointed rooftop dozens of thick stone chimneys bristled into the air like the quills of a porcupine, and were lost in their own aromatic mists of smoke and steam.

The pathway reached the building at a pair of enormous doors carved of dark wood and chased with beaten brass. A pattern of dogs, birds, and leaves zigzagged in and out like braided rope. Above the door, the words "Syllie Hall" were carved in odd letters that seemed half uppercase and half lowercase.

Cary could hear music playing and laughter ringing faintly from behind the doors. He was about to open one when they swung open and two brawling lads tumbled out, rolling and punching. Before the doors could swing shut again, he and Allie had slipped inside.

It was a tavern. The roof was high, braced with massive rafters covered with the same wild carvings as the door, crisscrossed with long timbers dangling chandeliers ablaze with candles. The floor was covered in sawdust and filled with long tables, where men and women ate, drank, and sang, toasting one another with upraised glasses, splashing one another as they did.

At the near end of the room was a grand oak bar with mirrored panels reflecting row upon row of bottles filled with liquids of every color. Below the bar was a long brass rail crowded with customers, all men, who chomped on fat cigars and spat into brass spittoons.

A burly bouncer with bared forearms, suspenders, a waxed moustache, and derby glared over in their direction as they entered. But there was a crash from the bar, and he turned away, giving them time to slip into the crowd.

Before a stone fireplace that blazed brightly, a group of musicians started a skirling reel, and couples began dancing to the music, legs flashing and skirts flying. They seemed to take as much delight in knocking one another over as in moving about the floor. Cary had to dodge them more than once as he and Allie threaded their way through the tables. They were nearly sloshed by a tipsy gent carrying a tray full of glasses of foaming ale.

"Why'n'cha look where you're goin'!" said Allie. Cary pulled her out of the way just in time to see him pitch forward to the floor. A passing dancer caught his tray as he fell, but otherwise nobody seemed to notice much.

"Disgustin'," said Allie, shaking her head. But Cary wasn't listening. Walking down the middle of a nearby table, carrying plates and salt and gravy and such back and forth were more of the Little People he'd seen in Lazy Fair. Most of them wore little white chef's hats or maid's bonnets. As Cary watched, one of them was knocked off a passing tray into a gravy boat. There was a chorus of laughter as he hauled himself out indignantly and washed himself off in a glass of water, drying himself carefully with a linen napkin. But Cary didn't have time to watch further, because Allie was pushing through a pair of swinging doors at the end of the room, motioning with her head for Cary to follow.

NINE

A BLAST OF STEAM hit Cary in the face, and he heard a thousand clatters, splashes, and clinks make an ocean of sound. He saw flashes of brightly burnished copper and brass and steel in the bright light of kerosene lamps, smelled soap and scouring powder, and felt the gurgle of pipes under his feet.

He and Allie were in a vast white-tiled room lined with shelves and cabinets and tables on one side and rows of sinks on the other. Dozens of young people, his age or younger, wearing white aprons, short-sleeved jackets, and little white caps, moved dishes to and fro in a frenzy.

"You, there!" shouted a tall young fellow in the center of the room. "What are you standing around for? Get those dishes over here, on the double!" Cary suddenly realized he was talking to *him*!

"Didn't you hear me? Now get moving before I . . . *Allie*!"

"Chester, ol' buddy!" said Allie. "Long time no see! How you been?"

"Allie, what are you *doing* here?" said Chester, glancing about nervously.

"We got 'Mashers on our tail, Chester," said Allie. "We came down here to try to shake 'em."

"Quick! Get over here in the corner, before somebody sees you!" Then his gaze returned to Cary. "I thought I told you to—"

"It's okay. Take it easy, Chester," said Allie. "That's Cary. He's with me."

"With *you*?" asked Chester. "Well, okay. Get him out of sight, too. Just a second." He turned to a young boy at one of the sinks. "How many times do I have to tell you, Freddy? It's *soak, wash, rinse*! You're getting suds in the cream pitchers!"

"I'm sorry, Chester," said the boy. "I forgot!"

"You forgot!" mocked Chester. "I ought to make a lesson out of you, put you on pots and pans for a month. Just be glad Eisenglas didn't catch you. Now hop to it!"

"Look, Chet," said Allie, "if this ain't a good time to talk, we can come back later. Just point us to the eats."

"You don't understand, Allie," said Chester, looking nervously over his shoulder. "Things have changed. You can't just—"

"What's eatin' you, Chester?" said Allie. "You're actin' like you're scared or somethin'."

"Scared?" said Chester. "Listen, Allie. You'd be scared, too, if you had the Eye breathing down your neck all the time."

"Who's the Eye?" asked Cary.

Chester's voice dropped to a whisper. "MacFinn's brought in a new chef, and he's been making life a nightmare around here. Eisenglas his name is. But we all call him the Eye."

"How come?"

"I hope you never find out, Allie. But if he finds you here, we could all be in a lot of trouble."

"This ain't like you, Chester. You never let nobody push you around before. Remember when you were workin' at that stand in the Fair? You always used to save me cakes and rolls and things and slip 'em to me when the boss wasn't lookin'. What's happened to you?"

"There's things going on around here you wouldn't understand, Allie," Chester was saying. "I don't want to see you get hurt. You'd better get out of here while you—" There was a horrible crash and a loud wail.

"Oh! I'm ruined, ruined!" moaned a skinny little girl with golden braids. About her feet were dozens of broken cups and shattered glasses.

"You little idiot!" said Chester, dashing over to her. "Can't you do *anything* right, Gretchen? You're hopeless. Hopeless!" At that, the girl burst into tears. "Now stop sniveling and pick up those damn monkey dishes before I—"

"What's the matter with you?" Allie exclaimed. "It was an *accident,* for pete's sake!"

"Stay out of this, Allie. This is none of your business!"

"If this is what you're gettin' like, Chester, I don't want to know you!" stormed Allie.

"Gimme a break, Allie," Chester pleaded. "You don't know what it's like around here—"

"Chester!" called a voice from next door. "We're running out of spoons again. The Eye is getting mad!"

"Okay, okay," said Chester, mopping his brow with an old towel. "Moira! You and Barney scout about in the dining hall. Aggie! Knock off those cups and start in on the silver. Get Bertrile to help you dry. And somebody help Gretchen here with these damn dishes."

A head popped in the door again. "It's cups he's yelling for now, Chester."

"Tell him I'm working as fast as I can. See what I mean, Allie? It's all I can do just to—"

"Atten-*tion*!"

The doors flew open and everyone snapped to rigid attention at their places. An immense figure stood in the doorway, a meat cleaver in one hand, a long kitchen knife in the other. It was the Eye.

He was as tall as anyone Cary had seen in Down Town, and half again as wide. He wore a starched white shirt with sleeves neatly rolled up to the shoulders, and an immaculate white apron. A florid oval of a face rose from his collar like an autumn moon. A few strands of black hair were plastered to his broad pink skull, and a great chunk of nose was set in the middle of his face like a chop on a plate. But the most terrifying thing about him was his eye.

Eisenglas's left eye was hardly there, just a tiny, squinting little pucker closed by a long scar. But the other eye was huge, gigantic, a staring nightmare as big as an egg, tinged faintly green by the thick monocle wedged in its pit.

Slowly, that eye roved about the washroom, coming at last to rest on Gretchen. With a tiny flick of his knife, Eisenglas gestured at her. "You," he breathed in a thick voice.

Gretchen dropped to her knees, pleading for mercy. Eisenglas glanced over his shoulder, jerking his great head slightly.

Without another word, Gretchen rose, took off her hat, apron, and jacket, and put them on a nearby table. A moment later, the Eye was leading her, weeping, toward a small door at the back.

"Chester," he whispered. "Dock everyvun an hour's pay for carelessness."

"But, *sir*—"

"And yourself two for disobedience. I trust this vill impress upon all of you the importance of diligence and hard vork."

"Yes, sir," said Chester.

"Good. As you vere." There was a moment of confusion as everyone returned to work. Without another word, the Eye turned and walked through the door after poor Gretchen.

"All right, Chester," said Allie angrily, planting herself in his path. "Just what's goin' on around here?"

"Come on, Allie," said Chester, raising his hands as if to push her aside. "I gotta go or we'll all be in trouble—"

"You ain't goin' nowhere until you explain yourself."

"Okay, I'll tell you what I know—which isn't much. But let's go somewhere we can talk." He took Allie's arm gently and began to walk with her across the room.

"Hey," said Cary. "Remember me?"

Chester and Allie turned, startled. "Huh? Oh, sorry," said Allie. "Come on, Cary. Let's find out what this is all about."

THEY PUSHED THROUGH a pair of brass-bound doors, and at once the damp, steamy air was replaced by overpowering heat. In the center of the room, a well-drilled army of bakers in puffy white hats sifted and stirred, kneaded and rolled, split and twisted dozens of loaves at once on a wide slab of white marble. Their faces were streaked with flour and flushed with heat, and perspiration poured down their florid cheeks.

A round dome of brick rose overhead, where the smoke and vapor congregated in a thick cloud. Around the walls were dozens of brick ovens set right in the walls. Whenever a batch of bread was done, a cook would carry it over to one of the ovens, pull down the iron door, and slide it on a wooden paddle into the flames.

The dance of the fire was hypnotic, and Cary thought he saw shapes moving in the ovens with the loaves. Yes! There were tiny imps tending and turning the bread, apparently impervious to the heat. When it turned golden brown, an imp would push the loaf out of the oven and into a waiting basket. Cary was reeling from the heat. If any place on earth, or under it, deserved the name of Hell's Kitchen, thought Cary, this was surely it.

Allie and Chester were already stepping through a door on

the other side of the room as Cary caught up with them.

"All I know is, they don't come back," Chester was saying as he unlatched a great steel door. A blast of arctic air gusted from the doorway. "Every time one of the kids gets in trouble, they disappear—and sometimes even when they don't. They're just here one day, and gone the next."

"Just like the Scamps!" said Allie. "I'll bet Brand's behind this!"

"Keep your voice down!" said Chester, waving them inside. They found themselves inside a great frozen meat locker. The floor was covered with damp sawdust, and great chunks of ice were stacked about the room. On hooks hanging from the ceiling were great swinging sides of beef, pork, and lamb that gave Cary the creeps just to look at them. "There. That's better," said Chester as he closed the door from the inside.

"What happens to the kids who disappear?" asked Cary.

"Nobody knows. It was real quiet at first. Mostly drifters, kids without families, but it's been getting real bad lately. One girl lost three of her brothers, one by one. Then, one morning, *she* was gone. I'm sure the Eye is behind it, but I've got no proof. I guess that's one of the reasons I'm so hard on the kitchen help. Better I should make it hot for them, than let Eisenglas get a hold of them."

"But why didn't you *do* something about it, Chester? Couldn't you tell his boss?" asked Allie.

"Who? Finn and Fianna? You've gotta be kidding. The Kingpin and his missus are so far out of this world that it would take the trumpet of doom to get their attention. Just so long as they get their meat and drink, they couldn't care less. Besides, it'd be just my word against his. Who'd they believe?"

"But you can't just let 'em take those kids away!" Allie protested. "You don't know what they could be doing to them. If you don't blow the whistle on the Eye, who will?"

"I've got to think of myself, Allie," Chester answered. "If I make trouble, it could cost me my job. And I've got my kid sister to worry about."

"And what if they come for you next?" said Allie. "Who's gonna look after your precious kid sister then?"

"I'm sorry, Allie, but what else can I do?"

"You can show a little guts for a change, *that's* what you can do," said Allie. "I don't know what I ever saw in you, Chester."

"But *Allie*—"

"C'mon, Cary," she said. "Let's get out of here. The smell is getting a little strong for me." And with that they left Chester in the cold room, exiting by a door on the other side.

They found themselves in the kitchen proper, a great gleaming place that reminded Cary of Captain Nemo's submarine. There were a lot of pipes and tubes crossing the ceiling, and hundreds of brass pans and iron skillets and the like hung on the walls and on iron racks suspended from chains.

Long, shiny glass cases along the walls held pastries and salads and fresh fruits packed in ice. Tanks of iceboxes dripping on the checkerboard floor stood next to basins of fish, baskets of vegetables, bins of grains, and buckets of beans. At a large wooden island in the middle of the room, a dozen cooks were chopping chickens and dicing carrots, whipping up puddings and peeling potatoes. And a dozen more toiled over a row of tiny cast-iron stoves, each giving off its own distinctive sounds and scents.

Cary turned to find Allie gone. A moment later, as he'd suspected, he found her at a side table piled high with cold cuts. As blithely as you please, she was stuffing her face and her pockets with the fresh meat slices. Cary looked around to see if they'd been spotted. In all the confusion, nobody seemed to have noticed them so far. But just then, the kitchen fell silent and everyone snapped to attention.

"Uh-oh!" said Allie with her mouth full. "Three guesses what that means! Quick! Over here!" Grabbing his arm, she pulled open a pair of doors set into the wall. Inside was a huge dumbwaiter, already laden with a host of platters. Kicking a few aside, she wedged herself into the upper shelf and waved to him wildly. He squeezed in beside her, pulling the cupboard doors shut, just as a great, looming figure entered the kitchen.

Through the crack in the door, Cary could see him as he passed down the row of chefs, cooks, waiters, and helpers, his one great eye sweeping over them like a searchlight. For a moment, that awful gaze fell on the dumbwaiter door, and it seemed as if he could see right through it. But then, to Cary's relief, it passed by.

"Atten-*tion*!" rasped Eisenglas's voice. He drew a great brass pocket watch from his apron, squinting at it. "Dinner vill commence in precisely three minutes and forty seconds. You all have your instructions. I expect strict punctuality and performance. I do not have to mention the consequences if you fail to do so. Now then! Places everyvun! Five. Four. Three. Two. *Vun!*"

The kitchen staff exploded into activity. Salads were set on trays and radishes popped on top. Soups were ladled out of a great tureen; baskets of rolls and boats of vegetables, chafers of fish and bowls of sauce, were readied. Then helpers carried the trays toward the rows of dumbwaiters. Cary's heart was pounding as they approached. There was a rumbling noise, and he and Allie were moving upward!

Someone must have activated the pulleys that moved the shelves, for they were plunged into darkness. The cables squealed as the dumbwaiter hauled the excess weight up the narrow shaft. Below, Cary could smell steaming soup; above, fresh-baked bread. Soon the din of the kitchen was left behind, and Cary could hear a babble of frenzied shouting and laughter overhead.

The dumbwaiter halted, and Cary jumped. There was a clatter of dishes, and it started again, and again stopped. Light spilled down from above.

"Next stop is us!" said Allie.

The elevator began to move again, bringing them even with the opened doors. A gawky young lad staggered back, speechless, at the sight of them as they clambered out.

Up a narrow, winding stairway came a parade of waiters, in

strict posture, towels over wrists and trays on shoulders, marching past the alcove where they were huddled. At the end of the
line, Allie fell into place, grabbing an empty tray, and Cary
followed, making double time to catch up.

The procession marched down a long, grand hall, through a
pair of high doors, and into an antechamber, where the waiters
lined up again, single file. Cary and Allie slipped away and
dashed through a small green door at the far end of the room,
ducking behind a velvet drape just inside the door.

In the warm dimness behind the drape, Cary heard Allie whistle softly and whisper, "Will you get a load of that!"

Pulling the drape aside an inch, Cary looked out on a richly
decorated formal dining room, with a high domed ceiling and
wood-paneled walls, carved into a frieze of stags and hounds,
maidens and youths, sprites, nymphs, naiads and dryads, dancing and capering in a timeless forest.

The ceiling overhead was so ornate, so layered with gilt and
silver, so filled with clouds and stars and comets and birds on
the wing, that Cary's head reeled. Under the interweaving mold-
ings were bronze vases and planters, filled with vines and leaves
and flowers, some carved, some real, and some that could be
either. There were paintings that looked like windows, and windows that looked like tapestries, and tapestries that looked like
paintings, and though it was indoors, there was a smell and feel
and sound about the room that made Cary feel like he was in the
deepest part of a forest on Midsummer Eve.

The light came from nowhere that Cary could make out,
seeming to glow from behind a statue or out of the petals of a
rose. On a wildly decorated carpet of forest green, there was a
great long table with small green-shaded lamps placed down its
center. Around the table were a dozen ornately carved chairs
covered in emerald velvet.

The two large chairs at the end of the table were empty. But
in the rest sat a half-dozen ladies and a half-dozen gents, although *sat* wasn't really the right word, since none of them was

still long enough to call it sitting. Instead, they jumped and
shouted, laughed and scowled, climbed up on the table and back
down again, clinked glasses filled with foaming brew, threw
papers and flowers and napkins, turned somersaults, and in
general turned order into chaos.

The men were all dressed in old frock coats and striped
pants, but their spats and vests were a blinding variety of colors. The women all wore long dresses, but the fabric was watered silk in a riot of mad colors: rose and lemon, flaming or-
ange and bitter chartreuse, periwinkle purple and robin's-egg
blue, complete with speckles. Some were short and some tall,
some stouter and some leaner, but their russet hair and
pale complexions gave them the appearance of a fine lunatic
family.

A harried-looking man in a green eyeshade and arm garters
was dodging in among them, clearing piles of papers and
overfilled ashtrays and emptying them all into the same deep
leather bucket, all the while glancing at his watch and shaking
his head. He was treated shamelessly, cuffed by the gents and
pinched by the ladies, but he bore it all with stoic calm. He'd
barely had time to clear away all the debris when a pair of
hulking men in outlandish livery, each bearing a battle-ax,
stepped through the door and struck their weapons three times
on the floor.

"All rise! All rise! All rise!" shouted the footmen. "Be up-
standing for Hizzoner the Kingpin Finn MacFinn and Her Ladyship the Lady Fianna!"

The gents all sat down at once, then rose again, and then the
ladies, all bashing and crashing into one another, jabbering and
chattering at the top of their lungs.

"Silence!" shouted the bailiff.

Through the drape behind the two empty chairs stepped Finn
MacFinn and Fianna, hand in hand.

Finn was dressed in a natty suit of soft brown leather. A bright
red vest and thick gold watch chain crossed his huge belly. He

had a flaming-red forked beard that flowed down his chest and a wild mass of red hair capped with a crown of twined wild flowers. His bright green eyes were at once merry and slightly mad.

Fianna might have been the prettiest woman that Cary had ever seen, if there hadn't been quite so *much* of her! Her round cheeks and lips were a rosy red, and her glowing red-gold tresses were plaited with an intricate mesh of golden chain. She was dressed all in green satin, and the faint pattern of entwining leaves on her ample gown seemed to move ever so slightly as Cary watched.

In Finn's hand was a pair of golden chains that restrained an immense pair of hunting hounds, all white but with red-tipped ears and fiery eyes. About Fianna's ankles, two overstuffed cats the color of fire prowled and growled. The animals settled quietly at their masters' feet as they stood before their great chairs. Then Finn thwacked the table thrice with a cudgel he carried under his arm.

"Silence!" he roared in a gruff and whiskery voice. At once the ladies and gents fell silent. "The Syllie Court is now in Preprandial Session!" The bailiffs struck their ax poles again. "Be seated!" said Finn.

The Ladies and Gents sat immediately, some in one another's laps.

"Any *Old* Business?" roared MacFinn.

There was a wild babbling of shouts and curses, and a rush of upraised hands.

"Order! Order!" shouted Finn. There was silence. "That's better. No Old Business. Any *New* Business?"

Again the group was up and screaming. Again MacFinn crashed his cudgel. "Good. No New Business. I move—"

This time the ladies and gents went wild.

"That's enough!" shouted Finn. "Order! *Order!*"

"I'll have the pea soup!" said Fianna in a voice that trilled like a husky thrush. "*I* move we eat!"

"A splendid suggestion!" said Finn. "All opposed?"

Nobody made a sound.

"All in favor?"

Cheers.

"Motion is carried!" cried Finn. "Make mine cock-a-leekie!" He snapped his fingers twice, and a waiter was at his elbow with soup. Finn dipped daintily at it with a tiny spoon, blew on it, then picked up the bowl in both hands and drank it down, leaving droplets sparkling on his red beard.

"More!" he roared, and the waiters began to descend, bringing appetizers, joints, timbales and salads, fruits, savories, and wines. The table was a melee of confusion, with breadsticks, haunches and chops, puddings and aspics flying about, glasses crashing in constant toasts, and silver flatware ringing relentlessly on the china plates.

Allie's eyes widened as she watched Finn MacFinn put away an immense slab of beef in only a few bites. She kept leaning farther forward as the waiters passed with their trays heavily laden. At last, the pace began to slow a bit.

"Here, Bran. Here, Sceolan!" called MacFinn. The two great hounds pricked up their red ears and sat up eagerly by the table. "Jump now! Beg!" said Finn, handing one a morsel. "That's a fella!"

"He's giving perfectly good food to a *dog*!" said Allie under her breath.

"Stop, Finn," scolded Fianna. "You'll only spoil them." Then her own great cats started clamoring and crying, and she passed them dainties from her own plate. "There now, Bigears. Yes, you too, little Sheecat. Dear little kitties, there's plenty for everyone—"

"I can't stand it!" cried Allie, hungrily watching the waiters as they scraped mounds of delicious, uneaten food off the plates. Then she was off, sneaking her way around the room behind the curtains. Though she moved with amazing stealth, it seemed to Cary that the drapes screamed out her presence. He craned forward to see better, fearing her discovery at any moment.

A skinny, streaked hand poked out from the drape behind Fianna's chair, plucking a chicken leg from a tray. A moment later the bone reappeared, picked clean.

Cary leaned closer, pushing the drape wider, trying to see around a marble column on which was displayed an ornate vase. As Allie dashed between the drapes like a moving shadow, Cary nudged the column and the vase atop it began to topple. Allie rolled her eyes as Cary reached out to steady it, barely catching it in time. His heart was hammering, but there was only a faint sway of drapery where Allie had ducked out of sight. He was about to do the same, when a hand closed on his arm.

"Aha!" screamed a croaking voice. "Got you!"

TEN

T HE BONY CLERK with the green eye-shade clutched Cary with iron fingers, dragging him from his hiding place toward the table. The Ladies and Gents of the Syllie Court were out of their seats at once, shouting and flailing about.

"What is the meaning of this intrusion?" roared MacFinn in a voice like thunder.

"I—" said Cary.

"Silence!" croaked the clerk. "Nobody gets an audience with the Kingpin without prior approval. And nobody gets prior approval! Bailiffs!" he barked with a snap of his fingers. "Clap this interloper in irons!"

The two hulking guards with the axes came toward Cary with a menacing stride.

"Wait!" shouted MacFinn. A moment later Cary was suspended in air as the two bailiffs carried him forward.

"Let me *go*!" he cried, kicking and thrashing. He looked about for Allie. She'd disappeared. Suddenly he was lifted up and hurled over goblets and dishes to land with a crash in the midst of Finn MacFinn's platter.

"Well, well!" said Finn with a wild gleam in his emerald eyes. "Aha! The main course!" Cary tried to roll free, but Finn pinned his shirt to the wooden table with a well-thrown fork. "You there!" said Finn, pointing a stout finger at the Bailiffs. "Spit this choice game for me! Tonight we feast royally!" There were cheers from the Ladies and Gents.

The bailiffs looked at each other for a moment, then shrugged. A moment later, the pole of an ax had been thrust through the back of Cary's shirt, and he hung upside down between two guards, turning slowly.

"Now, what have we here?" said Finn. "Who sent you here, boy? Who's behind you? Answer up, or I'll feed you to the hounds!"

At once Finn's two huge hounds had jumped up on the table and were looming over him, teeth bared, jaws dripping.

"No!" cried Fianna, pulling with her full weight on the dogs' golden chains. Cary sighed in relief. "I *told* you treats would only spoil them."

"Oh, very well," said Finn, disappointed. "Now, what do you have to say for yourself? Come! Speak up!"

"I—" said Cary.

"Lies!" roared Finn, and the Court echoed, "Lies!"

"But—" said Cary.

"Silence!" roared Finn, and the Court shouted, "Silence!"

"What'll it be?" said Finn. "All in favor of poaching, say aye!"

"Aye!"

"All in favor of fricasseeing, say aye!"

"Aye!" shouted the Ladies and Gents.

"The ayes have it!" shouted Finn. "Bring the braziers!"

"Wait!" cried Fianna. "Bring him here!" The bailiffs looked in puzzlement at Finn, who nodded and waved Cary forward. A moment later, Cary was in the air again, then standing before Fianna, a pair of ax poles poking his back. She stared at him with a perplexed expression.

"Whatever is it, m'dear?" asked Finn.

"I don't know," said Fianna. "I'm sure I've seen that face before."

"When? Where?"

"Let me *think*, Finn. Ah! I have it!" she said cheerily. "Bring the files!"

A moment later, the wizened clerk dumped the contents of the leather wastebasket in front of Fianna, who began digging through it, tossing wads of paper into the air.

"Now, let me see," she muttered. "Hmm. Dogs . . . Dentists . . . Jam . . . Kippers . . . Pies . . . Patronage . . . Parsnips (I never *did* like parsnips). No, that's not it. Oh, dear. *Aha!*" Her voice made Cary jump.

"Ow!" yelped Cary as a pike prodded his back.

"I should say *so!*" said Fianna. "Here, Finn," she said, handing a crumpled sheet of yellow paper to him. "You read it. I've forgotten how."

Finn pawed at a vest pocket, pulled out a tiny pair of half spectacles, and began to read in a booming voice:

"WANTED!

For Mayhem, Battery, Disturbing the Peace,
Creating a Public Nuisance,
Resisting Arrest,
Theft, Robbery, Pilferage,
Assault,
And Other Crimes Against Order:

CARY NEWMAN

REWARD for Information Leading to his Capture.
Notify Authorities IMMEDIATELY!
May be Accompanied by
Scamps, Tramps and other Lowlifes.
Believed ARMED AND DANGEROUS!"

Cary's picture was prominently displayed at the top of the poster. Suddenly the Ladies and Gents were up and screaming, "Fiend!" "Felon!" "Assassin!"

"Hmph!" said Finn. "It's marked Triple X, Priority, Urgent, and it's signed by Commander Brand himself!" There was a gasp from the ladies and gents. "Now out with it! Is this Cary Newman person you?"

"Don't answer him, Cary!" came a voice from above. "You'll only incinerate yourself!"

They all looked up. At first, all Cary could see was the shimmer of a thousand red-glass prisms on a majestic circular chandelier, lit by dozens of candles. Then he saw a smudged, striped face peering over the edge. It was Allie!

"Let him go!" she screamed. She held a candle in one hand, and was slowly burning through one of the four ropes that held the chandelier. "Anybody touches a hair on the kid's head, this comes crashin' down on all of ya!" *Including me,* thought Cary.

"Guards!" shouted MacFinn. One of the bailiffs climbed onto the table and tried to knock her down with his ax, but she ducked away in a shower of red glass. Suddenly, the rope burned through, and one corner of the fixture dropped a few feet, sending hot melted wax spattering down and casting shadows across the table.

Scrambling up the sloping chandelier, Allie held her candle to another of the ropes. "I ain't kiddin'," she called down. "Unless you want glass and hot wax for dessert, do like I tell ya!"

"Do like she tells ya!" shouted the Ladies and Gents.

"All right," said Finn. "What do you want?"

"I want you to leave my friend alone and let him go." Just then the chandelier gave another lurch and Allie had to grab on to keep her balance. The Syllie Court jumped back. Allie caught Cary's eye and motioned toward the door with her head.

"But—but we haven't hurt your friend," said Finn. "We were only having a little fun with him, weren't we, Fianna?"

"You call roastin' him alive *fun*?"

With all eyes on Allie, Cary began to edge away from the table toward the door.

"Oh, *that*," said Finn. "That's just our little way of making our guests feel at home, you know. . . ."

Cary was nearly at the door when Allie grabbed the loose rope and jumped down from the chandelier, swinging toward him like somebody in an old Robin Hood movie. She bumped against him hard, almost knocking him down, then dragged him out the door after her.

And straight into the arms of the Eye.

Eisenglas stood fixed between them and the exit, his single eye wide, a cleaver dangling from his belt. They turned to run the other way, and two great hands grabbed their collars, lifting them and carrying them back before Finn and Fianna. At Finn's feet, the two hounds, Bran and Sceolan, licked their enormous chops.

"Young people today simply have no manners," clucked Fianna. "You might at least have asked to be excused. What *shall* we do with you?"

"Leave them to me," said Eisenglas in a voice like a broken radiator. "I vill impress upon them the importance of proper manners."

"No!" said Cary. "He'll beat us or lock us up or something, just like he did with all the other kids."

"But why would he do that?" asked Fianna. "All of our kitchen help adore Chef Eisenglas. Why, just ask him yourself!"

"Boy, have you got it wrong!" said Allie indignantly. "Chester told me the Eye's been kidnapping kids for months now. I don't know what he does with 'em, but it must be something bad, 'cause they're never seen again."

A ghastly smile wreathed Eisenglas's face. "Me? Hurt my little children? Vot vould I do that for? All I vish is to make vonderful things for His Lordship und Her Ladyship to eat and drink. How could I do this vithout the help of all my young friends?"

"There!" said Fianna. "You see, that proves it! Shame on you for telling such terrible stories about such a nice man!"

"But he's lyin'! Can't you tell that? Ask Chester. He'll tell you the truth."

"Oh, dear," said Fianna. "Now I don't know *what* to believe. Whatever shall we do, Finn?"

Finn looked at Eisenglas, then at Cary and Allie, then back again. "We do as the children say," said Finn solemnly. "Eisenglas, bring this Chester here, so we can get to the bottom of this."

To Cary's surprise, the Eye smiled and bowed slightly, and left the room. A few minutes later he returned with Chester, who looked shaken and pale.

"Now, then," said Finn. "These two have made some serious charges against the Chef here—something about kidnappings or beatings or some such. What do you know about all this?"

Chester hesitated a moment, trembling, then spoke, slowly. "Chef Eisenglas is . . . the most wonderful employer anyone could have. He treats his kitchen staff like his own family. He's generous and gentle and always willing to help. I'm—I'm proud to work with him."

"But what about the charges these two have made?"

Chester glanced at Eisenglas for a moment. "Chef Eisenglas was too kind to mention it, but these two came here to make trouble. They were stealing food and stirring up the help and disrupting things and breaking dishes. I wanted to make them clean up the mess they'd made, but he said to go easy on them."

At this, the Eye nodded and smiled wider.

"Why you little *rat fink,* you slimy, low-down worm—" began Allie.

"But he's *lying,*" shouted Cary at the same time. "Can't you see he's afraid to talk?" All of a sudden everyone was shouting and carrying on at once, even the Syllie ladies and gents.

"Order! Order! Point of Order!" cried Finn MacFinn, pounding on the table.

"There's no point of order with a group like this," said Fianna with a sigh.

"Silence!" roared Finn. "Another outburst like that and I'll clear my throat!" At last the group fell silent. "That's better," said Finn. "Now let's take this one thing at a time. You!" he said, pointing at Allie. "Let's hear your story first. Just remember hanging is a lying offense—or is it the other way around?"

"He's been intimidated, Yeronner," said Allie.

"I have not!" Chester protested.

"Man, look at you, Chester," said Allie. "Anybody with two good eyes can see you're afraid for your own skin. You're scared witless of that—that *Cyclops* there. Everybody downstairs is terrified of him. Why don't you be a man for once in your life!"

But Chester refused to speak. "Chester told us the Eye was stealin' kids away for the least little thing and doin' who knows what with 'em," said Allie. "The last one was a skinny little girl called Gretchen, who got snatched just because she dropped a tray full of dishes—"

"Wait!" said Fianna. "Gretchen? A little slip of a girl with little golden pigtails?"

"That's the one."

"But she's my favorite niece's favorite nurse's favorite grandchild!" said Fianna with a shocked expression. "I promised her mother I'd find her a decent job and look after her while she was here. If anything's happened to her—"

"But this is nonsense!" said Eisenglas. "Your dear little

Gretchen is just fine. She merely had a little fainting spell and had to lie down for a while—a delicate constitution like yours, no doubt—"

"I'm as strong as a horse!" shouted Fianna.

"Eats like one, too," said Finn proudly.

"I won't stand for this!" said Fianna, growing flushed and flustered. "I demand that you bring little Gretchen right here this instant!"

"He can't," said Chester.

"What?" said Finn.

"I said, he *can't*," said Chester. "He took her away, just like he did all the others—"

"Quiet, you fool!" said Eisenglas. "You'll spoil everything!"

"I'm not taking the rap for you anymore," said Chester, "no matter what you threaten to do to me—or my sister."

"You'll regret this!" hissed Eisenglas, his face red as a beet.

"Then it's *true*!" screamed Fianna. "How dare you? Why you—you *monster,* you *beast.* I—I'll have you baked with an apple in your mouth for this!"

"Wait, m'dear!" said Finn. "This is all just hearsay. Let's here what the Eye . . . er, Eisenglas has to say for himself."

"Bah!" cried Eisenglas. "There's no reason to deny it anymore. The master plan is now unstoppable. There is nothing you—or anyvun—can do about it now!"

"What are you talking about?" asked Cary.

"That's all you vill get from me!" screamed the Eye.

"By Dan and St. Brigid, you've gone too far!" bellowed Finn MacFinn. "The brazen nerve! And under my own roof, too! Guards! Take this underdone bit of bratwurst away and marinate him a bit until he talks!"

The bailiffs came forward and seized Eisenglas, binding his arms and marching him forward at ax point. As he reached the door, he called back over his shoulder, "Do vith me vat you vill! In a few short hours all of you vill be calling *me* Kingpin around here!" And with that he was marched out of sight.

"Let's get outa here before they change their minds again!" said Allie. They began to edge once again toward the door.

"Not so fast!" called MacFinn. "We're not finished with you yet." He brandished the wanted poster in the air. "Now about these charges. Are they all true?"

"I—I guess so," Cary admitted.

"Well, why didn't you say so before?" said Finn with a huge grin. "Come, come! Sit down, both of you! Be our guests."

There were cheers from the Ladies and Gents.

"You mean you're not going to turn us in?" asked Cary.

"Turn you in? I should say not. Any enemy of Miles Brand's a friend of mine! Come, have tea. Have lunch. Stay for supper!"

"Thanks," said Cary, "but shouldn't we—"

"Sure we should!" said Allie. "We'd love to!"

"Well, then," said Finn, "pull up a chair. Pull up three! Now, then," he said to Allie as a waiter approached, "what'll you have?"

"What've you got?" asked Allie.

ALLIE DOVE INTO the food that was put before her like there was no tomorrow, and Cary found he was quite hungry, too. Finn and Fianna and the Syllie Court decided to join them, ordering up yet another meal, and washing it down with tankards of ale.

"Care for a drop?" asked Finn MacFinn, pushing a foamy mug in front of Allie.

"Not on yer life!" said Allie, pushing it back and reeling a little from the smell. "Smells just like the stuff my old man used to drink," she said to Cary under her breath.

"Just as well," said Finn, draining it in one gulp. "There's precious little of it left, what with Brand's blockade."

"Blockade?" asked Cary. "You mean he's got this place blocked off?"

"That's right, lad," said Finn. "Brand and his Badmashers are bleedin' Down Town dry. He's got the run of the markets, he controls the Broad Way, and he's even encroachin' on the Squares. Them as plays ball with him gets the gravy, the rest have to pay through the nose. It's getting to where you can't even cross the street without crossing a 'Masher's palm with silver. Most folks would rather pay up than make a fuss."

"We didn't see no 'Mashers when we got here," said Allie. "Just them goons of yours at the gate."

"We've managed to keep him out of Hell's Kitchen so far," said Finn. "He knows he'd get a warm welcome indeed if he showed his face around here again. So he's surrounded the place. Nothing enters or leaves unless his 'Mashers say so." Cary's heart sank. How would he ever get to Time Square now?

"So far he's let us send our baked goods to market—so long as he gets his cut. But he's putting the squeeze on us where it hurts—our beer and ale. It's inhuman, that's what it is!"

"It's a pity," said Fianna. "He was such a bright young lad, too."

"You knew Miles Brand?" said Allie. "I thought he just kind of *hatched* or somethin'."

"Oh, my yes," said Fianna. "He grew up in these parts. He had such promise, too—till he got too big for his britches, that is. The last and least of Mother Brand's baker's dozen and then all of a sudden he wants to grow up."

"Aye, he was a bad 'un," growled Finn. "Wanted to move Up in the world—that was his downfall. Gets a few inches taller than his friends and he thinks he's above it all. Next thing you know, he's strangling the life out of us. Broke his mother's heart, he did."

"How did it all happen so quickly? Didn't anybody notice?" asked Cary.

"The usual way," said Finn with a sad shake of the head. "Got a gang of Upstarts around him who thought they could change the world by main force. Oh, he talked a good game, all about how he'd seen the future, all shiny and bright. Pretty soon, he'd dazzled a bunch of young folk with his fancy ideas, and they forgot all about the old ways. Ran off to join his bully boys the first chance they got!"

"But why didn't anybody stop him, stand up to him?"

Finn got an embarrassed look on his face. "Well, you know how it is," he said. "People will always go along with something if they can avoid trouble, especially here in Down Town. And Brand has some kind of attraction about him I can't for the life of me fathom. By the time we all got wise, it was too late."

"I'll bet the Eye is his man!" said Allie. "He's usin' him to steal away kids, just like he did with the Scamps!"

"Why, whatever do you mean, dear?" asked Fianna.

So Allie explained about the way the Scamps had been disappearing. When she'd finished, Finn pounded his staff on the table and shouted, "It's an outrage! Something must be done about this!"

"It's Something in the Air," proclaimed Fianna. "I'm certain of it. People didn't want to grow Up when *I* was a little girl, I can tell you *that*! They even say," she said in a confidential whisper, "that he has High Friends in Low Places!"

"What does that mean?" asked Cary.

"Why, the Gnomes of Wall Street, of course," said Fianna. "I'm sure they're at the bottom of his rise to power."

"Now, Fianna—" said Finn MacFinn.

"It's the Last Days, MacFinn," Fianna declared. "Mark my words!"

"She's always going on like that," said Finn with a smile.

"I mean it, Finn!" said Fianna in dire tones. "Down Town used to be a peaceful place. Nobody bothered anybody. Oh, perhaps a donnybrook or two and a bit of petty thieving, but that was all. But now we've got children disappearing and Badmashers strutting all over the place and nothing is as it should be."

"Oh, it's not all that bad, Fianna" said Finn.

"It's the Beginning of the End, I tell you!" she said.

"Be that as it may," said Finn, "it isn't much use to these two fine young people." He lifted the wanted poster. "You certainly have made an enemy of Miles Brand. Whatever did you do to get him after you?"

"I don't know, exactly," said Cary. "I was just trying to get back home—"

"Very sensible," said Fianna. "And where *is* home, Corky?"

"*Cary*," said Cary.

"As you say," said Fianna.

"Cary's an *Up*towner," said Allie nonchalantly.

"But he can't be!" said Finn. "It just isn't done!"

"The Poet told him that," said Allie.

"An Uptowner!" exclaimed Fianna. "Fancy that! Do you suppose it's possible, Finn? Could young Kelly here be the One?"

"It's *Cary*," said Cary.

"No, m'dear," said Finn sadly. "Look at the boy. He may be an Uptowner, but he's only a wee thing, hardly there at all. It *couldn't* be him."

"*What* couldn't be me?" asked Cary, confused.

"Besides," Finn continued, "he hasn't got the Sign, has he? All the legends say he has to have the Sign."

"You don't happen to have a Sign, do you, Gary?" asked Fianna, hopefully.

"My name is CARY!" said Cary. "And I don't have any sign, and I don't understand what any of you are talking about."

"What about that golden whoosis you got, Cary?" asked Allie.

"You mean *this*?" said Cary. He took the microdisk from his pocket. In the light of the candles and chandeliers it flashed a golden green.

"Mother Mab preserve us!" cried Fianna. "It *is* the Sign! The Sign of the Promised One!"

To Cary's utter astonishment, the Ladies and Gents of the Syllie Court fell flat on their faces as one, bowing and crying aloud, "The Sign! The Sign! The Sign of the Promised One!"

"Get up! Get up, the lot of you!" roared MacFinn. "There's some sort of mistake here. Get up, I tell you!"

There was utter confusion as the Ladies and Gents untangled

themselves, dusted themselves off, and returned sheepishly to their seats. But their eyes never left Cary and the shining disk he held in his hand.

"That proves it, Finn!" said Fianna in a hushed whisper. "He's an Uptowner, and he has the Sign."

"It's not a sign!" said Cary. "It's just something I got from my mom by mistake."

"We don't know that's the Sign, Fianna," said Finn. "Nobody I know has ever seen the Sign. I'm as old as anybody in these parts, and it was before my time. Why, the Sign could be *anything*! Anything at all!"

"Hold it," said Allie. "Will *some*body please tell us what's goin' *on* around here? What's this Sign? Who's this Promised One anyways?"

"It's an old legend," said Finn. "Every town in Down Town has it, and everybody tells it differently. But they all say a lad left his village years and years ago to make his way Up in the world, promising he'd come back in the town's darkest hour. He's the one they call the Promised One."

"What's the Sign?" asked Cary.

"It varies," said Finn. "Some say it's a token or talisman or amulet or medallion. Round here they say it's a twenty-dollar gold piece—about the size of that thing there—that was all the money Hell's Kitchen could save up to send its best and brightest on his way. And one day, when we need it most, he's supposed to return in a blaze of glory, to pay us all back a hundredfold. Never paid much mind to it myself."

"I *told* you these were the Last Days," said Fianna. "The hour has never been darker. They even say Festival is coming. Not just *any* festival, mind you, but the Great Festival itself. If it was ever Time for a Sign, it's surely now. And here's this nice young fellow *bearing* a Sign, just like in the legends, to be our champion. I'm *sure* he's the Promised One, Finn."

"*Cary,* a champion?" snorted Allie. "Give me a *break*!"

A faraway light came into Finn's green eyes. "We could surely *use* a champion about now," he said with a sigh. "Fianna's right on that. The people of Down Town aren't used to all this trouble and change. They're looking for someone to lead them, to show them the way. Why, I'd do it myself if I were a hundred years younger. If some nice young fellow like you doesn't do it, they'll follow any rascal, like Miles Brand, who talks a good line or shows 'em a brass button."

"But I don't *want* to be a champion," said Cary. "Don't *I* have anything to say about it?"

"Of course you do," said Fianna. "In Hell's Kitchen nobody has to be anything they don't want to be. But these things work by strange rules. Why, you might be the Promised One after all and not even know it. With the way the folks of Hell's Kitchen are feeling about Miles Brand, all you'd have to do is *say* you're the Promised One and you'd have an army at your side in no time at all."

"Fianna, listen to what you're saying!" cried Finn, exasperated.

"Look, I'd rather not lead any armies, if it's all the same to you," said Cary. "I just want to find my way back Uptown, that's all. I just want to go *home*!"

"How are you going to do that, dear?" said Fianna.

"I'm not sure," said Cary. "The Poet said the closest Down Town comes to Uptown is Times—er—*Time* Square. There's someone there who's supposed to know how I can get home—the Watchman. We were headed that way when the 'Mashers spotted us. Do you know how we can get there from here?"

"The Watchman, eh? It won't be easy," said Finn. "Word travels fast in Down Town. These posters will be all over by now, and Brand will have his 'Mashers and spies everywhere. If I were you, young fellow, I'd stay here in Hell's Kitchen, where it's safe."

"But, Finn," said Fianna, "Hell's Kitchen *isn't* safe anymore, or that dreadful spy would never have gotten in here. And if this young man *is* the Promised One, then he has a mission to perform and will need all the help we can give him. And even if he isn't—"

"Very well," said Finn. "We'll help him—"

"But the only help I need is for someone to point the way out of here!" said Cary impatiently.

"Wait," said Fianna. "There's one more thing that must be done."

"What's that?" said Cary, not sure he wanted to know the answer.

"If I'm right about you, that Sign of yours is a thing of great power, Cary," said Fianna. "You may need it on your journey, and you wouldn't want it to get lost. I think I have something . . ."

She began rummaging through a small wooden chest of jewelry, throwing rings and bracelets up in the air. "Ah! Here we are!" she said at last, handing Cary a stout loop of chain with an attached ring that was just the size of the disk.

Cary stared at it for a moment, puzzled, then snapped the disk into the ring, like a picture in a locket.

"There," said Fianna. "That's much better!" Before Cary could protest, she was lifting the chain over his head and draping it on his shoulders. A cheer went up from the Ladies and Gents, and Finn and Allie joined in with laughter and applause. Then there was a roaring and rustling in his ears, and Cary again felt reality slipping away. That same golden-green light surrounded him and that same sweet voice was calling him again, frail, but more urgent than ever.

"Cary?" said Fianna, touching him lightly on the shoulder, her green eyes sparkling. "Wake up, Cary."

"You're dead on your feet," said Finn. "Why don't you get some sleep? You'll need your wits about you if you're going to elude the 'Mashers. We've guest rooms aplenty in the Inn, so you might as well get some rest."

Cary found his eyelids drooping, and he turned to discover Allie yawning, too. He wanted to press on, but he felt bone weary, and the idea of sleeping in a real bed again was very tempting.

"I—I guess I could use a couple of hours' rest," said Cary, fighting to stay awake. "How 'bout you, Allie?"

"Huh?" she answered, hand over mouth.

So they made their way by candlelight up a spiral staircase to a little bedroom under a sloping eave. Cary and Allie were almost dropping from fatigue. Opening the door, they saw the huge expanse of a wide feather bed and, at its head, only one small, plump pillow.

With a mischievous look, Allie dove for possession of the pillow, and Cary leapt after her, sinking at once into the soft down. Allie grabbed hold of it first, rolling over on it, and wrapping her arms and legs around it, laughing giddily. Cary tried to pull it from her, but no amount of tugging, teasing, or tickling could wrench it from her grasp. At last, Cary, still laughing, let go and flopped over on his back in exhaustion, gasping, "Okay! You win!"

Cary lay there in silence for a few moments, feeling sleep pulling at him. "Say, Allie," he said, rolling over, "shouldn't we get undressed or something?" But instead of a reply, all he heard was snoring.

As Cary's head sank into the soft bedding, the swirling green rushed back, and the voice called out, *Cary? Cary? Hurry. There's very little Time. . . .*

ELEVEN

JOHN NEWMAN couldn't sleep. At first he'd told himself Cary was just blowing off steam, trying to make them worry about him. He'd succeeded at that, certainly. But now, with every hour that passed, John knew it was more likely something unpleasant had happened to his son, and the knot of fear in his gut grew tighter.

John felt helpless and frustrated with waiting. He'd done everything he could to track Cary down—calling friends and relatives, the local news, police stations, airports, bus and train stations in all five boroughs and upstate—even calling in a favor with a friend in the Police Commissioner's office to be sure they took Cary's disappearance seriously. But so far there was no word.

Whatever excitement he'd felt before about his work had turned to ashes. With Cary lost in this unforgiving city, it was hard for John to rouse himself to the defense of even so worthy a cause as the public parks. But there was nothing more he could do for Cary until morning, and it didn't look like he was going to get much sleep. Finally, downing the last of his cold coffee, he turned exhausted back to the papers on his desk.

His only hope to stop the city from signing over responsibility for the parks system to the Excelsior Corporation lay in finding a key document in the city's files. There were references to it in several places in the city's records, but the document itself was nowhere to be found.

APPPL had lost an important battle when the city allowed Excelsior to build its headquarters over the Plaza on the Park. As a quasi-public corporation, they claimed exemption from the usual rules and regulations. But his suit on behalf of APPPL contested that exemption. John felt there was an important issue at stake here—the common law doctrine of stewardship. He'd based his brief on the premise that public lands were held in trust for all the people, and were not assignable for profit.

Judge Kiernan's law clerk had told him confidentially that the judge had been very impressed with his arguments, calling them masterful reasoning. The problem was, there was no clear legal precedent to support his premise, no official document confirming the city's responsibility for stewardship of its public lands. Even one such deed might have swayed him to issue a temporary injunction.

But there wasn't a damn thing John could do about it without precedent. He'd scoured the city's oldest land records, but he'd come up empty-handed. To his surprise, the documentation wasn't anywhere in the archives. Nor were there any copies in the libraries and museums. It was as if every single one had disappeared at the same time. He suspected, though he had no proof, that all of the key documents were now in the hands of

Excelsior's lawyers. Finally, having exhausted all other leads, he'd tapped his office computer into the deed files in Albany, on the slim chance that duplicates were on file there. The search had been going on all evening, but so far—nothing.

If Viv were here to help him, like she had in college, she'd probably find it in no time. She loved this kind of archival detective work. It was infuriating. Logic and reason were on his side, but that didn't seem to matter here. Well, if life were reasonable, he'd never have lost Viv. Or Cary.

John laughed at the bitter irony. He was angry at the city for treating its people just the way he'd treated Cary, hiding from its responsibilities, leaving the painful decisions to others.

But you couldn't hide forever. Sooner or later, the world caught up with you. Of course, you didn't have to take responsibility in the first place. There were plenty of people willing to take it from you, if you were willing to play by their rules. But if you did accept a trust, like the city had for its public lands— or like he had for Cary—then whatever it took to uphold that pledge, no matter how painful or difficult, was what you had to do. You didn't have to be perfect, but you had to do your best.

If he'd only admitted it to himself, John had known all along what was expected of him as a husband and a father. Not to give Vivian what she asked for, more possessions and money. If he could provide those things, fine. But if other things were more important to him, then it was his responsibility to tell her so, for them to work it out between them. No, he had to give her what she *needed*—faith and trust, strength and support. And neither of them had the right to deny their son what *he* needed most at this time in his life—love and guidance, confidence and respect. If by some miracle John ever got another chance with his wife and son, he promised himself he'd do better next time.

He felt like picking up the phone and calling Vivian right now. But he'd promised her he'd only call if he had news of Cary, and he didn't want to upset her needlessly. Besides, it was after midnight. She was probably asleep.

VIVIAN NEWMAN TOSSED in her old wooden bed, troubled by strange dreams. Cary was running down an endless corridor lined with hundreds of doors, chased by a tall, dark figure she couldn't quite see. A voice behind one of the doors was calling, "Cary! Cary!" But it wasn't her voice.

The door opened, and behind it was a forest path that led to a grove of tall trees by a lake. Cary's pursuer was getting closer, would see him just around the next bend unless she did something. *"Cary! Look out!"* she called. The dark figure chasing him turned to face her, and in that moment, Cary was gone.

Then she was sitting upright in bed, trembling and shivering despite the hot and humid night. Some sound had waked her. Cary? No, just some night noise in the street below. She glanced over at the bedside clock. Half past midnight. She closed her eyes and tried to go back to sleep. It was no use. Pulling on her robe and slippers, she padded into the kitchen to make a pot of coffee.

Sitting at the kitchen table, Vivian fought hard against despair. John hadn't called her at seven with word about Cary. Or at eight, for that matter. And when she'd called John, at eight-thirty, there was no answer at either the apartment or the office. Finally, at quarter of nine, when she was almost out of her mind with worry, he'd called. Cary had never shown up.

She'd gotten mad again at John for not calling, though to be fair to him he'd had reasons. To her surprise, he responded by being understanding rather than cold and distant. If he'd been more like that before—and if she'd kept her temper a little more often—maybe they'd still be together, and their son wouldn't be lost somewhere in this big, heartless city.

What had happened to them? They'd been so excited and alive when she was studying urban history at Barnard and he was

at Columbia Law. Those endless late nights studying together
or solving the world's problems or just lying quietly in each
other's arms had been magical.

Then came Cary. She hadn't planned to get pregnant in college; it just sort of happened. Not that she'd minded, really.
Cary was a bright, delightful child who seemed to find wonder
in each little thing. Then, after John's parents died and he took
over the firm, they'd moved in with John's grandmother in the
family home upstate.

It seemed like a sensible idea at the time. Even though Linda
was remarkably spry and active for a woman in her eighties, the
house was getting to be too big and expensive for her to manage
all by herself. Cary would have a lovely old home in the country,
a good school system, and a doting great-grandmother to help
look after him while Vivian finished her degree at the local
college.

But then Linda had her stroke, and Viv dropped out of school,
suddenly finding herself with two dependents to take care of—
three, if you counted John, who could barely pick out socks by
himself or make his own breakfast. And suddenly the magic was
gone. Vivian felt alone and isolated in that big old house, out
of place in that stodgy neighborhood with its self-satisfied
housewives and their silly organizations. John's grandmother
grew thinner and vaguer and more demanding, and Vivian had
to admit that it was a relief when she finally passed away.

Then the bills started to mount up. There was Cary's school-
ing, of course, and piano and sailing lessons, membership in the
Club, repairs on the house and pool, the cars, clothing for herself, and John, and Cary, who went through shoes weekly it
seemed. And Linda's medical bills, and the expenses of the
funeral, and all of her debts, which were considerable.

John didn't seem to know how to cope with it. He'd never had
much sense of money, probably because he'd had it around him
all his life. He never cared about making an impression, wearing
the same suit all week if nobody noticed, and ignoring people

who could be of use to his career. And he was always throwing himself into lost causes, while his paying clients took their business elsewhere. In no time, things got worse.

That's when the fights started, if you could call them that. They were mostly one-sided—hers. Every day John grew more remote, more distant and withdrawn. Vivian tried to get through to him, to get any kind of reaction out of him, any sign that he understood what he was doing to his future, to his marriage, to his relationship with his son. But he just listened with infuriating calm, and spent more and more time at work and less and less with her and Cary.

At last, Viv had to go to her own parents for a loan, though she'd rather have died. It was all the proof her mother needed that John was a washout as a husband. "It's not too late to make a decent match, dear, even with a child. After all, you've still got your looks and your figure."

Finally it began to affect Cary, too. He became more sullen and moody, like his father. He started doing badly at school. Oh, he was bright, of course. Any son of theirs would have to be. But he didn't seem to be living up to his potential. He neglected his homework, daydreamed in class, even got into fights. He seemed to prefer to spend his time curled up with a book or taking long rambles in the wood across the street rather than playing with the neighborhood boys. And lately, he'd grown increasingly hostile.

It was partly her fault, she admitted, for pushing them both so hard to be what she wanted. She hadn't really paid enough attention to what they wanted. She realized that in some ways she didn't even know who her son was. Could he handle himself all alone in the city? She didn't know. And John. Even though she knew what he did, she always had dismissed his work as "saving the snails and whales."

If they could just start over again, maybe things would work out. She'd try her best to be less unreasonable, less demanding, more supportive of what mattered most to John, if John were only willing to face reality, to open up more, to express his feelings, to show her some sign he cared. But she knew better than to hope for that. . . .

There was a rush of summer wind, and Vivian found herself drifting. Something was nagging at her, like a memory she could barely recall. She found herself picking up her copy of the report she'd prepared for Mr. Janos. She turned to the last page, to a copy of an old document she'd uncovered, the oldest in her files.

It was a yellowed sheet of parchment, an addendum to the ship's log of one Captain Jan Van Addaam of the Dutch East India Company, dated 1609, describing a treaty with the local Indian tribes that predated Pieter Minuit's purchase of the island. It was engrossed in a bold calligraphic hand by Van Addaam, and in the lower left, below faint lettering in Old Dutch script, was a graceful drawing of a young tree.

The tree! She'd seen that tree before. Of course! It was the same tree she'd seen in her dream. But what did it have to do with Cary? Was it some weird sort of psychic hunch about what had happened to him?

Suddenly, she wanted more than anything to speak to John, to ask him if he had news, to tell him about her dream, just to hear the sound of his voice again. But she knew John would think she was foolish. He'd said he would call her if there was news.

She knew she should try to get some sleep, just in case. But sleep wouldn't come. Pouring herself another cup of coffee, she sat down on the old velvet couch by the window, to wait for the dawn.

TWELVE

CARY AWOKE WITH A start. At first he had no idea where he was. In his house? In the brownstone? *No. In Down Town. I guess that proves this isn't a dream,* he found himself thinking. *I've never heard of anyone dreaming he's been dreaming before.* But what had he been dreaming?

A green place, like a forest or a wood. A waterfall rushing down into a wide lake. A tree. A tall green tree stretching far out of sight. And that same sweet, rustling voice calling him, pulling him almost physically toward it. There was something he almost remembered, something important he'd forgotten—as important as his birthday or his own name. But he couldn't make it come clear.

Shaking his head to clear away the dreams, he threw off the

covers and lowered himself to the floor. He was splashing his face with cold water from a porcelain basin when Allie poked her head in the door. "About time you was wakin' up," she said. "I been up for hours and had breakfast, already. I didn't sleep much anyway. I had some pretty weird dreams."

"What kind of dreams?" asked Cary.

"Nothin' that concerns you," she said testily.

Cary suddenly realized there was something different about her. Her patched denim overalls were soft and clean, and she smelled of soap instead of the streets. Under them she wore a brand-new white blouse embroidered with flowers. There were still markings on her face and hands, but the smudges of dirt that had covered them were gone, revealing glowing skin. And her wild tangle of hair, though still ragged-cut, was now dark and glossy, with her one braid neatly plaited with a new white ribbon.

"What're you starin' at?" she asked with a crooked grin. "Ain't you never seen a lay-dee before?" And with that she linked her fingers under her chin and pranced about in a circle, batting her eyes at him until he burst out laughing. "C'mon," she said at last. "I'll watch ya eat!"

Finn and Fianna, minus the Syllie Court, were waiting for them in the great dining hall. They seemed to have started on lunch already. As Cary expected, Allie did more than watch, putting away twice as many pancakes and sausages as he did.

"Well, Cary," said Finn MacFinn when they'd finished breakfast, "we seem to have found a way to get you up to Time Square without being spotted."

He walked a few paces to a rich tapestry behind the table and pulled it aside. Behind was a tiny oak door set into the richly carved wall. Pulling an old key from his watch pocket, Finn unlocked the door to reveal a narrow flight of steps leading steeply up.

"That's your way out," said Finn. Allie peered dubiously into the tiny space.

"Are you sure?" she asked.

"Certainly," said Finn. "It's a secret passage. Our oldest maps show it leads to Time Square, though you'll have to pass through a few other places first in order to get there."

"What sort of places?" Cary asked suspiciously.

"Oh, you needn't worry," said Fianna. "I'm sure they're all the right sort of people. We've sent word you'll be coming, and they'll be waiting to show you the way."

"Sort of an underground stairway, you might say," said Finn, pleased with his own joke. "Now off you go!"

"Taara's blessings on you," said Fianna. "If you are who I think you are, you'll need them." She bent over, giving him a kiss on the brow. Allie snorted. "And as for *you,* my dear," said Fianna. "You're part of this, too, you know. Look after Cary, won't you? And yourself, too, of course!" Then she swept Allie up in her pudgy arms and kissed her once on each cheek. Allie squirmed and blushed and rolled her eyes, all the while smiling that crooked smile of hers.

Cary and Allie squinched into the staircase, bending over constantly to avoid bumping their heads.

"Imagine," said Allie as they ascended in the darkness. "Thinkin' you was some kinda champion or somethin'. All you did was flash that thingumajig of yours, and now they're making you out like you're some kind of hero or somethin'. Some people got no sense."

"I don't like it any better than you do, Allie," said Cary. He wasn't being one hundred percent truthful. He *did* get a kind of kick out of everyone thinking he was special. "But what if I *was* the Promised One? Then what?"

"You, the Promised One? Don't make me laugh! It's bad enough *those* jokers think you're somethin' you ain't without *you* startin' to believe it, too! I know *somebody's* got to stand up to Brand and his goons before they take over the place, but *you*? Get serious. If you can't save yourself, how're you supposed to save the world? Let's just get you home. That's been hard enough. Now save yer breath for climbin'."

MILES BRAND SCANNED the map that formed in the mirror before him. Against a black background, gray swaths diagrammed the limits of his territory. Clustered about them were glowing red dots that indicated the locations of the Badmashers and his army of spies and saboteurs. The wide blue areas were the Freeholds, the parts of Down Town still outside his control, and the green patches were the Squares, those chaotic areas of light and life between the orderly zones of Brand's domain. They were the main passages from one level to another in Down Town.

Sooner or later, the boy would have to cross one of them, and Brand felt sure he knew which one it would be. He'd received a report from a spy inside Hell's Kitchen, a careless bungler named Eisenglas who was now expendable, that they were traveling upward again.

Brand's finger touched the map at a narrow wedge of green. Time Square. They were sure to reach it soon. And when they did, his 'Mashers would be waiting.

The gray glove curled into a fist.

THE STEEP STEPS and stooped posture gave Cary a crick in his neck and a pain in the backside, but he trudged on, trying the handles on the little doors that appeared here and there along the stairs. At last, the stair stopped at a little landing with a small door made of frosted glass and chicken wire that was painted in black letters that said

ANTIQUARIUM
KEEP OUT!
_____

Authorized Persons *Only*

"That means us," said Allie. "Let's go."

She pushed open the door slowly to reveal an almost endless corridor lined with dusty shelves. Their feet clattered and echoed on grimy marble floors, and bright bare bulbs cast sharp shadows ahead of them and behind them.

On the shelves were a curious combination of books and bones, artworks and artifacts, manuscripts and memorabilia. Through the shelves to each side, Cary could see hundreds more, and through small gaps in the floor and ceiling, he saw tier upon tier of corridors above and below him.

Cary walked slowly down the long hallway, staring in wonder at the contents of the shelves about him. It seemed as if all the products of dozens of different civilizations had been jumbled up together and then placed at random here.

One whole section was filled with nothing but bits and pieces of statues: arms, legs, lips and noses, onyx owls, blossoms of lapis lazuli, alabaster toads. Another was packed with yellowed maps and old rolled scrolls. A third contained hundreds of tiny mechanical parts, each separately tagged and numbered in black ink. And here and there among them were cases filled with even stranger artifacts—stuffed geese and Winged Victories, bas reliefs and incunabula, bronze plaques and clay tablets.

At last, the corridor ended in a wide open area where a massive iron stair led downward into darkness. Beyond, Cary could see another corridor as long as this one stretching far away, and two more to the left and right. Down the center of the stairwell stretched thick brass tubes, and to one side, stout cables carried wooden baskets up one side and down the other, laden with all manner of outlandish objects.

In an alcove by the stair, a wood-paneled office had been built. A large wooden rolltop desk sat against one wall, and beside it was an old-fashioned crank telephone.

The tinny bell of the telephone began to ring, a whirring noise from far away grew suddenly louder, and a blur in blue flashed in front of them.

"Antiquarium, Belinda Billings speaking." She was dressed all in blue, except for a dusty white apron with bulging pockets. Her brown hair was shot with white, and bright-blue eyes flashed behind wire-rimmed glasses. Her long sleeves were rolled to the elbows, and bright-blue button shoes protruded from her skirts, ending in quaint, ornate roller skates!

"1066. Hastings," she said breathlessly into the receiver, and hung up. "Now, then," she said, turning to face them. "What can I do for you?" A buzzer sounded, and a light began blinking on a panel above the desk. "Just a moment," she said, touching the light. A small glass cylinder dropped into a large wooden basket out of a brass tube that snaked down from above. She unscrewed the cylinder, pulled out a little colored slip of paper, and peered at it.

"It'll keep," she said. "Now, how can I help you?"

"I'm Cary Newman," said Cary hesitantly.

"Newman?" she said. "It seems to me I've heard that name before. Ah, yes. *Cary* Newman. The Promised One—or so they say. Rather small for the job, aren't you?" Just then the phone rang again. "Just a moment. Yes? . . . The Diet of Worms, 1521." She slammed the phone on the hook.

"You'll have to forgive the interruptions," she said. "I keep asking for help from the folks Upstairs but I never get an answer. I suppose I should have learned by now. 'Let old Billings run the Antiquarium all by herself,' they say. 'How important is it, anyhow?' Ha! Had to pay for my roller skates out of my own pocket, would you believe it?"

"What's a Auntie-Queerium?" asked Allie.

"Antiquarium," Belinda Billings corrected. "The Antiquarium is where all those odd little things that nobody wants anymore are kept, just in case somebody might want them someday. You know what Down Town is, don't you?"

"Yes," said Cary. "The Poet said it was a place for old memories."

"Quite so!" said Belinda. "Well, the Antiquarium is sort of a

Down Town in miniature. It's essential to have one, you know.
There's more to history than any one of us can ever recall. It's
easy for our memories to distort it for good or ill. But curios and
documents are the bones of history. You never know what old
thing might supply just the newfangled notion you've been looking for all along. These stacks and shelves and cases and cabinets are connected to all of the great libraries and museums
Uptown. Every so often someone Upstairs will need some forgotten fact or artifact, and I'll have to round it up."

"You don't mean you manage all these miles and miles of
things all by yourself, do you?" asked Cary.

"That's exactly what I do mean, young man," said Belinda.
"It wasn't so bad at first really. It's either feast or famine down
here. You'll go for days without a query and then suddenly
there's a flurry of them. Had a few dozen Pages in the old days
—that's young helpers like you two—to catch the overflow and
keep the collections shipshape. But they all began disappearing not so long ago. I didn't notice at first, what with one thing
and another. But one day I found myself all alone down
here."

"Maybe they were snatched, too!" said Allie.

"Snatched?"

Allie explained about Brand's order to round up the Scamps,
and about the kids who disappeared from Hell's Kitchen.

"But that's *terrible,*" said Belinda Billings. "Oh, botheration!"
she said suddenly as a single light lit up on her board. A single
glass cylinder dropped into her basket, and she opened it to read
the gray slip inside.

"Oh, dear," she said, shaking her head. "I'm afraid you two
will have to run along."

"Why?"

"This," said Belinda, holding up the slip. "I've never shirked
my job before, and I don't plan to start now. But this request
is impossible."

"Why?" asked Cary. "What do they want?"

"You," said Belinda gravely. "This time it's from *Down*stairs, as far down as it goes. Now be off, both of you! I can't very well send you down if you're not here, now can I?"

"I guess not," said Cary. "How do we get out of here?"

"I'm afraid the only way out of here is by way of the Morgue."

"The Morgue?" said Allie and Cary at once.

"I'm afraid so," she said. A dozen lights on the board started blinking. "Quick. Through here. You'll find the door at the end of this corridor."

"Thanks," they said at once, and were off down the long wood-paneled hall.

A black door waited at the other end, painted in white with the words:

UNDERWORLD

MORGUE

Cary warily opened the door, half expecting to see piles of dead bodies. Instead, he found row upon row of metal shelves with stacks and stacks of old, yellowed newspapers that sprinkled dust on them as they brushed past. At the other end of the hall was a door that said "Newsroom." It led to a row of cubicles made of wood and frosted glass, overhung with old-fashioned electric bulbs in wire cages. The door to the largest was half open, and Cary could see a broad wooden desk piled high with yellow sheets of paper and a shiny but old-fashioned bare-bones typewriter.

Behind the desk was a wooden swivel chair, and seated in it was a muscular young man with neatly parted hair and gartered shirt sleeves, sporting bristling muttonchop whiskers. He was peering at a copy of a freshly printed newspaper through a magnifying glass. Across the top was written

THE NEW YORK UNDERWORLD

"WE GET TO THE BOTTOM OF THINGS"

The man in the chair looked up suddenly at the sound of their footsteps and called out, "You there! Come here!"

With a dubious glance at Allie, Cary drew closer.

"Stop the presses!" the man shouted, pointing an ink-stained finger at Cary. "Haven't I seen that face someplace else?"

"It's always been right here as far back as I can remember," said Cary.

"Don't crack wise with me, mister," the man said. "You're talking to Sam Hill here." He rapped his knuckles on a partition that was painted with the words "Saml. P. Hill—Editor and Publisher—New York Underworld." "I smell a four-star extra!" He flipped through a pile of paper on his desk, pulling out Cary's wanted poster. Allie looked like she wanted to run, but Cary stood still.

"Yessirree. Here it is!" Sam Hill shouted in triumph. "Hmmm. Mayhem, is it? Felonious assault! Shocking, that's what it is. Disgraceful!"

"I'll say it is," said Allie. "It's a frame-up. A fix!"

"*Is* it now? I was talking about the printing. Worst job I've seen in years. Smudges and streaks and spots, half the words misspelled. Must be scab labor. But a *frame*-up, you say? That's what Finn said. That *is* news. Have a seat, why don't you? And bring your lady friend with you. Cigar? No, I s'pose not. Come, come. Sit down."

Cary rolled his eyes at that "lady friend" remark, but took a seat all the same, nudging Allie into the chair next to him.

"Now. Let's hear your story. Is it true what I hear about you being the long-lost Promised One who's supposed to deliver Down Town from the clutches of Brand and his 'Mashers? If it's true, this could be the scoop of the century. You wouldn't care to give us an exclusive, would you? I can see it now. Front page, all eight columns: THE INSIDE STORY: 'I WAS FRAMED BY BRAND'S 'MASHERS'—PROMISED ONE ISSUES CALL TO ARMS. What do you say? We couldn't pay you much for it, but think of the glory—"

"Hold it!" said Cary. "I never said I was the Promised One. I'm *not* the Promised One, at least as far as I can tell. This whole thing's getting out of hand! And I don't have time to sit around making up stories. I just want to find the Watchman and get back Uptown, where I came from, without getting beaten or killed, before my mother gets too worried about me. Why does everybody keep pushing me into things?"

"Listen, young fellow," said Sam Hill. "It doesn't much matter to me whether you're the Promised One or not. I can play the story either way. But Finn and Fianna seem to think you're something special, and in my book, that's news. So what do you say, Cary? Just the bare bones. You won't even have to write a word. I'll get my best rewrite man on it. Hang that! I'll do it myself!"

He whipped a little black notebook out of his pocket and pulled a blue pencil from behind his ear. "All right, let's have it. Immortality awaits you."

So Cary began to tell his story again, and Sam Hill wrote down every word. When he told about the disappearing kids, Hill shouted, "I knew it! I should have listened to Old Bert sooner. He *told* me it was getting harder to find cubs and copyboys to work in the newsroom. It's obvious to me there's some sort of plot at work here."

"What kind of plot?" asked Cary.

"Something big, that's for sure. It's hard to say when you've got nothing but rumors and whispers to go on, but when you sit in the editor's chair long enough, you begin to smell things *before* they happen. There's a whale of a hullabaloo blowing up, and it's gonna be a monster."

"A *what*?" asked Cary.

"A fracas. A rumpus. Now I can see after hearing your tale how you don't see yourself as any knight in shining armor. But my nose tells me the whole thing swings around you, like it or not. I know us members of the fifth estate are supposed to be impartial and all, but considering the trouble they give me, I for one wouldn't mind seeing Brand and company taken down a peg or two. And you can help."

"Him?" said Allie incredulously.

"Yup," said Hill. "You just whistle, and I'll put the power of the press behind you. Everybody in Down Town reads my paper. If you're looking to spit in Brand's eye, I can whip up a bell ringer of a campaign for you in no time flat. Just say the word, and you'll have more recruits than you can beat off with a stick."

"But how can I say I'm what I'm not?" asked Cary. "And what happens when the people of Down Town find out I'm just a kid?"

"Now, now," said Sam Hill. "Nobody's asking you to go against your grain. If you say nix, it's nix. And I'll go with what I have. But if you *want* to be a hero, I can make you one overnight. That's all I'm saying."

"But I don't *want* to be a hero!" said Cary.

"Whatever you say," said Hill. "I'll play the story straight, because I like your face—and the humility bit is a great angle. But it's still gonna stir up a hornet's nest, let me tell you."

"Terrific," said Cary. "Now, could you tell us how we can get to Time Square from here?"

"I'll do better than that," said Hill. "I'll send you there myself with the four-star final. But you might as well get the Cook's tour of the place while you're here. It's on your way after all. Now let's get hopping," he said, checking his pocket watch. "I've got an extra to put out!"

As THEY PASSED a half-dozen desks filled with reporters in derbies and shirt sleeves, Hill ripped the pages from his notebook and dropped them on the first desk. "That's your lead, McCarthy. Four stars, full eight-banner with double banks and lots of play—streamers and dingbats, the works! I want sidebars, shirttails, and dope stories in five each. Make 'em up if you have to. The Lobsters can patch it later."

"Yes, sir!" said McCarthy, who began to type at once.

"What language was he speakin'?" asked Allie. Cary shook his head.

Under a huge burnished brass clock in the middle of the room hung a large sign reading COPY. Below was a great semicircular desk where a small, white-haired man sat snipping up yellow sheets of typed paper with a pair of scissors that hung on a black silk ribbon about his neck. The chairs surrounding the tables were mostly empty, but here and there were tired-looking youngsters in knickers, sleeping with their heads on piles of foolscap.

As Sam Hill came near the desk, he held up four fingers. The white-haired man, who must have been Old Bert, gaped a moment, held up four trembling fingers of his own, and looked back questioningly. Sam nodded and Old Bert shook his head, then struck a gong four times with a little metal hammer.

At once all the copyboys (and copygirls, too—Cary could see a few flying pigtails) were awake, dashing to and fro to shouts of "Copy!" and "Rewrite!" Sam Hill folded his hands behind him and beamed proudly.

"Shame you couldn't be here for a full edition," he said wistfully. "You've missed most of the excitement. There's nothing like a newspaper at five minutes to deadline to get the blood moving. Pandemonium, that's the word. Sheer pan-*dee*-monium!"

At the back of the room, Cary saw a tangle of machinery and heard a steady rattle clank and smelled the sharp tang of hot metal. A row of tall machines stood side by side. At the side of each steamed a metal crucible filled with gleaming molten lead. The machines had keyboards something like typewriters, but they looked to Cary more like metal looms.

Men with green eyeshades and rolled-up sleeves sat at the machines, tapping away at the keys, reading yellow sheets

brought to them by the copyboys and copygirls. At the end of
each line, a slug of warm metal dropped down into a slot.

Just then, the lid on a small wooden case labeled "Hellbox"
popped open, and a small creature about the size of a kitchen
imp popped out. It was dressed in a red frock coat with a pair
of tails. Actually, *three* tails, Cary noticed: two on the coat and
one thin forked one that stuck out from underneath. On its head
was a little hat made of folded newspaper, with a pair of tiny
horns sticking out of it.

Dozens of the little imps were climbing all over the typecases
and machines, assembling headlines out of type from the racks
and fitting in lines as they were finished, and carrying the cases,
six abreast like pallbearers, back to the pressroom at a trot.

"What are those?" Cary asked.

"Don't tell me you've never heard of printers' devils!" Hill
chuckled. "Why, with the labor shortage, we could hardly run
the Underworld without them. It might take a bit longer this
way, but you get a better grade of work."

"Where do they come from?" asked Cary.

"I don't know for sure," said Sam Hill, "but it's my guess they
were once printers themselves, Upstairs. When all those newfangled contraptions put them out of business, they came down
here. They're good, hard workers. Cheap, too. They live mostly
on newsprint and printer's ink." Then the floor began to trem-
ble as if an earthquake had struck.

"Ain't it a sweet sound?" shouted Sam Hill over the din.

"What is it?" shouted Allie back, hands clapped over her ears.

"That's the presses starting up! This way! You can ride up
with the papers.

Beyond the typesetting room was a wide loading dock, where
horse-drawn wagons were pulled up. To the right was a wide
stone slab with four chains, one at each corner, that met high
overhead at a great hook, suspended from a cable that vanished
into the fog and steam above.

"That's your way Up," said Sam Hill with a wave of his hand.

"Hop aboard." Cary hesitated for a moment, then stepped down onto the slab, with Allie following. Moments later, bales of freshly printed newspapers were stacked all around them.

Suddenly the platform was moving upward. The mists grew denser, and it was harder to see Sam Hill on the loading dock. Just before he vanished from sight, Cary could hear him shouting, "So long! See you in the papers!"

THIRTEEN

T HE PLATFORM CAME to a halt in a hiss of steam and a cloud of smoke. Cary opened one eye, then the other, and his heart leapt. He stood on a brightly lit street corner at the foot of a tall tower that sat on a narrow block formed by the crossing of two wide avenues. Cars and buses sped past, and the street was lined with gaudy signs and gleaming lights.

"Times Square!" cried Cary. "I'm home!" Then his heart fell into his shoes. For it wasn't the Times Square of his own time, but one that looked like a Charlie Chaplin movie, with old-fashioned cars and ads for things that didn't even exist anymore, and lots of people in outdated clothes and hats.

He and Allie were surrounded by bales of newspapers. Cary glanced down and was surprised to see his own face, done up

as a line engraving, staring back at him. He noticed in shock that
the headline read CARY NEWMAN AMBUSHED BY BADMASHERS IN
TIME SQUARE! Sam Hill must have meant it as a warning!

"Hey! Get a load of that, willya!" said Allie.

Cary looked where she pointed. On every kiosk, lamppost,
and street sign, Cary's likeness looked back at him. The poster!
They were back in Brand's territory for sure.

"Get down!" said Allie. "Outa sight!"

Cary dropped behind a stack of papers and peered over.
There, on the other side of the street, two 'Mashers were scan-
ning the street.

"What do we do now?" he asked in a whisper.

"We run for it," said Allie.

"Where?" asked Cary.

"There!" said Allie. On the building behind them was a great
round clock with roman numerals and hands that stood almost
straight up. Directly below it was a little shop with a miniature
of that clock above it, and a sign on its door saying

THE WATCHMAN
ONE TIME SQUARE

"Let's go!" said Allie.

"Right in front of them?" asked Cary.

"You got a better idea?"

"Nope."

"Then let's get movin'!"

They'd nearly reached the door of the shop when one of the
'Mashers turned, looked away, did a double take, and looked
back. Just then the door of the shop opened and they ducked in.
As the door was swinging shut, Cary heard whistles blowing.

The door closed behind them, shutting out the street noises.
Looking about the little shop, Cary saw hundreds of timepieces
—watches and hourglasses, clocks of every size and description,
all meting out the minutes. There were clocks on every available

surface: on the glass window shelves, on racks and casements along the walls, and in a long glass-fronted case that stretched along the back of the shop.

"About Time you got here!" said a voice at Cary's side. A thin little man stepped from behind a walnut grandfather clock. He was dressed in a vest and a bow tie with a tiny clock pattern, and an enormous jeweler's loupe was screwed into his left eye. He looked the two of them up and down, as if they were watches in need of mending, then grabbed each by an arm and shoved them toward a huge clock by the wall. Taking a key from a bristling chain on his belt, he unlocked the clock and pushed them inside, locking it after them.

"Wait a minute!" cried Allie. "You can't—"

With a stern look, he lifted a finger to his lips. Then he pulled a gleaming pocket watch from his vest, opened it, looked at it intently, then counted down from five to one on his fingers. There was a pounding on the door.

"Just a moment," he shouted over the din. "I'm coming!"

With a slow, shuffling gait, he made his way over to the door. Cary tried to make out what was going on through the glass front of the clock, through Allie, who kept stepping on his feet, and through the swinging pendulum that threatened to shorten his nose. It was hard to see, but there was no mistaking the hulking forms of the Badmashers at the door. Slowly and patiently, the Watchman spoke to them, and at last, after what seemed like hours, the door of the shop closed and the Watchman came back to unlock the clock and let them out.

"What's the big idea?" began Allie.

"No Time for that now," said the Watchman, tapping his pocket watch. "You've come from Uptown, and you want to get back there, no?"

"Yes!" said Cary in astonishment. "How did you—"

"It was in the book."

"What book?" asked Cary.

"This book," he said, jotting down a short note in a great

black book. "My almanac. Everything that happens is in it, somewhere—or some*when,* I should say."

"But we just got here!" said Cary.

"Well, that proves it, no?"

"You're talkin' in circles!" said Allie.

"True," he said. "A hazard of my profession. I'm a watchman,
you see."

"No foolin'," said Allie, with a glance at the clocks.

"No, no," said the Watchman. "You misunderstand. I don't
mean I am a watch *repair* man, although I am that, too—just to
keep in touch, you see. But I am also a *watch* man. I watch for
things."

"What kind of things?" asked Cary.

"Oh, holidays, seasons, centuries, history. They all go in the
book. And every day I read my book to see what is supposed to
happen. It's simple, no?"

"No," said Cary.

"Well, let's see what it says for today: 'Sunny, chance of rain;
darker toward evening.' It says that today may or may not be the
beginning of the Great Festival. If so, then it should start in"—
he peered at his pocket watch again—" exactly three minutes,
thirty-three and a third seconds from now. That's just one of the
things I'm supposed to watch for. You're another."

"Me?" asked Cary.

"Yes, you," said the Watchman. "It says in the book that you,
or someone like you, would be here now, or very soon. Since you
are here, you were *meant* to be. It's very simple. You have the
Sign, I presume?"

"Not you, too!" said Allie.

"What sign?" asked Cary.

"The Sign of the Time, of course," said the Watchman. "It
says right here that you will be carrying it."

"But—"

"You might as well show it to him," said Allie. "He already
knows ya got it."

So Cary pulled the disk and chain from his shirt. The Watchman examined it through his loupe, shaking his head. "Not at all what I expected," he said at last. "But then, times change, don't they? Well, no matter. It will serve. And now you will be asking me how you can return to your Uptown world, no?"

Cary's opened mouth shut. He *had* been just about to ask that question.

"You can't," said the Watchman.

"But the Poet said that if anyone could tell me how I could get back home, it would be you," said Cary.

"And he was right," said the Watchman. "If anyone *could,* it *would* be me. But no one can. At least not now. So it isn't. And I can't."

"But why *not*?" said Cary.

"Any number of reasons. First, there's a band of 'Mashers waiting just outside the door to stop you if you try. Second, if there ever was a way for you to get back Uptown, it's closed, at least for the moment. And last, you can't go back because you're not ready to go yet."

"How do you know?" asked Cary angrily.

"Because there's nothing in the book about it. If you were meant to return Uptown now, it would say so in the book. It doesn't, so you're not."

"*I don't care about your old damned book!*" Cary found himself saying. "Look. I never *asked* to come to Down Town." As he said it, he wasn't sure. "Well, maybe I did; I don't know. But ever since I got here people have been pushing me and pulling me this way and that. They tell me how *they* think things are, and what *they* want me to do, but nobody ever asks me what *I* want!"

"Welcome to the human race, kid," said Allie.

"What *do* you want, Cary?" asked the Watchman.

"I don't know," said Cary. "I know everybody thinks I've got to have some kind of purpose in life, to make some big decision —like being this Promised One they're all waiting for, or something. But I don't *want* to have a purpose. I never promised

anybody *anything.* And I don't want to make any decisions. I just
want to go *home!*" He knew he sounded like a three-year-old
throwing a tantrum, but right then it seemed like the only thing
he could do.

"But you *do* have a purpose—or will. It's only a matter of
Time," said the Watchman. "And you have made promises, you
know," he said with a wave at Allie. "And you've already made
your decision, you know," continued the Watchman. "Or will,
in Time. It's much the same thing."

"No, it's not!" Cary protested.

"Yes, it is. It's only a matter of Time, young man—what *is*
your name, by the way?"

"Cary," said Cary, astonished. "I thought you knew everything."

"Oh, no," said the Watchman. "I only know *when* things will
happen, not to whom or how. Maybe I'm not making myself
clear. Do you know why clocks are round? They *are* still round
where you come from, aren't they, Cary?"

"Not all of them," said Cary.

"Perhaps that's part of the problem," said the Watchman. "I'll
tell you why clocks are round, Cary. They're round to remind
us that things go in circles—up one side and down the other and
back round again. That's the way it is with Time. If you wait long
enough, certain things come round again, regular as clockwork:
mornings and evenings, springs and winters, being born and
passing away. If you watch long enough, as I have, you get to
know the rhythms.

"You can't tell just how things are going to happen each time,
just as you can't know for sure what the weather is going to be
like on the first day of autumn, even though you know that
sooner or later it has to get colder. Perhaps your Uptown world
has forgotten some of that, Cary—trying to keep it summer
when it's time for fall, or making winter in the midst of spring."

"But what does all that have to do with *me*?" asked Cary, that
hollow, burning feeling growing once again inside him.

"A fair question, Cary," said the Watchman. "I can only tell you this. There are little circles and big circles, lifetimes and millennia. And, once in a while, two of them come together. That's why you're here. The little circle of your life has gotten tangled up with one of the biggest circles there is. Until you get them untangled, you won't be able to get back where you belong."

"But why did it have to be *me*?"

"It *didn't* have to be you, Cary. It still doesn't, if you're willing to turn your back on the Past. But I don't think you are, or you wouldn't be here now. Something called you here. And something is keeping you here. There's something you have to do, something that's part of one of those bigger circles. Until you do it, it won't be Time for you to leave."

The hollow feeling inside Cary's chest grew stronger, until the ache was almost a pleasure. The clocks all around him seemed to be ticking to the beat of his heart.

"What do I have to do?" he asked at last, barely breathing.

"Only you can answer that, Cary," said the Watchman. "Only you know where you should go next. I only know you've come as far Up in Down Town as you can go for now, and there's no way out of here. To find your way back, to find your place on the circle, you'll have to go back into the Past, just as the hands of a clock must go down to six o'clock before they can come round again to seven. You're at sixes and sevens now, Cary, and the only way Up for you is Down, as strange as that may seem."

Time stopped. Somewhere deep inside Cary, something very small or very large shifted slightly. The Watchman was right. There *was* something he had to do. A small, quiet voice had been trying to tell him something. He could hear it whispering to him now. If he could only be still and listen, he was sure that voice would become clear. But his mind kept chattering away, as if it wanted to keep him from hearing. Then he remembered the Poet's poem. He started saying those jumbled lines under his breath.

While his mind was distracted, a vivid image appeared before his eyes.

"There's a place I've got to get to," said Cary. "A green place, a very *old* place, with tall trees and falling water."

"That would be the Green Wood, Cary," said the Watchman, "the oldest and largest of the Squares."

"Squares?" asked Cary.

"Even an Uptowner should know that the city is built around Squares, Cary. They're the open places that keep it alive and breathing. Time Square is one of them, despite all the noise and bustle. But the Green Wood is the most important Square of all. It makes it possible for Down Town to exist, by holding in Time. A part of it can even be found Uptown, Cary; what you call Central Park. If that's where you're going, you'd best be on your way. There's very little Time left," he said with a glance at his watch. Cary noticed the case was engraved with a wide-spreading oak tree. The hands on the watch pointed straight up.

Cary turned to face Allie. "You don't have to go with me," he said. "I can make it alone now."

"You ain't gettin' rid of me that easy," said Allie. "I promised to help you get back Uptown, and that's what I'm gonna do. A Scamp don't go back on her word. Besides," she said, "everybody says I'm part of this, too. If there is some big muckadoo brewin', I ain't about to be left out of it. An' that's final."

"Okay, Allie. Which way to the Green Wood?" Cary asked the Watchman.

"Straight up the Broad Way. Here. Take these. You'll need them." Out of an old chest the Watchman had taken a pile of old clothes. He handed Allie a long white coat with a fur collar, and an outlandish hat with a long veil. To Cary he gave a beat-up tuxedo jacket and an old top hat.

"What're these for?" asked Allie.

"Festival will begin at any moment," said the Watchman. "In all the noise and confusion, you'll stand more of a chance of escaping if you're wearing these."

With a shrug, Cary pulled on the oversized coat and placed the hat on the top of his head. Allie put on her overcoat and hat, and gazed with satisfaction at her reflection in the mirrored glass of a standing clock.

"You'd best be going!" said the Watchman, stuffing wads of cotton into his ears. "Time's a'wasting!" He held open the door of the shop, and Cary and Allie dashed through it. As it closed, Cary could hear all the clocks chiming at once.

THE CHIMING INSIDE was echoed by the deafening booms of the great clock above them, hammering out the hours. From all over Down Town, gongs and bells answered, and there was a roar from hundreds of exultant voices. Ticker tape and confetti began to fall from the windows above like multicolored snow, and from everywhere at once appeared hordes of revelers and merrymakers blowing horns and banging drums. It looked to Cary like New Year's Eve at high noon.

The Broad Way stretched out ahead of them at a wide angle to the other avenues, and Cary could see a trace of green at its end a dozen blocks away. He found himself running, nearly bowling over other pedestrians as he streaked along the crowded sidewalk.

"Whoa, speedo!" cried Allie. "Wait for me!"

They zigged and zagged about the dazed, crazed celebrants who clogged the streets in ever-increasing numbers. At the end of the block was a wide intersection filled with people. As Allie started to cross, Cary grabbed her wrist, pulling her back. A group of Badmashers stood on a wide traffic island, peering intently in all directions.

Cary looked back the way they'd come. One of the Badmashers was looking back and forth from Cary to the wanted poster on a nearby pole.

"Come on, Allie!" said Cary. "Let's run for it!" A screeching whistle spread the alarm in all directions.

"Did somebody call a cab?" rumbled a deep bass voice.

A brand new Model A had pulled up within inches of Cary's toes. It was covered in black-and-white checks. The driver reached out and opened the passenger door. A black-and-white checked interior beckoned invitingly.

"Well, *do* you want a ride or don't you?" the Cabby asked again. "He told me you'd be waiting here right about now. I guess he was right at that."

"Who was?"

"The Watchman. Called me this morning and told me to be on *this* corner at exactly *this* time and take whoever was there wherever they wanted to go. How long you been waiting?"

The Cabby was a burly black man with a bushy beard that seemed checked with a pepper-and-salt pattern. A dapper derby with a checked band was perched rakishly on his head, and he wore a checked suit, black shirt, white shoes, and a checkered bow tie. Even his smile was checkered with gold and silver teeth.

"We just got here," said Allie.

"Ooo-eee!" said the Cabby. "That's what I call cutting it *close*!" He gave a loud, rumbling laugh and then said, "I wouldn't stand there all day if I were you. Festival's just started, and cabs'll be hard to get a hold of. Besides, there are some gentlemen in black headed this way in a powerful hurry, and I don't think you want to wait around to greet them."

Cary glanced over his shoulder. A group of 'Mashers were marching in their direction.

"He's got a point, Cary," said Allie, hopping into the backseat. "Get in!" She yanked on his arm, and he fell across her as the cab peeled off in a screech of tires, the door hanging open. At the last minute, a 'Masher caught hold of it, but Cary slammed it hard on his fingers and he fell off.

"Looks like I came along just in the nick of time," said the Cabby. "But then, the Watchman always *did* have a knack for timing. Where to?"

"The Green Wood," said Cary. "And fast!"

"*Fast,* you say?" said the Cabby with a laugh. "Hold onto your head, son, so we don't leave it behind!"

They were thrown back against the seat as the Cabby floored the accelerator. The buildings and people whirled by as the Green Wood grew rapidly closer. Then, from behind them, came a wailing scream and a flashing light. A black limousine was following them, overflowing with 'Mashers inside and out.

"Step on it, willya!" said Allie, anxiously. "They're *gainin'* on us!"

"Don't worry your head about it," said the Cabby. "There's nothing can catch my little cab. Watch my dust!"

The cab leapt ahead, leaving the coach behind in a dense cloud of smoke. When Cary looked back, it was nowhere in sight. But just then, the Cabby said, "Uh-oh, trouble!"

Ahead, Cary could see the Green Wood only a block or two away. The Broad Way entered a tunnel at the corner of the wood, near a wide circle with a giant statue of a man holding a globe in one hand and a pair of calipers in the other.

But across the roadway, there was a wooden barricade in front of the entrance to the wood.

"Hold tight, children!" called the Cabby. "This calls for some fancy footwork." Turning the steering wheel hand over hand, the Cabby swung the cab up onto the curb and into a brick wall. Cary covered his eyes, waiting for the crash. But at the last minute the cab swerved and bounced off the wall, heeling up onto two wheels, throwing Cary on top of Allie again. It reeled back toward the barricade and knocked it apart. The 'Mashers scattered to avoid being run over.

The cab dropped back down with a painful crash. A moment later they were roaring toward the tunnel. The cab jounced down the steep grade, its tires jolting on the old cobbled street. Cary heard the Cabby call out something he couldn't make out. Then they were in the tunnel.

FOURTEEN

T_{HEN} THE WORLD reappeared in an explosion of lush green.

Cary and Allie had tumbled onto a luxurious carpet of soft moss, dotted with red and yellow flowers. They lay in the midst of a grotto that glowed with green life. The cab had disappeared.

A gurgling rivulet bounced over a rocky cascade and disappeared behind a fold of rock. A winding rock stair led upward, and verdant light spilled down the steps to touch Cary's fingertips.

Cary got slowly to his feet, then held out his hand to Allie and helped her up. Together they climbed the winding steps. When they saw what lay beyond, they stopped in awe, stunned with wonder.

They were in the midst of the deepest, greenest wood Cary had ever seen, only a hundred times deeper and greener. Tall, gnarled trees with ivy entangled in their branches formed a canopy of greens and golds. Birds of various colors—coral and crimson, sapphire and brilliant yellow—darted among the leaves, filling the air with their warbling.

A winding path led off into the trees, and from it came a gentle whisper of water and soft breezes. It drew Cary irresistibly, and he found his feet following it.

The path led across a wooden footbridge over a sparkling stream. In the gap between the branches overhead, Cary saw high above a mist-wreathed rock ceiling so far away it looked almost like the sky. The mists shifted, and Cary thought he could see the full moon, tinged greenish gold. Just then, some swift creature—a bird?—crossed the sky, and the moon broke into silver-gold glimmers and was gone. It was as if a great lake hung over them like a cloud.

The trees parted, and Cary and Allie found themselves at the edge of a wide paved walkway lined with slim white birches. Here it was like a park, but wilder and more alive. The foliage was denser and more tangled, the rocks craggier, the brooks barely keeping within their banks. Animals walked without fear across their path: pheasants and woodchucks, rabbits and foxes, beavers and geese, bobcats and deer, and even a great lumbering shape that might have been a bear.

Even the man-made things seemed part of it all. A gas streetlamp was encircled with carved bronze vines that bloomed with real blossoms. The feet of the park benches looked like paws and claws and talons, which seemed to shift restlessly as they passed. Even the statues that lined the path seemed to turn with them, changing attitudes with the shifting of the light.

Then one of them bent and touched Cary lightly on the shoulder. "Well, how do I look?" said a familiar voice. It was the Poet, standing on a vacant pedestal, striking a heroic pose. Cary saw that they were passing a pavilion with a plaque that said POETS

WALK, surrounded by statues of famous poets, just a little larger than life-size.

I was just trying it on for size," said the Poet sheepishly. "I'm not quite ready for immortality yet. I see you did find your way after all, Cary. I was sure you would. Shall we go?"

"Go where?" asked Cary.

"To Taara," said the Poet. "That *is* why you came, isn't it?"

"What's Taara?" asked Allie. "Another one of your poems?"

"Taara, a poem?" said the Poet. "I suppose she is, in a way. No, Taara's the oldest living being in all of Down Town. She's been waiting for you to find her."

"But if you knew all along where I was supposed to go, why didn't you tell me before?" asked Cary.

"I told you you came here to find something you already had, to learn something you already knew, Cary," said the Poet. "Until you *knew* you knew, there was no way I could tell you. Come. I'll take you to her."

Cary and Allie followed the Poet along the rambling path that threaded its way past lakes and lawns, through fields and thickets, deeper into the Wood. On a warm breeze came the sultry scent of ripe bananas and the sound of far-off drums. A moment later, Cary caught the musky spice of new-mown hay and the heady smell of heather, laced with the melancholy lilt of a flute. Then the air grew cooler and thick with the fragrance of pine.

"There's a bit of every sort of wilderness here," said the Poet, as if in answer to his unspoken question. "Whatever the peoples of Down Town brought with them from their old countries. It's as I said, Cary. What you find here depends largely on how you come, and what you bring with you."

They began a descent into a deep valley. The farther down they went, the fewer traces of human handiwork there were. The neat park paths gave way to forest tracks that were hard to make out in the wild half-light. But the rustle of the trees grew stronger as Cary walked, and he thought he could hear his name in the soft murmurs of the trees.

The trail they followed divided, and before the Poet could show them the way, Cary turned onto the left-hand one, almost overgrown with greenery, drawn by a force he could not name. They were clambering down steep rocks now. Allie was close by his side, and he could hear her soft breathing, but the Poet was huffing and puffing to keep up with them. More than once, Cary's hands or feet lost their grip, and he skidded a few feet, but the deep urgency within him drove him on.

They broke through a patch of thicket on the crest of a bluff that overlooked a wide valley. Below them, a torrent of water gushed forth, dropping over roots and rocks to form a great mere below. On the far shore of the pool was a thick grove of trees. Cary found himself scrambling down the hillside and running along the path that circled the pond, his pulse hammering in his ears.

The path ended in a broad clearing. Cary stopped, as if held by an unseen force.

Here was the place he'd been dreaming about. There was the great waterfall and the wide lake. And beyond, the grove, at once forbidding and inviting. He held his breath, and he could feel the world turning under him. He let it go, and a whispering breeze rustled the leaves and cooled his skin.

"I'll be leaving you here," said the Poet.

"But why?" said Cary.

"This part of your journey is over now, Cary. You don't need me to show you the way anymore," he said. "You know where you're going. And when you know the way, there's sure to be others who will help you find it." And with a wave, he was off. Cary watched him for a time, until he merged with the green of the trees, then started down the lane into the heart of the grove.

The trees began to lean over them, and it grew darker, almost like twilight. Allie, who'd been strangely silent, kept staring about her, wide-eyed.

"What is it?" asked Cary at last. "Haven't you ever seen trees before?"

"Not so many all at once!" she said in a hushed whisper. Then she stopped. "Look!" she said. There, ahead, stood a dark figure, blocking their way.

"Well, there you are at last!" said a cracked and rasping voice. "Kept me waiting long enough!"

It was an ancient woman, wrapped in a mottled brown robe marked with strange round designs. Her hands were dark and thick and gnarled like tree roots, and her shoulders were stooped and humped. Her face was incredibly old, pulled tight against the bones of her skull. Her skin was nut-brown and leathery, like a miniature hillside, cut deep with gulleys and ravines. Two white braids lay against her cheeks like snowfall on a hillside. Her lined neck and sharp features reminded Cary of a snapping turtle. But though there wasn't an ounce of softness in her face, there was gentleness in her deep-brown eyes.

"Come here where I can see you," said the old woman sharply, squinting her eyes. They stepped forward, and she peered at them closely. "So young," she muttered, almost to herself. "So very young. Well, come along." And she reached out to grasp Allie's arm.

"Not *me*," said Allie, *"Him!"*

"You?" said the old woman. "It can't be. This one, young as she is, at least has some of the old blood in her." Her hand brushed the feather in Allie's hair lightly. "But you—"

"I was called here," said Cary, startled a bit at the sound of his own voice.

"What?" said the old woman. "Who called you?"

"I don't know for sure," said Cary. "A voice, like the sound of the wind, calling my name. I *had* to come. I was told I would find Taara here. Is that you?"

The old woman made a strange noise that Cary realized was laughter, old and unaccustomed laughter. "Me? Taara?" she said at last. "No, young one. I am only Unami, keeper of Taara's grove. It's strange that one who comes to Taara should not know her. Perhaps the calling was not meant for one of you

alone. Perhaps you two, together, are the one she seeks. Come."
And with that she was hobbling off deeper into the grove. Cary
and Allie followed after.

A moment later, Unami held up her hand to halt them. "This
is a place of great power, young ones," said Unami. "Here it is
as it was when the world was young. Here, in this place, an oath
was sworn between your people and mine," she said, looking
deep into Cary's eyes. "A pledge to be honored above all others,
that this one place shall be free to grow, unharmed and un-
spoiled, as long as the waters run and the trees stand under
heaven."

Unami's hand clutched Cary's shoulder. "A promise was
made here, years ago, young one, a promise from which all
others flow. It must be remade by each generation, with its
words, and with its heart. So long as that oath is kept, the earth
is yours, to do with as you wish. But it is said that if that oath
is ever broken, Time itself will stop, and a great darkness will
descend forever upon the world. Do you understand, young
one?"

"I think so," said Cary.

"Good," said Unami with a hint of a smile. "Then I have not
lingered here in vain. Come along then, both of you. Taara
awaits you."

As he passed, Cary felt a prickling at the back of his neck and
a tingling in his fingertips. A moment later, he found Allie's
hand in his.

At the end of the pathway, Cary and Allie stopped, unable to
move. Before them was a scene of unearthly beauty. An aisle of
tall trees met overhead in a tangled arch that flashed and spar-
kled with the glimmer of fireflies. From among the trees a thousand pairs of eyes watched them. The wind stirred, and the
murmur of the trees rose to a rushing roar as if in greeting, then
died down to a hush.

The colonnade of trees ended in a circular clearing. At first,
all Cary saw was a wide umber shadow. Then his eyes followed

the dark shape upward, and all at once it came clear, a tall, slender tree hundreds of feet in height, whose tops were lost in the mists above and whose bottom was a wide skirt of thick, twining roots. As they drew closer, Cary could see a great white owl, with a fierce beak and great jutting horns, slumbering in one of the lowest branches.

The wind moved again, and the air felt charged with electricity. The sighing of the great tree's branches was like a great choir singing a hauntingly familiar hymn. Just then, the moon broke through the cloud lake above, and the tree was bathed in a soft, milky radiance. A breeze stirred the back of Cary's hair, swirling lightning bugs with it, and he felt a sweetness inside him that was almost more than he could bear.

The owl's eyes opened. It turned its great head back and forth, twitching its feathery horns and moving its claws. Then the mists moved and the moon vanished, and the wind grew colder, and Cary had to blink his eyes three times to clear them of the green-gold blur that clouded them.

Unami stood next to the tree, steadying herself with a gnarled hand. She lifted her chin high and began to speak. "This is Taara, young ones," she said in a hoarse but piercing voice. "She has stood here, in this place, for longer than any living thing, since the time when the only people here were hunters and fishermen who strayed far from their homes. Her roots now reach deep into the earth, and her branches, high into the air. The birds of the air and the beasts of the land and the fishes in the water are her eyes and ears, telling her all that happens here.

"I have listened to her since the days when we were both young and green. In those days, she spoke often about earth and water and sky, when there were still those who knew how to listen. But I fear neither she nor I have the strength to speak again. Now her roots cannot find water, and her branches cannot find air. She has grown old and tired and forgetful, as I have. She speaks only to me now, in dreams even I do not understand. I fear it may be too late—"

"But I *have* to speak with her, Unami," said Cary. "I don't know why exactly, but it must be important, or she wouldn't have called me here, would she?"

Unami was silent for a long time. She seemed to be listening to the rustling of Taara's leaves, the chirping of the birds, the wind on the water. At last she nodded, as if at an unheard sound.

"There is a way," she said at last. There was a weary sadness in her voice that touched something in Cary. "It will take all of our strength, but it can be done. It is good that your young friend here has a great heart and the blood of the First People. That will make our medicine circle stronger."

"What's a medicine circle?" asked Cary.

"It's a way of touching the spirits of things," said Unami. "It is not usually done with ones so young as you, but now we have no choice. And it is said that to make a Great Circle, such as we must make, each within it must be willing to give up something dear to them some day. I do not know what will be asked of you, young ones, or when, but I know it will be asked. Are you willing?"

"I'm willing," said Cary.

"Me, too," said Allie.

"Good," said Unami. "Then come, sit next to me here, next to Taara." She lowered herself stiffly to the ground, pulling her blanket tighter about her and shivering a bit, though it didn't feel very cold to Cary. They seated themselves beside her, cross-legged, in the curve of one of Taara's great roots.

"Now," said Unami. "Be still. Very still. Feel the weight of your body against the ground, the heaviness of your arms and legs. Hear the wind as it caresses your cheek. Smell the scent of the earth, and taste the inside of your mouth. Be aware of yourself, with all of your senses. When you are ready, you will know it."

Cary found it hard to sit still. All sorts of places on him itched or ached, and he had a hard time getting comfortable. But then he began to listen to the soft wood noises, and feel the earth

beneath him, and it stilled his buzzing brain, just like the Poet's poem had.

His eyes had drifted shut. When he opened them, Unami had taken from under her cloak a carved wooden pipe, tipped in pale stone, and a small leather pouch, ornamented with beads. From the bag she took a pinch of pungent herbs and filled the bowl, then lit it with a spark struck from two small stones, blowing on the fire to kindle it.

Then she drew deep on the pipe, blowing out a cloud of milky smoke that smelled of the essence of the forest. Then she passed it to Allie, who inhaled deeply, then shuddered, as if restraining a cough, and passed the pipe to Cary. The warm smoke stung his throat as it entered his chest, and he began to feel light-headed. As he handed the pipe back to Unami, she began to chant in a low rhythm that seemed to pulse with the blood in his temples. Unami placed the pipe in the center of the circle, and as the three joined hands, Cary felt his body tingling and shifting.

His eyes closed again. When he opened them again, the Green Wood looked somehow different.

It was as if he were under water, only the water was the glowing light that came from above. There was a liquid sound in his ears that sounded something like singing and something like water falling. It was Taara talking to him, he was sure, but Cary couldn't understand.

He looked across to Allie, who sat before him motionless, eyes closed. She seemed to be glowing somehow, brighter even than the moonlit leaves. Suddenly he'd touched something in her, and her thoughts were his thoughts. He pulled away after only a moment, but not before he'd been nearly drowned in a rush of feelings: old, scarred-over memories of pain and sadness, worry about what might happen to the Scamps without her to take care of them, tender feelings about someone called Scotty that caused a small hurt inside him—and her feelings about *him*, too, that made him blush with embarrassment.

Then, through Allie's eyes, he was seeing Unami, wondering if she would ever be that old and wrinkled. A moment later, he was touching Unami herself. At first all he sensed was the dimness of her sight and the dullness of her hearing, the painful stiffness in her limbs, the shortness of her breath, and a sharp, aching twinge in her chest. But then, the sound of her chanting filled his head, and he was looking up at Taara, as if he had eyes in the back of his head.

At first, he saw her as before, as a tall tree. Then, for just an instant, he saw her as a woman, an ageless, beautiful woman with brown skin and hair of golden green, frozen in a timeless dance. He strained to make out her face, but it disappeared in a fold of bark.

Then the soft sighing song became a deafening roar that made pictures in his head instead of sounds in his ears. First, he was looking down on the circle from a great height, seeing all three of them grow smaller and smaller. Then he was seeing all of the Green Wood, but in all directions at once, as if his very skin was able to see.

Then he saw the ground, but it was a seeing of roots and limbs that reached out under the whole of the city at once, into every crack and corner. For a moment he was seeing every part of Down Town that was touched by the sight or scent or sound of Taara, or her younger offshoots in the farthest parks and Squares. It became too much for him to understand, and for a moment he sank into warm darkness.

Then, in that warm darkness there was another darkness, a gray, cold one, like the chill numbness that had filled him when Miles Brand's eyes met his. Cary felt the gray coldness seeping into his own roots and branches, slowing his blood and stealing around his heart. He was filled with a great weariness, and he wanted just to let go, to slip into the darkness, to sink into the soil and sleep. . . .

He pulled back in fear and was suddenly in his own body again. Across from him, Unami was ashen pale, her skin waxy and almost translucent. Next to him, Allie's youthful life-force beat strongly inside her, giving him strength. And about his own neck, the disk on its silver chain was burning with an eerie heat.

He lifted it to the light and peered through it. Light glistened off its myriad rings, and it shimmered like a rainbow in his hand. He looked closer, and he seemed to be drawn into those many circles, deeper and deeper. He felt as if he were falling into the heart of the disk.

Through the disk's center, he saw the Green Wood as it had once been, centuries before—much the same, except that Taara was a green and slender sapling, growing up among the fallen stumps of her elders, and Unami was just a girl, barely Allie's age. As he moved outward through the surrounding rings, Taara, Unami, and the world all aged, and history whirled past, from the earliest settlements almost to his own time.

But as the rings grew wider, and Taara and Unami grew older, that cold darkness began to close in. It surrounded all of Down Town, and suddenly the city felt fragile, delicate, like an egg-shell in an iron fist. Suddenly he saw the Green Wood devoid of green, the sky dark and stormy, the trees bleak and bare of leaves, shrouded under a wide white blanket of snow. Only the warmth of Taara at its heart kept it alive. And that warmth was fading, fading. . . .

Cary held on tightly to the disk, the only other source of light and warmth in all that cold and darkness. Then, suddenly, a flower of burning heat bloomed in his chest, and he surrendered to the darkness.

CARY FOUND HIMSELF lying facedown in the soft grass, the palms of his hands throbbing, his head still spinning. The air had taken on a slight chill, as if a northern breeze were whispering of winter. The coolness roused Cary, and he stirred slightly and groaned.

Propping himself on one elbow, he rubbed his eyes and shook

his head. There was a harsh, burnt taste in his mouth. Between his parted fingers, he saw Allie lying still on the ground.

"Allie," he said softly.

She didn't move.

"*Allie!*" he said again. "Are you all right?"

The color came back into her cheeks, and her eyes fluttered. "What? Oh, yeah, I'm okay, just a little dizzy, that's all." Then she turned to him with the strangest expression on her face—a look of sadness, mingled with something else he couldn't place. A moment later she got to her knees, then sat down again.

"Wow!" she said a moment later. "That was really something, y'know?"

"What did you see, Allie?"

"Well, at first I felt as if the world had turned sideways, and I was in one corner, looking down at everything at once—even me, not caring what was going on but just, you know, *watching* everything. Then this voice started filling my head, only I couldn't understand what it was saying. And then I began to see everything so clearly, like I never saw anything before. I saw flowers that grew outa nowhere, clouds that looked like mountains floating over bubbles of air that shimmered like rainbows. And one of the bubbles got larger and larger until it burst with music that kind of tinkled down like busted crystal. Oh, I know none of this makes sense, but it sure did then. . . ."

"It makes sense to me, Allie," said Cary softly.

"I'm glad it does to *somebody*," said Allie, "because then I felt like I was being pulled out of bed, only instead of my bed, I was being pulled out of my *body*. And I had my arms out, and I went sailing straight up into the air. It felt so *real,* I can still feel the breeze as I went soaring. All I had to do was just tilt my head and I went zooming off in that direction, backward and forward, up and down. And I wasn't afraid of crashing or getting hurt or anything."

Allie's face clouded. "Then it started getting scary. I was no longer in control. I kept zoomin' all over the place. And then I was headin' toward this dark cloud that filled the whole sky, and I could hear the Scamps calling my name over and over, fainter and fainter. I tried to break away but I couldn't; it took everything I had to get away. Then I flew back here and I saw my body lying there on the ground, and yours, too, and Unami's, only she looked *different,* like she—"

"Like she was dead?" asked Cary quietly.

"Yeah. Like she was dead, Cary. It really scared me. Pretty creepy dream, huh?"

"It wasn't a dream, Allie," said Cary. A cold certainty told him what he'd find if he looked behind him. He turned and walked toward the still figure in the grass.

The old woman lay unmoving. Her eyes were open and her lips were half parted, but there was no sign of life in that still face, just old skin over old bone. Allie came up behind him and put one hand on his shoulder. As they watched, a fly landed on Unami's face, rubbing its legs at the corner of her mouth. Allie shuddered and turned away, crossing her arms over her chest and rubbing herself up and down.

"Isn't there anything we can do for her?" said Allie at last.

"No, Allie," said Cary, feeling more grown-up than he ever had before. "She gave up the thing that was most dear to her, just to make our circle. She had a purpose in life, a task to do, and now it's over. So do we. Come on, Allie, it's time to go."

"But we can't just *leave* her here like this!" said Allie.

At that moment, the wind blew cold about them, and a single red-tinged oak leaf drifted down to land beside Unami at their feet.

"Taara will take care of her, Allie. We've got our own work to do. Now come *on.* There isn't much time left."

"What are you *talkin'* about?"

"I know what I have to do now. Taara told me."

"You mean that wasn't all just a dream? All that stuff about the Scamps bein' in trouble and the black cloud and all was *true*? Even—"

"What, Allie?"

"Nothin'. Skip it."

"No, Allie. *Tell* me."

"I said skip it, didn't I?" she said sullenly. A great gust of cold wind swirled about them, and red and golden leaves began to fall like snowflakes from above. "Now, let's get goin'. If you're gonna go off and play hero, I'm stickin' with you. You'd be hopeless by yourself."

"Thanks, Allie," said Cary. "I really appreciate it."

"There you go *thankin'* me again. Save it, willya? It's bad enough I'm takin' orders from trees without you gettin' all mushy on me, okay?"

"Okay, Allie," said Cary. "Hey, look!" Where Unami's lifeless body had lain only moments before, there was nothing. Nothing except a small land turtle with leathery skin and dark-brown eyes, and a pattern on its back that reminded Cary of Unami's robe.

FIFTEEN

As CARY WALKED slowly away from Taara's grove with Allie silent by his side, a chill wind dug its fingers deep into his soul. There was a melancholy sadness in the song of the birds, and the brilliant green of the trees seemed to fade before his gaze. He pulled the old coat the Watchman had given him tighter about him.

In the middle of his chest, where the disk lay, Cary felt a sweet pain. It felt a little like fear or sadness, but there was an excitement to it as well. The skin of his face felt tight against his bones, and his muscles felt charged with a restless energy. Turning his face into the strengthening wind, he began to walk more quickly.

"Cary?" said Allie quietly after a time.

He turned to face her. "What is it, Allie?" The wind had mussed her hair, and she'd turned the soft white collar of her coat high up about her chin. There was a look in her eyes that Cary had never seen before.

"Oh, it's nothing. It's just—well, I'm sorry for what I said before about you bein' the hero type and all. Maybe you ain't the Promised One everybody's been waitin' for, but you got guts all the same. And—and I just want you to know that whatever you gotta do, I'll stick with you, no matter what. Okay?"

"Okay, Allie," said Cary. "That means a lot right now."

"There's just one thing I gotta ask."

"What's that, Allie?"

"Just what is it that you *do* gotta do?"

Cary smiled. "I don't know exactly," he answered. "All I know is that there's a place I have to find—a cold, dark place way down in Down Town. When I get there, I'll know what to do next— I think."

Allie shook her head. "Not much to go on, is it?"

"Nope," said Cary, "but it's all I've got."

IN THE MIRROR on the wall, Miles Brand watched as scene shifted to scene. He'd lost his quarry in Time Square through an uncanny combination of treachery and luck. It seemed the boy had a positive gift for finding those few Down Towners remaining who dared to defy his power, to aid him in his escape.

This time he'd vanished into the Green Wood, a region so dense with the noxious vapors of grasses and trees that even his own 'Mashers dared not venture there. But again, time and fate were on Brand's side. He had learned from Zenovac the most probable course the young man would now take and had stationed his ablest lieutenants along that route, ready to intercept him.

And the beauty of his plan was this: Zenovac assured Brand

he did not even have to capture him. He only had to ensure the boy went where Brand intended him to go.

SOMEHOW CARY AND Allie found their way to a broad stair that led up and out of the Green Wood. At the top of one long flight, they paused a moment to rest, and Cary looked back at the wide panorama below him. The whole landscape was afire with autumn colors now, and a few brown, shriveled leaves had begun to fall. Far away, beyond a lake of silver, was a high stand of trees that must be Taara's grove. The sight filled him with a restless impatience, and he started quickly up the steps again, with Allie close behind.

At each landing the walls and lamps and benches became more modern and the land around them more tame and well groomed. At last, the steps wound through an arching bower overhung with ripe grapes. Allie plucked a few and tossed her head back to eat them, frisky as a colt. Beyond was a stone wall with a sign on it saying TO THE PLAZA, with an arrow pointing left.

They turned the corner, and once again Cary thought he was Uptown for a moment. A monumental fountain decorated with shells and nymphs stood before a grand, opulent hotel by a wide avenue stretching away before them. Horse-drawn carriages made their way about the circle, picking up and unloading elegantly dressed passengers, dressed in light fall coats.

Allie began to glance around nervously.

"What's wrong?" asked Cary.

"I dunno," said Allie. "There's somethin' about this place that gives me the creeps. Like we was bein' watched or somethin'."

"*There* you are!" boomed a merry voice. "Lovely day for a ride, isn't it?" Cary turned to see who was speaking. An open carriage painted in black-and-white checks had pulled up before them. The pied horse was covered with a checked saddle blanket. The driver tipped his derby and smiled, revealing gleaming checked teeth.

"It's the Cabby!" said Allie. "How did *you* get here?"

"How did *I* get here?" the Cabby asked. "I was just about to ask you the same thing! Didn't I just drop you at the other corner a minute or two ago?"

"Nope," said Allie. "That was more like *hours* ago. . . ."

"Looks like he's up to his old tricks again," said the Cabby.

"Who is?" said Cary.

"The Watchman. He told me to stop at this corner, too! Guess he thought you'd need help again."

"But we ain't bein' chased by 'Mashers now," said Allie.

"I don't know about that," said the Cabby. "Sounds like *something's* coming."

At first, Cary couldn't hear anything. Then a clanging sounded faintly, growing louder, accompanied by a clip-clop sound. A moment later, a bright-red fire engine rounded a corner, steam belching from its smokestack, pulled by two coal-black horses. Though they wore old-fashioned fireman's hats, there was no mistaking its crew.

"'Mashers!" said Allie. "I *told* you we was bein' watched."

"Well, children, shall we depart?" Cary and Allie had barely clambered aboard when the Cabby cracked his whip in the air, and the horse reared up and, with hooves striking sparks, took off at a gallop down the avenue.

The street was lined with elegant town houses and shops, and most of the people were dressed in grand finery. The buildings and the people looked far more old-fashioned than they had in Time Square. There were no motorcars at all, and very few lights. From behind them, the clanging grew louder. The fire engine was gaining on them!

"Look out!" Allie cried. The two 'Mashers at the back of the engine had uncoiled a great hose. One pumped up and down on a wide handle, while the other pointed its nozzle at them. A moment later, a great spray of water knocked off the Cabby's derby, spraying Cary and Allie at the same time.

"That did it!" said the Cabby. "Time to take a little evasive action!" Hauling hard on the reins, the Cabby pulled the coach in a tight curve onto a narrow little side street that bore the name Jump Street. "Oh, I almost forgot to ask. Where are you headed?"

"I'm not sure," said Cary. "Somewhere way down in Down Town. At the very bottom. That's all I know."

"Well, I'm not sure I can take you all *that* way, but I'll surely do my best. But to shake off those 'Mashers, we've got to take a little detour uptown first."

"You can take me back *Up*town?" asked Cary eagerly.

"No, I'm sorry. I meant uptown in Down Town. That's a different thing altogether."

"It'll take forever in this horse and buggy," said Allie. "We would've made better time if you'd kept your old flivver."

"But this *is* my old flivver," laughed the Cabby.

"What do you mean?" asked Cary.

"Hold tight. I'll show you!" And with that the Cabby reached forward and flicked down a lever on a little clockwork meter on the dashboard. The world blurred, and suddenly the cab had changed, back to the Model A that had first picked them up. It was driving along a treelined residential street across from a park.

"Hey! What's goin' on here?" said Allie. "Lemme outa this thing!"

"Relax," said the Cabby. "Nellie won't hurt you. This is just how we get about—by jumping."

"*Jumping?*" asked Cary, wondering if the Cabby had flipped his lid.

"You've played checkers before, haven't you?" asked the Cabby.

"Yes, but—"

"So you know that a checker can go from place to place by jumping from square to square, right?"

"Yes, but—"

"Well, this is a *checker* cab. It can go from Square to Square too, but it does it by jumping from Time to Time, see?"

"I don't think so," said Cary.

"Let me see if I can explain it," said the Cabby. "You might say Down Town is made sort of like a layer cake, with one era right on top of another. The easiest way to get from one layer to another is by way of the Squares. My cab, Nellie, can take a kind of shortcut from one Square to another, but she can only do it by jumping from one Time to another. Like just now, we jumped from the Plaza—that's one of the Squares, too—right up to Saint Nick's Place. That's Nellie's home turf, so it's the place she thought of first."

"But why did the cab turn into a car from a—a *horse*?"

"Well, that's the only way the Watchman could make his meter work, turning Nellie into something that fits the Time."

From a small chapel across the street came a choir of voices singing a sweet, sad tune. A moment later, Cary heard the blare of a cornet. From the window of the cab he saw a round man with a fringe of gray hair playing the same tune mournfully on a street corner in front of a funeral parlor. Down the steps, to the beat of a bass drum, a coffin was being carried into the street by four stocky, white-haired men. As the coffin reached the street, the slow dirge of the horn picked up the beat of the drum and began to wail. Soon a clarinet and trombone joined in, playing Dixieland jazz.

The cab was now puttering along a wide street filled with people. The air was laden with music. From a saloon on the corner, a piano tinkled ragtime, while three boys on a stoop harmonized *a capella*, making complex rhythms with only their hands, feet, and old spoons. Farther along, a lone saxophonist warbled a weird version of the tune in wild and anguished tones.

As they crossed to the next block, the street was filled with dancers, and the Cabby had to tap his horn in order to pass. The air was sweet with the scent of blossoms and perfume, tinged with the frostiness of an autumn evening. The faces on the street were the same swirl of chocolate and ebony and tan, but the music had a Latin lilt. A man surrounded by hand-clapping onlookers beat out a sprightly tune on a steel drum. Beyond, two men in bright-colored shirts played maracas and congas, while women in flashing skirts kicked their red heels high.

"I'd love to give you the grand tour," said the Cabby, "but something tells me you're in a bit of a rush. So hold on, here we go again!"

Cary's head spun again, and this time he felt like he was falling. The cab shifted under him, and when he could see again, the soft seat had been replaced by a padded bench. And where the front seat had been was a high perch, where the Cabby now sat steering the car with a little tiller. It looked like one of the earliest electric models.

Ahead of them on the street was a large crowd, dressed in severe formal attire, grouped around a raised dais draped in red, white, and blue bunting. Atop it, a stout gentleman in mutton-chop whiskers spoke to the crowd in a loud voice. Behind them, a large marble building gleamed at the busy intersection. It looked a lot like the 42nd Street Public Library, only there was no roof, and the pedestals where the lions should have been were empty. Police in old-fashioned helmets and long coats were directing traffic. One spotted their cab and waved them over.

"Don't you know you're supposed to have a flag on that contraption?" he said. "There ought to be a law against these horseless carriages on busy streets, where someone could get killed—"

But before he could finish, there was a shrill piping, and Cary saw a group of police running toward them, blowing whistles. Under their blue topcoats and hats, they wore black gloves and dark eyeglasses.

"Jump for it!" cried Allie.

"I'm not sure I can!" said the Cabby. He yanked on the tiller and made a sharp U-turn in the street. "Hang on for your lives. This could get tricky!"

Then they were falling.

It was as if the pavement had melted away, and they were dropping like a stone. Cary's eyes swam, and they were in a coach again, this one an enclosed brougham with a terrified Nellie flailing her hooves in space.

A great shape loomed below. It looked like a pyramid with its top cut off, only the middle was a pair of what looked like square, stone swimming pools joined side to side. Strollers about the edges pointed up as they came plummeting down.

The Cabby hauled on the reins, and their descent slowed a bit, like that of a falling parachute. "Whoa, girl! Slow down!" shouted the Cabby. But it was too late. The spooked mare was hurtling down toward a gleaming glass building below.

Cary saw another horse and carriage hurtling toward them. To his surprise, they, too, were checkered. Then he realized they were looking at their own reflection.

"We're going to crash!" he cried.

THERE WAS AN explosion of flying glass, and Nellie came clattering to the ground, nearly throwing Cary from the carriage. When the coach stopped moving, Cary opened his eyes.

They were inside a vast glass building stretching for a block or more in each direction. It looked like nothing so much as an outsized greenhouse. They seemed to be in a fair or museum or exposition of some sort. Each of the chambers of the great glass structure held some sort of display: paintings and drawings, sculptures, inventions and devices.

The area they were in was given over to a beautiful display of flowers and greenery, marred a bit by a bunch of trampled geraniums and a large horse-and-buggy-sized hole in one of the panes of glass. Nellie had pulled the coach slowly forward, stop-

ping to drink from a small marble fountain and lazily crop the flowers around its border.

"Stop!" shouted a loud voice. A man in a tailcoat and top hat with a red ribbon across his chest was striding in their direction, sputtering and fuming and not making any sense at all. He waved at the wreckage they'd made, and his face turned red above a tight white collar. Behind him a group of dignitaries in a variety of exotic costumes chattered to one another in half a dozen different languages.

They were starting to draw a crowd. Two tall uniformed guards were coming toward them. At first Cary thought they were Badmashers, but they seemed to be the usual sort after all.

"What do we do now?" asked Allie.

The Cabby simply tipped his hat and bowed several times, which caused the dignitaries to tip *their* hats and bow; he then tipped his hat again and bowed again three or four times. When he had everybody tipping and bowing, the Cabby jumped in the carriage, shook the reins, and Nellie started to trot down the long center aisle of the building.

"What *is* this place?" asked Allie, as they passed through a pair of wide glass doors at the other end.

"The Crystal Palace. The marvel of the age. Home of the Great Exposition of Progress and Culture. That place behind it where we came down is the Croton Reservoir at Fifth Avenue and Forty-second Street. It holds all of the drinking water for the city."

"I thought the Public Library was on that corner," said Cary.

"It is, up there," said the Cabby, with an upward motion of his thumb. "Or rather, it will be, after this place burns down. That's the first time Nellie has ever jumped straight down before. I'm not sure how much of that sort of thing she can take. It takes a lot out of the old girl, changing Time and Place and Shape all at once."

The Cabby pulled out onto a broad boulevard and turned south. "I don't see any of Brand's henchmen hereabouts," he said. "We'll let Nellie rest up a bit, then change to something a little swifter at Herald Square. Giddyap, Nellie!" The mare gave him a sad look over her shoulder, then started off slowly.

To their right, the Broad Way joined the road they were on, and the Cabby moved the flag on his meter again. Nellie snorted wearily, and the low buildings about the square before them were replaced by tall, imposing facades. At one end of the Square was a large monument flanked by two carved stone owls. Across from it was a pair of department stores decorated for the holidays. The streets were crowded with shoppers bustling about in the wintry air. On one corner, a sidewalk Santa Claus gave them a broad wave.

The street was overshadowed by a great elevated railway, and the cars on the road were as modern as any Cary had seen, as modern as the sleek checkered roadster they now rode in. As the Cab turned swiftly onto the Broad Way again with a squeal of tires, Cary heard an ominous wailing behind them and saw a flashing red light in the rearview mirror.

"Uh-oh," said the Cabby. "Company!"

"How do they *find* us all the time?" asked Allie. "It's like they could *smell* us or somethin'!"

"Can't you go any faster?" asked Cary anxiously.

"Sorry," said the Cabby with a shake of his head. "My foot's to the floor as it is." The engine was making a laboring sound that was almost a whinny. "But don't worry. There's another Square coming up soon. I'm sure we'll lose them there!" While they spoke, the long dark car had closed half the distance between them.

The wind was raw now, and fat flakes of snow were starting to drift down. Allie moved closer to Cary, as if to share his warmth. Cary rolled up the window, shutting out the cold and the deafening noise. The red light grew nearer in the mirror.

The Cabby moved the flag again, and the cab shuddered in protest. "Come on, girl," he said. Then they were falling again, slower this time, drifting out of the mist like a snowflake, down toward an enormous, fantastical wedding cake of a building that filled an entire city block. Its roof was studded with fanciful towers and a lavish roof garden, and at its center was a tall spire topped with a beautiful bronze statue of a nude woman.

Nellie touched ground, gently this time, as a vintage Model T, just as a lavish coach pulled up before a gilded gate. Liveried footmen rolled out a red carpet and opened the door, and a stout, distinguished-looking man in a white suit stepped out, a lovely lady on his arm.

"What is this place?" asked Cary. "It's beautiful!"

"And who's the swell bein' treated like royalty," asked Allie.

"It's Madison Square Garden," said the Cabby with a chuckle. "Nothing like it before or since. And that's the fellow who de-signed it."

"But I thought Madison Square Garden—" began Cary.

"That place over on Eighth? It isn't in the same league. For one thing, it's not here at Madison Square where it belongs, and for another, it's *round*!"

The Cabby started Nellie puttering slowly down the Broad Way, this time at a slower pace. The sky had begun to darken, and the lights came on, and people were hurrying by in their winter coats and hats. Shivering, Cary pulled the thin little lap robe up over their knees.

Far behind, Cary thought he saw a group of mounted figures galloping after them. Ahead, a broad green park appeared, decked with large banners reading "Solidarity" "Brotherhood" and "Union." As they pulled past, Cary saw a crowd of people shouting and chanting by torchlight while a shirt-sleeved orator on a soap box spoke loudly with upraised fists.

"This is *Union* Square, in case you hadn't guessed," said the Cabby. "It was named for the Union Army in the Civil War, but these days it's mostly used by *labor* unions for speeches and demonstrations." As the cab pulled up, the demonstrators closed around them. One of the leaders knocked on the window.

"Let me handle this," said the Cabby, rolling it down.

"Which side are you on, brother?" said the union man.

The Cabby pulled a card from his hatband. "International Amalgamated Livery Association, Local Number 303," he said with a smile. "What's the buzz, brother?"

"There's talk of a general strike against Brand and his goons. You heard anything?"

There was a clatter of hoofbeats, and four dark figures dressed as mounted police came riding into the circle of light, brandishing nightsticks.

"No time to talk, brothers," said the Cabby, edging the car forward. "We've got 'Mashers after us!"

"You get going!" called one of the leaders. "Now's our chance to give Brand's bulls a taste of their own medicine!" With a loud cry the demonstrators surrounded the 'Mashers. Just as the cab began to roll away, two of the riders broke through.

"Okay, Nellie," said the Cabby softly. "One more time, and then we can rest." He pushed the flag on the meter hard to the left. Nothing happened. He hammered on the meter, and the cab gave a bray of protest. Then, just as a nightstick smashed hard against the window, cracking the glass, the cab gave a violent jolt, and they were spiraling down and down. For a moment, Cary blacked out.

They were sitting in an open carriage again, a grand old-fashioned one, in the midst of a lush and beautiful park surrounded by splendid mansions. Poor Nellie, looking weary and cold, limped to a trough to drink. A thin sheet of ice had formed on the top of the water.

They sat for a while in silence, waiting for Nellie to drink her fill. Allie had wrapped herself up in the checkered blanket to keep warm. "We'd better get going," said Cary at last, "before they find us again. Do you think Nellie can make it?"

"I'm not sure," said the Cabby, patting Nellie's flank. Her sides were lathered with foam and steaming, and her chest heaved. "I've never worked her this hard before. We'd better

not do any more jumping for a while." The Cabby clucked his
tongue and jerked on the reins, and she slowly raised her head.

He began to walk her slowly down the avenue at a slow,
halting pace. After several blocks, she stopped at a wide green
that blocked the end of the road. At the center of the green was
a beautiful white marble arch. The snow had begun to fall steadily now, and there was an eerie quiet about the place.

"Giddyap!" said the Cabby, touching her lightly with his
buggy whip. Nellie just turned, looking at him with a mournful
expression, and bent down to crop the snow-covered grass.

"Well, folks," said the Cabby, brushing snow from his hat,
"I'm afraid that's it, for now at least. She won't be going anywhere at all until she's rested a bit, and maybe had a feed bag
of oats." He stepped forward and stroked Nellie's nose. "We've
never been this far down before, Nellie and me. I'm not sure
what she'll do when she gets closer to the Wall."

"What wall?" asked Cary.

"The Great Wall," said the Cabby. "The one that separates
Wall Street from the rest of Down Town. That seems to be
where you're heading. I'm willing to take you as far as I can when
she recovers, but I don't know when or how far that will be. If
you're in a hurry to get there, I'm afraid you'll have to go it
alone."

Cary sat still for a moment, listening to the wind whistling in
the trees. Then he stood up. "I understand," said Cary. "Thanks
for taking us this far. But I do have to be going. Come on, Allie."
He stepped down from the carriage, patting Nellie on the flank.

"Are you crazy?" said Allie. "Neither of us knows where we're
goin'," she said, arms folded, teeth chattering. "And besides, it's
gettin' *cold*."

"I promised Taara I'd go," said Cary quietly, looking up at
her in the carriage. "You don't have to go with me if you don't
want to. You've got your Scamps to worry about."

"Oh, no ya don't," said Allie. "That trick won't work. I ain't
comin' with ya just 'cause you make me feel guilty."

"But I'm not *asking* you to come with me, Allie," said Cary. "Really I'm not."

"All right, all right!" said Allie, jumping down from the cab. "You win. Lead on, MacDuck!"

SIXTEEN

THE BOWERIE. That's what the street sign said. All Cary could remember about it was that it was supposed to be filled with drunks and bums begging for spare change. On the near corner was a domed building with the word "Wintergarten" in spidery black lettering over the door. The doors flew open, and Cary heard music and raucous singing, and a group of red-faced young men came reeling down the steps, arms around one another, singing a drunken tune out of key.

But the road that stretched before them was quite pretty, really, a sort of country lane lined with heavily laden fruit trees and rustic houses set far back from the road. The light was the color of an autumn afternoon. The air was cold and crisp, and tinged with the sweetish scent of apples that had fallen like the leaves beneath the trees.

Allie bent to pick up a windfall and polished it on her coat, tossing another to him. Its tartness tasted good, but it felt like ice as he bit into it, and it hurt his teeth, causing him to shiver.

"You're finally gettin' cold, too, huh?" said Allie, who was now bundled up in both coat and blanket.

"A little," said Cary.

"Well, no wonder," said Allie. "Look!"

They'd come to a crossroads. A weather-beaten fingerboard pointing left read TO THE WHINTERLANDS, and then, below it, were several smaller signs reading ISTRIA, BOHEMIA, SILESIA, KARELIA, SLOVENIA, and several other names that Cary couldn't read.

"This way," said Cary, turning onto the left-hand road.

"Are you sure?" said Allie, teeth chattering. Cary nodded. "Just askin'," she said.

The road descended slowly into a wide valley. After a time, a town came into view on the horizon. At first, they saw only a few small farms with a cow or two and some chickens running loose, and fields filled with frost-covered stubble. Then they saw a cluster of buildings and heard the whirl of festive music. As they came closer, a few fat snowflakes began to fall.

The streets seemed deserted, and Cary began to look about nervously. Then they turned onto a narrow street filled with dozens of pushcarts tended by women in kerchiefs and men with long beards and dark coats. The little carts were heaped with clothing and notions, jewelry and trinkets, and the air was filled with the sound of haggle and barter as shoppers, filled with the festive spirit, looked for bargains. The street was so crowded that Cary and Allie had trouble threading their way through the maze of vendors.

Beyond, a group of shops—butchers', bakers', tailors', and the like—surrounded a square that was lightly dusted with snow. A tall fir tree at its center was hung with foodstuffs and trinkets, and around it a small winter carnival was in progress.

On the near corner, a young man in a fur hat played a sad song on a strange-looking stringed instrument while a young woman with a tambourine danced about a fire. She was covered all over in ragged scarves and leggings and wore a half-dozen skirts and petticoats that flashed brightly as she danced. Every now and then, the man would hold out his hat to catch coins from those who were watching. Nearby, a crowd had gathered around a hulking, bearded man, who turned a little hand organ while a big black bear capered at the end of a slender chain.

Farther on was a tall booth with faded blue drapes painted with a golden sun and a silver moon. As they passed, a man in a poked hat popped out of the top, holding in each hand a pair of crossed sticks, from which four strings dangled. The curtains parted to reveal a pair of life-size puppets, who seemed to be made all of wood, with white clown faces and red cheeks and big buttons on their colorful costumes. The two bowed and curt-seyed, pirouetted and turned, and Cary was amazed at how lifelike they looked. Just as the two were about to kiss, the puppeteer loosed their strings, and they collapsed in a heap. But, as the curtain swung closed, Cary thought he saw one of them wink at him.

Then, from behind, came the hammer of hoofbeats, and Cary's heart began to pound. He pulled Allie out of sight behind a pile of trash.

The merchants looked up at the sound and began swiftly packing up their wares and rolling their carts out of sight. Then, at the end of the street, four dark figures appeared.

Four riders all in black were galloping toward them on jet-black horses. One held an upraised torch in his hand, another, a coiled whip. As they charged along the narrow street, their horses kicked at the remaining carts, shattering them. The lead rider dipped his torch, setting the wood ablaze, and soon the flames had spread to the nearby buildings, traveling toward the spot where Cary and Allie hid. Allie wouldn't move. She seemed dazzled by the fire.

"Allie!" said Cary. "We've got to get out of here!" At last, she shook herself, and they began running in the opposite direction. The riders spotted them, wheeled their mounts around, and were after them. At the corner, Cary turned sharply, pulling Allie with him. He heard the crack of a whip close behind them and began running as hard as he could.

When the riders rounded the corner after them, there was a chorus of cries from the balconies overhead. "Go away!" shouted a young woman with a child. "Get out!" said a vegetable seller, pelting the horsemen with potatoes. From the steps of a small synagogue, an old man in a cap and shawl cried, "Stop! Stop!"

The merchants wheeled their carts in a barricade in front of the horsemen and began throwing anything at them they could get their hands on. Old pots and pans, shoes, and dishes began raining down on the horsemen. Their frightened horses reared and wheeled about, nearly throwing the riders, and Cary and Allie were able to escape down a side street.

Before them, the block came to a dead end. A row of tall buildings with elaborately carved facades stood before them. Above each of the doors was a strange word: "Livonia," "Latvia," "Lithuania." From behind, Cary could hear the drumming of hooves.

"In here, Allie!" he cried. Without thinking, he yanked hard on the door under the word "Estonia," praying under his breath that it would open. To his relief, it did, and he and Allie went through, closing it behind them just as the riders neared.

THEY WERE SURROUNDED by snow, sunk into a deep drift up to their knees. A fierce, bitter wind cut through them, and all they could see before them was a snow-covered hillside at the edge of an evergreen forest. Cary and Allie stared at each other, stunned, and turned to see the door they'd come through. It was gone. Their tracks started in the middle of the snowbank, as if they'd been dropped from the sky. The sky was over-cast, and the cold gripped them hard through their light cloth-ing.

"Now what, big shot?" said Allie through her teeth. Her face was flushed with the cold, and there was an edge of panic in her voice.

"What do you mean, 'now what'?" said Cary sharply. "I thought you knew everything about this place, Allie."

"Don't give me that. You're the one who's s'posed to have all the answers. I'm *freezin'*, Cary. My ears are burnin', and my feet are gettin' numb. What does your precious Taara say we're s'posed to do now?"

"I don't *know!*" said Cary. "Look. Ever since this thing got started I've been doing what everyone else said I should do. Now I'm just going by—by *feelings,* that's all."

"Yeah, well my feelings tell me I'm gonna *die* out here. So use that magic whatsis of yours to get us someplace warm—and maybe some dry clothes while you're at it—but *do* something for pity's sake, before we both freeze to death!"

"I told you, I don't *know* what to do. I've just got to have faith in Taara. I've got to believe she wouldn't steer me wrong. I'm sure we'll be all right," he said, sounding surer than he felt. "Wait! Listen!"

˙ In the distance, he heard the tinkling of bells and the sound of merry laughter. A moment later a beautiful sleigh pulled by a strong white horse came whishing past, not two hundred yards away. It was filled with young people drinking and singing, who waved as the sleigh went by.

"Hey! Wait a minute!" cried Allie. "Don't leave us!" Then he and Allie were running after them and hollering at the top of their lungs for them to stop, but the people in the sleigh just waved and smiled and soon were out of sight. Allie fell to her knees in the snow.

"Have faith," she said softly. "That's a laugh. I'm tired, Cary. I'm *cold.*"

"You can't give up, Allie. We'll follow those sleigh tracks. They must lead somewhere. All we have to do is keep walking." The cold was beginning to creep into his back and chest, and he found himself shuddering uncontrollably.

"*You* keep walking," said Allie. "I'm just going to go to sleep here for a while."

"Allie! Get up!" There must have been something in his tone of voice, for her eyes opened again, and she got slowly to her feet. Step by step they began to make their way along the sleigh tracks down the hill.

As Cary grew colder, his vision began to swim, and a deepening sense of despair began to grow in him. Suppose Taara didn't have a plan for him? What if it were all the ravings of an old Indian medicine woman? No! He had to believe. To keep himself going as he trudged through the snow he tried reciting the Poet's poem under his breath:

> "Deeply breathe and widely—
> (*No.*)
> *Breathely* deep and *gridely* win,
> Let the healing air—eeling hare—
> (*No.*)
> Let the *steal*ing hare *eel* in;
> (*That was it.*)
> A fear's a funny—
> (*No, that wasn't right.*)
> A *sear's* a *sunny* foe, and so,
> You know the way, so—
> (No!)
>> You *woe* the *nay*, so get it low!
>> (*That's right!*)
>
> Breathely deep and gridely win . . ."

Cary suddenly realized he was being shaken.
"Look, Cary! Smoke!" Somehow their path had diverged

from the sled tracks toward a stand of trees. Above them rose
a thin thread of dark smoke. Then they were both loping
through the snow toward a small thatched cabin nestled at the
base of the trees. They each fell once or twice, and their shoes
and clothes were soaked, but the thought of a warm fire drove
them on.

The cabin door had a wide wooden latch that was warm to the
touch. Cary fumbled with it for a moment with numbed fingers,
and then Allie was trying to help. All at once the door flew open
and sent them rolling across the room within.

It was very dim inside the room, but a glowing warmth came
from a small wood-burning stove near a door at the far end of
the room. High up on one side a quartz window admitted what
light there was. On either side of the room was a long bench with
wooden pegs over it, hung with clothes. Sitting down on the
bench, Allie began to quickly untie her shoes.

"What are you doing?"

"Gettin' rid of these shoes. They're ruined!"

When she'd pulled them off she tossed them in an old wooden
barrel nearby. There was a splash, and Allie jumped back, spat-
tered.

"Hey!" she said, tasting the tip of her finger. "It's beer!"

"But what are you going to wear?"

"How about these?" She held up a large pair of fur-covered
boots, embroidered with colored thread. "Here's another pair!"
she said a moment later. "And coats and hats, too. They look
like they'd keep us plenty warm. Looks like Taara answered our
prayers after all!"

"Put those down, Allie! They're not yours. They probably
belong to those people we saw in the sleigh."

"Then we should take 'em just to pay 'em back for leaving us
there to die in the snow," said Allie.

"Sh!" said Cary. "Listen!" A pair of voices could be heard
through the wall.

"There's somebody in the next room!" said Allie. "Do you

think they heard us talkin' about takin' the boots? We'd better get outa here."

The far door opened, and a man was standing there, watching them.

A naked man.

He was young, and squarely built, with a mane of thick, blond hair dripping with water. With barely a glance at Cary and Allie, he dipped a wooden ladle in the beer barrel and drank deep, wiping off the foam from his lips with the back of his hand. Allie covered her mouth as if suppressing laughter. But whether it was at the man's lack of clothes, or the thought of her shoes in the beer, Cary couldn't tell.

"Noh mis te ootate?" said the young man, wrapping a towel about his waist.

"What'd he say?" asked Allie.

"Oh, you two don't speak the language," said the young man. "Sorry. I'm Mattis."

"I'm Cary," said Cary. "And this is Allie."

"Kaari? Aali?" said Mattis. "Those don't sound much like Estonian names."

"Uh, they're not," said Cary, figuring he'd better play along. "I'm—er—Slobodian on my father's side. Allie here is my—"

"Cousin!" said Allie, getting into the spirit of things.

"Half-sister!" said Cary at the same moment.

"Slobodian!" said Mattis, sounding impressed. "You *have* come a long way for the wedding. Are you friends or family?"

"Friends!" they both answered in one voice.

"That's nice," said Mattis. "Of the bride or the groom?"

"Bride!" said Allie.

"Groom!" said Cary.

"Both!" said Allie. "We—we went to school with them!"

"Oh, I see," said Mattis with a strange smile. "You're here to take *saun,* aren't you?"

"That's right," said Cary eagerly.

"Well, I'm cooled off enough for another round myself. Let's go."

"In there?" said Cary.

"That's right. It's nice and hot now. I started it up early this morning. Now off with your clothes, before the rest of the wedding party gets here and takes all the best spots!"

"Right now?"

"Of course," said Mattis. "Unless you're here for some other reason."

"Oh, no," said Allie. "That's why we're here all right."

"Allie! What are you saying?" hissed Cary under his breath.

"If they find out who we are, they'll turn us over to the 'Mashers for sure!" she answered.

A minute later she was unbuttoning her overalls and stepping out of them. As she pulled her shirt off over her head, Cary found himself staring at her. Though she was skinny, she was definitely—well, *female*. With all that they'd been through, he'd forgotten that.

Cary quickly turned away, thinking she might get mad at him or something for staring at her like that. Hesitantly, he began to take off his own clothes.

His mom had gotten mad at him a couple of weeks ago when he'd seen her drying herself after a shower. She'd been talking to him through the bathroom door, but he wasn't really listening; his mind had been a million miles away somewhere. When the door had opened, and he'd given her a blank stare instead of an answer to some question she'd asked him, she'd suddenly gotten uptight and slammed the door on him like he was an intruder, waking Cary out of his daze.

He couldn't figure out what had happened, why his mom had started treating him differently all of a sudden. He and his mom and dad used to shower together when he was younger, especially when they went camping. But whatever it was that had made his mom mad, it was suddenly very important to Cary not to make Allie mad at him in the same way. Stepping out of his trousers and shorts, he reached quickly for a towel.

"Not bad!" said Allie with that crooked grin of hers, looking him up and down. He wondered just what she'd meant by that. Then he realized that she was treating the whole thing as a joke, so he began to relax a bit.

"You won't need that towel in the *saun*," said Mattis, heading for the door.

"Uh, that's okay," said Cary. "I'm used to it."

"No need to be bashful on my account," said Allie. "You ain't the first." When Cary looked surprised, she laughed and added, "I had six brothers, y'know. Now come on!"

They stepped through the little door, and Cary was washed with waves of heat that made Hell's Kitchen feel like Christmas. There was a hissing sound that came from a small square stove in the middle of the floor, with a glowing fire below and a stack of stones on top. Several rows of benches hugged the walls, going up like steps toward the ceiling. On one of the benches was a row of wooden buckets filled with water and what seemed to be tree branches. Mattis had seated himself cross-legged on one of the lower benches, and Cary and Allie sat down beside him.

Cary had expected something like a steam bath, but the air was dry, very dry, and baking hot, and spicy with the scent of the burning wood. The sweat that formed on his back and sides evaporated almost instantly, and Cary felt the last of the cold being cooked out of his bones. The wooden bench under him was almost too hot to bear. The disk that hung about his neck began to burn. A moment later, the towel about him began to feel hot—*too* hot—until it was burning his skin, so he reluctantly let it drop, and hung the disk on a nearby peg.

"*Kas need kakks on sinu sugulased, Mattis?*" said a deep voice from the shadows.

Cary and Allie turned quickly, startled, toward the sound. In the glow of the embers, they saw a dark figure seated in the corner. It was as if he had materialized out of the darkness. He was much older than Mattis, with dark hair combed straight back over his head. He had piercing, deep-set eyes, and the way the fire lit his face made the little smile on his face look sinister and menacing.

"Looks like a vampire, don't he?" said Allie, sounding like she was only half joking.

"*Välis maalased, Uno. Andressi leerivend ja leeri ōde!*" Mattis responded in the same language. Cary didn't understand anything but their names. A moment later, the old man laughed out loud.

"What was that all about?" asked Allie.

"This is Vana Uno," said Mattis at last. "One of the elders of our village. I was explaining to him your little joke."

"What joke?" asked Allie.

"Why, the one about going to school with the bride and groom," said Mattis. "After all, Mari is forty if she's a day, and Andres is ten years older!"

"Oh, *that* joke," said Allie with a feeble smile. "Pretty funny, huh?"

"You mean he can't understand what we're saying?" asked Cary anxiously, wondering if he'd heard them planning to steal the boots.

"Only a little," said Mattis. "Uno speaks six languages fluently, but he's always had trouble with yours. Says it makes no sense to him." He got up and splashed a bucket of water on the stones. A cloud of steam rose and evaporated, and a moment later, it was hotter than ever. Next thing Cary knew, Mattis had poured the rest of the bucket over Cary's and Allie's heads, to cool them off a bit, leaving them sputtering in surprise.

Uno spoke again. Mattis nodded, then got up and picked up one of the dripping branches from the buckets of water. Uno turned his back and bent forward, and Mattis began lashing the old man on the back and sides with the wet leaves.

"What are you *doing*?" asked Cary, astonished.

"Just using a *vihk*, a birch branch, to get the circulation going," said Mattis. "What do they use in Slobodia?"

"Radishes," said Allie with a perfect dead pan.

"*Radishes!*" said Mattis. "Imagine that!"

When he explained that to Uno, the old man chuckled again. Then Uno dipped the branch in the bucket and proceeded to lash Mattis's back with it. As the limb moved, it stirred the air, making it even hotter. Cary had trouble breathing, and his face and hands felt like they were burning. He leaned over and shut his eyes, determined to bear it as long as he could. A moment later, Mattis was tapping him on the shoulder.

"Well, I've had about enough for now," said Mattis. "And we're getting low on wood. Care to take a break?"

"I thought you'd never ask," said Cary, getting up. "How 'bout you, Allie?"

"Naw," she said, eyes closed. "I'm just gettin' warmed up."

"Okay," said Cary. "I'll be back in a couple of minutes."

Grabbing the disk, Cary followed Mattis out the door. The outer room was a blessed relief after the intense heat of the *saun.* He wrapped another towel about himself, and the next thing he knew, a mug of beer was in his hand. Cary was so thirsty, and it looked so wet and cool, that he drank it down.

"Let's get some wood," said Mattis, finishing a beer of his own. He'd stepped into a pair of shoes, but otherwise, he was walking out into the snow stark naked!

"But we'll freeze out there!" said Cary.

"Nonsense!" said Mattis. "You're so hot now you won't even notice the cold. Here. Put on these boots and follow me."

Reluctantly, Cary pulled on the boots and followed Mattis out into the snow, glancing around to see if anyone was watching. The late afternoon sun blinded him after the dark room. To his surprise, he found himself steaming like a cup of hot cocoa, and the cold air felt refreshing to his overheated skin. When they'd reached the woodpile, Mattis turned to him, holding up a big ax, and said, "Now, let's have some answers. Just who *are* you anyway?"

SEVENTEEN

CARY HAD NEVER felt more helpless in his life. Here he was, half naked in the snow, far from home, about to be murdered by a madman with an ax. And he couldn't even run, because that would mean leaving Allie behind.

"I'll tell you anything you want to know!" said Cary. "Just please, don't kill me!"

"*Kill* you?" said Mattis. Then he realized he was holding the ax and put it on the ground with a slight smile. "Look, I'm not going to hurt you. I just want to find out what's going on," he said. "I didn't want to make a scene in front of Uno, but it's obvious to me that you aren't Estonian, that you've never been in *saun* in your life."

"Then why did you make us go through it?"

"To get the truth out of you. The *saun* is a sacred, special place to my people, Cary, the soul of our traditions. It's the place of births and deaths, and even weddings. Oaths sworn there are binding. And besides, it's hard to lie when you haven't got any clothes on, especially in a hot room surrounded by others like you. I have to admit you did pretty well for a couple of amateurs. Now tell me what you're doing here."

"I'm not exactly sure," said Cary hesitantly, not sure of how much to reveal. "Allie and I are on a kind of—mission I guess you'd call it."

"What kind of mission?" said Mattis, suddenly wary. "If you're here to spy on us—"

"No, nothing like that," said Cary. "We're just passing through really. We came here by accident—I think. It's kind of hard to explain—"

"But if you have nothing to hide, why did you lie to us?"

"I'm sorry about that," said Cary. "It's just that I was afraid you'd turn us in."

"Turn you in?" said Mattis. "To whom?"

At first Cary was afraid to tell Mattis the truth, but considering the fix he and Allie were in, he really had no choice but to trust him.

"You see, Miles Brand and his Badmashers are after us—"

"Who?" asked Mattis. He'd obviously never heard of them.

"They're sort of a gang of thugs who're trying to take over all of Down Town," Cary explained. "They dress all in black and—"

"Black Riders!"

"What?" said Cary.

"They sound like the Black Riders," said Mattis, "old enemies of ours." They were standing at the edge of a small wood behind the *saun*. A half-dozen tree trunks lay in a heap on the ground, covered with snow. "But why are they after you?" he asked.

"I don't know exactly," said Cary, "but they've offered a reward to anybody who turns us in. They seem to be able to find us wherever we go. They almost caught us this time, but we escaped through some kind of weird door—that's how we found this place."

Mattis's face grew grave when Cary mentioned the door. "If they do find a way to follow you here, we're all in trouble." As Mattis spoke, he picked up a large log in his arm and gestured for Cary to pick up another. Together, they carried them to a wide tree stump that was scarred with hundreds of ax marks.

"Why?" asked Cary.

"The Black Riders forced us out of our homeland not so many years ago," said Mattis. "We fled here because we thought we would be safe here. We always hoped that someday we might return." He set a half log on end up on the big stump and, taking a step back, brought the ax down hard on it, splitting it in two.

"I've always had a feeling that the Black Riders might find us someday, even here. Now I'm sure of it," Mattis continued, splitting the log in half again. "If you could find your way through that door, sooner or later, others will, too. I've tried to tell the others that we have to be on our guard, but nobody ever listens. They'd rather just drink and laugh and take *saun* all day, without a care for tomorrow."

"What about Uno?" asked Cary.

"He should understand better than anyone," said Mattis. "He's the only one of us old enough to really remember the Black Riders. But he's stuck in the old days—his memory of the old days, that is. He wants to remember only the good things about the past, and none of the bad."

Mattis gathered up the kindling he'd made and piled it to one side. "Uno forgets that life goes on and things change," he continued, "that the old has to make way for the new, just like the old trees here have to come down so the new ones can grow. He won't admit that somewhere, beyond that door, the world we left behind is growing and changing, too, and we can never go back to it again."

Cary's eyes were caught by the column of smoke rising up out of the chimney. It drifted up in a thick column, then branched out like a tree—like Taara! The sight and smell of the smoke blended with the whisper of the wind through the pines, and Cary found himself drifting again. "Here," said Mattis, handing Cary the ax, "you have a try."

"But I don't know how," said Cary.

"There's nothing to it," Mattis replied. "Just relax and follow through with your whole body—like this." Effortlessly, he raised the ax above his head and split the log in two.

Mattis set another log on the stump and stepped back. Cary tapped the log a couple of times with the blade of the ax, to get the feel of it, then lifted it over his head. Suddenly he stopped. Looking down at the wide, scarred tree stump, he couldn't help but think of Taara, and he shuddered, letting the ax drop behind him.

"What's the matter?" said Mattis. "Getting cold?" Cary nodded. "Well," said Mattis, "you can't keep warm unless you have wood to burn. Get chopping!"

Cary picked up the ax again, staring at the log. For a moment, he couldn't move. Then an understanding came to him he couldn't express in words. The wind whispered in his ears, and suddenly the ax was falling.

The next thing Cary knew, Mattis was saying, "Whoa! That's plenty!" Cary didn't know how long he'd been chopping, but there was now a sizable pile of kindling before him. The effort had warmed him, but now the wind howled, and Cary felt the breeze begin to cut through him. Mattis loaded Cary's arms with the wood, then filled his own arms, and together they went back into the *saun.*

The warmth of the outer room was delightful. As his eyes adjusted to the darkness, he saw that Allie and Uno had forsaken the *saun* and were seated on one of the benches, playing checkers. She was wrapped in a long robe, and Uno wore a loose pair of drawstring trousers.

"I'm beatin' him," said Allie proudly. Then Uno promptly jumped six of her men. "Hey!" she cried. "How'd you do that?" Uno just raised his large eyebrows and smiled.

As Mattis and Uno began speaking earnestly to each other in Estonian, Cary pulled Allie aside. "I had to tell Mattis the truth about us, Allie," said Cary.

"What'd you do that for?" she said. "How do you know he won't rat on us or something?"

"I just *know,* that's all. Besides, Allie, we've got to trust somebody around here or we'll never get where we need to go."

"I told Uno about the Black Riders," said Mattis. "At first, he wouldn't believe it. He can't understand how you found this place."

"I don't know," said Cary. "All along, I've just been doing what I thought Taara would want me to do."

"Taara?" said Uno, looking at him intently. *"Kusi mis ta Taarast teab?"*

"Taara?" asked Mattis. "What do you know about Taara?" Cary didn't know what to say.

"Oh, she's just this tree Cary talks to," said Allie breezily. "She's the one that sent us here."

"Allie!"

"Is that true?" said Mattis. "You've talked to Taara?"

"Yes," said Cary finally. "It's true. How do *you* know about her?"

Uno interrupted, interrogating Mattis. He seemed very excited.

"What was that all about?" asked Allie at last.

"It's difficult to explain," said Mattis, looking puzzled. "Taara is an ancient Estonian spirit, the being from whom all life flows. Uno says it must have been Taara's power that led you here." The old man spoke again.

"He wants to know how you managed to open the door into Eesti," said Mattis.

"I don't know. It just opened, that's all."

"But it's only supposed to open for our people. What's your last name?"

"Newman," said Cary.

"What about your mother?"

"Her maiden name was O'Reilly."

"And her parents?"

"They're mostly O'Neills and Carrigans on that side of the family," said Cary. "Though I think I have a Dutch uncle in there somewhere."

"What about your father's mother?" asked Mattis.

"She's a Bradford," said Cary. "And *her* mother's name was Palmer—I think."

"What about your great-grandparents?" asked Mattis, in response to Uno's promptings.

"What's the big deal?" said Allie. "What *difference* does it make?"

"Well, Grandad wasn't really a Newman," Cary confessed. "His name was something long and unpronounceable, Novo-something-or-other. The story in the family is that the man at Ellis Island took one look at it and said, 'Well, you're a Newman now!' I'm not sure about Grandmama's name." Cary tried to remember. "Ullmister, I think," he said at last. "Linda Ullmister."

"*Ülemiste Linda!*" said Uno in astonishment. "*Kas se noor Tasuja võiks töesti olla meie Kalevipojapoeg—Issand Jumal! Ta ei räägi isegi Eestikeelt; ta polegi tõeline Eestlane!*" Mattis shook his head, and for several moments there was a heated discussion.

"*Now* what's he so fired up about?" said Allie.

Mattis found himself staring at Cary, almost as if he'd seen a ghost. "A young Estonian named Tassuja once led our people in an uprising, centuries ago, against the Teutonic Knights. At the time, some said he was our legendary champion Kalevipoeg, son of our epic hero Kalev, come to life again. Since then, there's been a story among our people that whenever the Estonian people are in grave danger, Kalevipoeg will be born again among us to lead us against our oppressors."

"But what does that have to do with me?" asked Cary.

"I know this sounds strange," said Mattis, "but in the legends, Kalevipoeg's mother's name was Linda. She was called Ulemiste Linda, after the lake of tears she wept for Kalev after his death. Uno still holds to the old beliefs, Cary. He says the blood of Tassuja runs in your veins, and you must be the champion our people have been waiting for for so long."

"Oh, no," said Allie. "Here we go again!"

"What do you mean, Allie?" asked Mattis.

"Everywhere we go, everybody's got some kind of story about how Cary is their long-lost son, their hero and champion."

"Maybe it's true, Allie," said Mattis.

"What're you talkin' about?"

"I've never put much store by the old stories myself," said Mattis thoughtfully. "I've always believed it was events and ideas that were important, that men arise when they're needed to bring them to being. But there's too much here that can't be explained any other way. Maybe Cary *was* sent here by Taara to warn us—"

There was a shout from outside the *saun*. At once, Mattis and Uno were on their feet. Cary and Allie followed them out the door.

The sleigh that had passed Cary and Allie in the snow had pulled up in front of the *saun*. The white horse was prancing nervously and pawing at the snow, while the young men and women in the sleigh cried aloud to Mattis and Uno.

"They're coming!" said Mattis. "Juriado and his friends saw four Black Riders coming this way only a few minutes ago. They've been riding as fast as they can, warning everyone they could find. It looks as if you were right all along, Cary. We all owe you our thanks."

"Why should you thank me?" said Cary. "I brought them here. I put you all in danger. I'm no champion. I'm a curse on all of you." Uno had been watching him as he spoke, and when Mattis finished explaining what Cary had said, Uno spoke again.

"No, Cary," said Mattis. "Uno says we've been dreaming of the past too long. You only woke us up. The Black Riders always come, sooner or later, and we must be ready when they do. As for you, Uno feels we should help you in any way we can. Find some boots and clothes that fit you, and I'll take you as far as I can in the sleigh."

"But what about you?" said Cary.

"Don't worry about us," said Mattis. "This is a time of great changes. You have something greater to do than saving one people. It's up to us to help you fulfill your mission. And it's here that we have to make our stand. They took from us the land where we lived, but they can never take from us the land where we die. Now go!"

Cary and Allie dressed quickly, wrapping themselves up in thick fur coats. "Y'know," said Allie, when Cary had finished dressing, "in that getup, you *do* look kind of like a champion at that!" He couldn't tell if she was kidding or not.

The young people from the sleigh had gathered around Uno, listening. A few moments later, they were grabbing up axes, sticks, whatever was at hand, to prepare for the Riders. A moment later, four dark specks appeared against the far horizon.

"Get in the sleigh!" said Mattis.

Cary jumped into the sleigh, pulling Allie up after him. Mattis joined them, and with a jingle of harness bells, the white horse began to pull the sleigh faster and faster across the snowy countryside.

The white banks of snow and the dark stands of trees whirled past as the surefooted horse pulled them across the fields. Cary looked back to see the Black Riders gaining on them once again, slowly but surely.

Far behind, they could see the villagers gathered to stop the Riders. One horse went down, but the others broke through and soon were gaining ground on them again. Just then, Mattis shouted over his shoulder, "Get down!" and Cary and Allie dropped down just as the sleigh swung under a low stone bridge and started down the bank of a frozen river.

Allie clung tightly to Cary and the sleigh, as if expecting it to crash through the ice, but it held firm under the horse's hooves. When they looked up again, they saw the Black Riders picking their way slowly down the bank, their horses balking at the ice.

They sped along for several minutes. Then, to Cary's surprise, Mattis pulled up on the reins, slowing the horse to a trot. The Black Riders began to close the distance between them, and Allie cried, "Can't you go any faster?"

"Sh!" said Mattis, cocking his head as if listening for some unheard sound. Cary listened, too, but all he could hear was the whistling wind and the musical tapping of the horse's hooves on the snow. That must have been what Mattis was listening for as well, because he began to turn the horse in a complicated pattern across the snow-covered ice. Then, when the Black Riders' horses were almost upon them, Mattis snapped the reins, and the sleigh was flying across the ice again, a blustery wind blowing about their ears.

The Riders were close behind them now, barely two or three lengths away. Then Allie pointed, crying, "Look!"

Then Cary understood Mattis's strange maneuvers. He was listening to the ice! Sprays of water began to erupt from the hooves of the Black Riders' horses, and chunks of ice began to fly into the air. One after the other, the Riders broke through the ice, their black horses neighing in terror. As the sleigh rounded a bend in the river, the last Rider disappeared from sight.

The river grew wider, and the sleigh streaked along the ice, with no sign of pursuit. Then, there was a blood-curdling howl, and three dark shapes detached themselves from the line of trees on the nearby ridge and began to run on all fours down the snowbanks in a rapid, loping gait. Wolves!

The creatures were larger than normal wolves, with jet-black coats and glowing red eyes. In a few short strides they were behind them, leaping and yapping at the back and snapping at the horse's legs. The horse shied and whinnied, and one of the wolves tore into its flank with its sharp teeth.

Mattis stood up in the sleigh, leaning over the harness for a moment, pulling a pin out that let the horse loose. Freed of the weight of the sleigh, it shook itself loose and clambered up the bank, speeding away on fleet legs. Two of the wolves followed it, but the third turned after the sleigh, which was now speeding downriver under its own momentum.

"What'd you do *that* for?" Cary shouted.

"Here!" Mattis answered. "Give me a hand!" He reached behind him for a tall wooden pole. Standing up in the seat, he pushed the pole down into the floorboards at Cary's feet. Then Mattis began to unfurl a large sheet of canvas with a wooden rod in its edge, fixing it to the pole. A sail!

Cary pulled himself forward in the sleigh. Mattis had climbed out onto one of the sleigh's sides to secure the rigging, and Cary began to help him. The mast and boom weren't all that much different from those of the sailboats he'd sailed on the lake near home. Cary's hands were clumsy in the cold as he fumbled to knot the lines in place. The wolf was growling and snarling at the sleigh as it slowed down, leaping at Allie, and she pulled herself as far back from the side as she could.

A gust of wind hit the sail, swinging the boom around hard, catching Mattis unawares. He clung to the sail, but the wind pushed him over the side. Then the sleigh hit a rough spot in the ice, and Mattis dropped. Cary tried to bring the sleigh to a stop, but it kept moving. From far behind, he heard Mattis call, "Follow the river!"

SOMEHOW THEY WERE still sailing. Cary didn't have time to think, just did what came naturally. He found his eyes fixed several yards ahead of the sleigh, moving the lines almost instinctively.

Soon the wolf's howls were lost in the wailing of the wind.

"Say, you're pretty good at this," said Allie.

"I used to sail with my mom and dad a lot when I was younger," said Cary, never taking his eyes from the ice ahead. "Here. Take this rope and keep it tight."

As he went forward to adjust the boom, the boat began to drift toward the riverbank. But he got the lines untangled quickly and was back in time to steer them off the bank.

"Look out!" shouted Allie. There were windmills along the river now, and ahead, the ice was filled with skaters zipping back and forth across the ice. Cary swerved the sleigh around them as Allie hollered, "No brakes! Out of the way!"

The river began to bend sharply, and Cary moved up on the outer rail to make the sleigh heel around the curve. Beyond, the river narrowed and the banks grew straighter, with high stone facings that turned the meandering river into an arrow-straight canal.

Dead ahead was a dark patch in the ice. Cary swerved as best he could, skirting its outer edge, but it was worse up ahead. Cracks started to form, mostly at the edges, but soon spreading across the width of the canal. Then a gust of air sent the sleigh skidding out of control, and they slid into the dark blue water with a chilly splash.

But the sleigh was watertight, with sides high enough to keep out the water, as long as they didn't rock it too much. They'd both gotten soaked, and Allie's teeth were chattering again, but otherwise they seemed all right. Cary shifted the sail about to catch a change in the wind, and a stiff breeze over his left shoulder sent them skimming down the canal on a long tack.

Cary's next tack took him over to the far side, where gondolas, sampans, junks, and other exotic craft were tied up. Allie pointed out a huge paper dragon with dozens of dancers inside making its way down a side street. Then the wind freshened, and they left the sound and smell of fireworks far behind.

The walls of the canal grew still narrower, and Cary had to be careful not to run up against the docks. The buildings here looked much older than any he'd seen before. Up ahead, the canal ended, emptying into a small lake with shells piled about its shores.

The sky grew darker and more ominous here. Thunderclouds had begun to gather, and there was a circle of large black birds overhead, ravens perhaps, or buzzards. Far ahead, where the water met the land, a great black wall loomed up, cutting the world in two, vanishing into a dark, murky cloud bank high above. The air became charged with electricity, and the sky was lit with lightning and filled with the crash of thunder.

The wind shifted suddenly, as the water began to seethe with running whitecaps. "Duck, Allie!" cried Cary as the boom swung across the sleigh-boat, striking her head. He rushed over to her, and the sails went slack, but she waved him away.

"I'm okay!" she said in a thick voice. "Keep your mind on what you're doin'!" A moment later she asked in a hushed voice, "Cary? What's a Collect?" A buoy had floated by with the words "Stop! Collect! Proceed at your own risk!"

"That!" cried Cary, fighting with the lines to swerve them in time. A short distance ahead was a great roaring whirlpool. It frothed and churned, spinning down in foaming green and white into a funnel of darkness below. About its sides Cary saw bits and pieces of wood and cloth—wreckage of its earlier victims. He felt a powerful undertow as he fought to bring the sleigh-boat's nose into the wind.

They began to drift sideways toward the spinning water. Cary hauled in tight on the sheet, and the boat skimmed along the edge of the maelstrom and around to the other side. Slowly, they began to pull away.

Cary's arms were getting sore. He pulled the sail taut, close-hauled to the wind, and the sleigh-boat jumped a bit, putting distance between them and the whirlpool. Then Allie's arms were around his, pulling with him as the boat heeled way over onto its side, lifting one of its runners up into the air. They moved up to the rail, as the boat turned nearly sideways.

Then the wind slackened, and the sleigh flopped over with a sickening lurch, dropping them down into the icy water. Cary fought for air and came up in darkness. He was under the overturned sleigh. He dove again, coming up outside. For a moment there was no sign of Allie, and Cary began to panic. Then her head broke the surface.

"This way!" he cried as she went under again. Fighting against the current, he swam toward her, put his arm under her chin, and pulled her back to the sleigh.

"I s'pose this ain't the time to tell ya," she gasped, "but I can't swim!"

They hauled themselves up onto the flat bottom of the sleigh just as it was caught in the curve of the whirlpool, whipping them around at furious speed. They were flung against the side of the funnel and watched in horror as the water dropped away beneath them. The roaring was so loud they couldn't hear, and when Cary looked up, it was dark overhead.

Faster and faster the vortex whirled, shaking and cracking the sleigh. The funnel narrowed, and the air was close and hard to breath. With her free hand, Allie put one arm about his shoulder and shouted something Cary couldn't hear. Then the boat began to break up, and the last thing Cary remembered was the touch of Allie's lips against his cheek.

EIGHTEEN

PAIN. THAT'S THE first
thing he noticed; deep,
dull, aching pain in almost every part of his body: arms, legs,
head, back, even his teeth.

And then cold. The rough stones that pressed against his back
were as bitter cold as the draft that blew across his damp body.

And dark. He opened his eyes, saw nothing but utter darkness, blinked, and closed them again, wondering if he'd gone
blind. He tried it again moments later, but not knowing whether
or not his eyes were open made his head hurt worse.

And noise. Somewhere nearby was a roaring sound that
pounded in his skull. And a smell—a thick, musty, smoggy,
choking smell that made him gasp for breath.

Later, he opened his eyes again. After several minutes of

staring, Cary thought he could make out a faint light from far overhead that came through a sort of grating. He tried to get up, but the pain was too great. Everything hurt at once. Then he thought of something that made him forget the pain.

Allie.

He groped around with his hands, found nothing. He tried hard to listen for her breathing. Nothing. Finally, bracing his palms against the clammy stones, he forced himself up.

Sharp, searing pain shot through his left leg, and he collapsed again, his breathing hard and labored, tears in the corners of his eyes.

Come on, Cary, he told himself. *Get up. It's not like you've never been hurt before.* He remembered a time he'd gotten banged up when he swerved a bicycle to avoid a passing car, and the day Darryl Holzinger and his buddies had beat him black and blue. He'd gotten over those, hadn't he? *Get up, dammit!* he swore. *Allie could be hurt really bad.*

A part of his vision from the Green Wood came to him unbidden—Allie lying still, her neck at a horrible angle. That's all it took. He forced himself to his feet, blinking back the pain and reeling dizzily, trying to steady himself on the slimy stones.

He could see a little better now. He was in a big, curving storm drain with a culvert worn down in the middle. Back behind him, a steady cataract of water spilled down from some impossible height into a shallow pool at his feet. High up in the arching pipe, a grille let in a hint of light.

Cary walked toward the pool. Every step was jolting agony. It seemed only a few feet deep, but he couldn't tell in the inky darkness. As he neared, the din of the falling water grew almost unbearable.

There was no sign of Allie on the narrow ledge that surrounded the pool. Maybe she'd recovered before he had and gone on ahead, Cary told himself. *Or maybe she's lying at the bottom.* He had to find out. He plunged in. The numbing water came up well above his knees. By the time he was satisfied the pool was empty, his legs were losing feeling.

He hauled himself out again, his clothes heavy with the cold water. The frosty air seemed almost warm by contrast. He let himself sit for a few moments, just so the blood could return to his legs, then found he'd dozed off. *Wake up!* he chided himself. *Got to find Allie!*

His leg had stiffened. It hurt to bend it. He limped slowly down the length of the drain, looking deep into the dark water. Wait! What was that up ahead? There was a dark shape by the side of the gulley. He started running, heedless of the pain, stumbled a bit, and fell, banging the other knee, as he dropped beside the dusky form.

It was Allie.

She lay on her back, one arm over her chest, head thrown way back, just like in his vision. *First Unami, and now Allie,* Cary found himself thinking. But he wouldn't let himself believe Allie was dead. He touched her gingerly. Her clothes seemed drier than his; her skin was cool but not cold.

He bent his head to her chest, trying to hear her breathing or pulse, but the noise of the water was too great. He patted her cheeks, gently at first, then roughly, but she didn't stir.

"Allie!" he called. "It's me, Cary. It's okay now, we're safe. Wake up, Allie."

She didn't move.

Cary did everything he knew how to do—rubbing her wrists and loosening her collar, pressing her chest with the palms of his hands, clearing her throat with his finger, even covering her mouth with his and pinching her nose while he tried to blow air into her lungs. Her chest lifted a bit, and there was an acid taste to the air, but Cary wasn't sure she was breathing.

Finally, he arranged her more comfortably, legs outstretched, arms folded over her stomach, head to one side, pillowed on his coat, and sat down cross-legged on the wet stone, his head in his hands.

He sat like that for a long time, unmoving. At first he just let the despair wash over him. But then the sadness inside him turned sharper.

What am I supposed to do now? he asked himself. *I didn't ask to get into this mess; it just happened to me.*

Up to now, there'd always been someone to tell him what he should do. Not anymore. It was up to him. Whatever happened now would be because he *did* something. He'd have to be his own hero.

If it was just me, I could give up. But there's somebody else to worry about now. Allie. It's my fault she's in this mess with me, and I'm the only one who can get her, and me, out of it.

Cary opened his eyes and looked down at Allie. Her lips were slightly parted, and he thought they'd been closed before. Was she breathing? Damn this light! He couldn't tell for sure. Well, one thing was certain. They couldn't stay here. Cary knew you weren't supposed to move an injured person if you could help it, but he was afraid if he just left Allie here she . . . Well, that was out of the question.

He slipped an arm under her head, then slid another under her knees. Bracing one foot under him, he stood up.

To his surprise, she was very light. He remembered what Grandmama said about bodies being lighter when the soul leaves them, and shivered. Allie weighed hardly more than a puppy, or a box full of groceries. He started walking.

The storm drain met another that led downhill at a right angle. Cary hesitated, shifting his burden slightly. There was an icy draft blowing up the tunnel. But he kept walking. He had to.

The tunnel seemed to go on endlessly. At last, when Cary's arms were beginning to ache, the drain ended abruptly at a tiny ledge overlooking an overwhelming space. Cary peered over, and reeled with vertigo, almost losing his grip on Allie.

It was a tremendous, circular shaft as wide as a football stadium. Pipes of all sizes and shapes poked out of its walls, discharging a variety of foul-smelling liquids that mingled in the air

and splashed down into a deep, dark pit far, far below. Surely
that couldn't be where Taara meant him to go. But where else
was there to go besides down?

He looked around the walls of the shaft and saw only other
dank outflows like this one. No, wait. There, about a quarter of
the way round and about twenty feet down was an iron balcony,
with what appeared to be a well-lit passageway leading back
from it. But how was he to get to there from here, especially with
Allie?

There was a series of rungs, made of metal, that looked like
they led down to the balcony from a ledge at about his level. But
he couldn't be sure if the ledge he was standing on curved
around to meet it. Still, what choice did he have. Down? He
looked down into the roiling waters below and a giant snout of
palid white with pale pink eyes and hundreds of sharp teeth
surfaced for a moment, then submerged. *No way!*

All of his old fears of falling came back at once, and he felt like
he was toppling over. Holding Allie tightly, he pressed his body
against the stone and closed his eyes, waiting for the dizziness
to pass.

Come on, Cary, he told himself. He guessed he could probably
make it around himself, edging along the ledge the way police
and firemen did in the movies to reach people about to jump.
But how was he going to take Allie with him? There would be
no way to hold on, carrying her in his arms.

Almost before he knew it, he'd made his decision. He shifted
her head and torso over his shoulder, fireman-style, twisting his
knee badly, and slid one foot out onto the narrow ledge. It
wasn't really all that narrow, Cary told himself. Wider than that
reservoir wall, for sure.

It was pretty easy going at first, though Allie was getting a lot
heavier, and his knee did hurt him a lot. But big knobs of brick
stood out that made good handholds when they didn't get in the
way, and there was nearly always room for his feet, except where
pieces of the stone had broken off. But then Cary saw his mis-

take. There was no way he could have known from where he'd
been standing, but the ledge he was on wasn't the same level as
the one that reached that balcony. It was about ten feet up, and
dead-ended here at a big square pillar. Now what?

He couldn't put Allie down. He couldn't go back. He couldn't
go ahead. Desperately, he stretched one hand around the pillar,
groping for some sort of handhold. Nothing. He edged closer,
and Allie's weight almost threw him off balance. Then his hand
found a sort of hollow in the stone that might have been meant
as a foothold. And another one above it. Pressing his cheek
against the stone, swinging one arm and one leg around the
pillar, he wedged his toe into the crack, grabbing hard with his
free hand.

Then slipped and fell.

TIME SEEMED TO slow down. As if in slow motion, he watched
his hand come loose from the stone, felt Allie begin to slip from
his shoulder. Somehow he was incredibly calm. He knew he had
to keep his center of gravity near the wall. He knew he had to
fall flat on his back, palms down, so as not to break anything.
And he knew that if he kicked his feet up in the air, he'd drop
faster, reaching the balcony below before Allie did. If there was
a balcony. His only regret was that he knew Allie was going to
hurt him when she came down on top of him. But there was
nothing he could do about that. So he kicked out and dropped.

Time sped up. His shoulders hit metal with a stinging pain,
then his back and palms, and finally his feet. Seconds later Allie
was crashing down on him and he was wrapping one arm around
her and grabbing the handrail with the other. She rolled toward
the edge, then rolled back, and Cary thought he heard a grunt
or rush of breath as he squeezed her. He'd made it. Maybe Allie
was going to make it, too.

No time to think about that now. Cary hefted Allie back up on his shoulder again, feeling a twinge in his ribs. *Probably cracked.* Tossing Allie over his shoulder again, Cary clambered down the metal rungs almost without thinking, losing his grip for only an instant. One hand after the other, that's the ticket. Just keep climbing. Allie doesn't weigh that much. That screaming pain isn't yours, it's somebody else's. Just one more rung. And another. And another.

When his feet touched the metal balcony, he almost lost his balance. Then he swung around to the entrance and found a five-sided shaft of shiny black stone. He pulled Allie into the corridor, a few feet from the edge, and propped her up against the sloping wall, sitting down beside her. A sudden wave of nausea came over him, and he felt his gorge begin to rise. *Some hero!* he found himself thinking. *Saves the damsel in distress, and then tosses his cookies!* Then his gut was racked with waves of sickness, and he spewed over the metal railing, surrendering at last to darkness.

DREAM SHAPES MOVED through his half-conscious mind; great, hulking forms too strange to be human, and a sound like a soft cry. When his head cleared again, Cary's muscles were trembling, and his eyes had trouble focusing.

And Allie was gone.

Cary looked around desperately, but saw nothing. Then he noticed something white clinging to the edge of the tunnel near his head. A white feather, twined with ribbon and a hank of dark hair. Cary put it in his pocket. He didn't want to think about what that meant—that someone, or some*thing,* had torn it from her in a struggle. He had no idea how long he'd been out, or why they'd left him alone. But whoever, or whatever, had Allie must be long gone by now.

Cary lurched to his feet, expecting the pain in the knee but not the ache in the ribs that gripped him like a giant fist. *Got to find*

Allie, even if it kills me, thought Cary. *Which it might.*

The other end of the tunnel was blocked by a grating. Cary kicked it out with his good leg, then dropped down a few feet to the ground below. He was standing on a deserted street. Behind him were a row of abandoned buildings, their windows dark and broken. Before him was the Wall.

It was made of hundreds of monstrous black oblong stones fitted so closely together a knife blade wouldn't fit between them. It rose so high above Cary's head that it was indistinguishable from the black sky. There was no way around it, and no sign of a door.

Cary started limping along the Wall. As he ran, he began to make out immense carvings in the stone, all joined together by an interlocking design of dollar signs.

At last, Cary came to a pair of enormous doors set into the Wall, tall enough for giants, with a pair of huge golden knockers hanging from them seven feet or more above the ground.

He stared at the doors in frustration; then, taking several steps back, ran forward and threw himself at the left-hand ring. He grabbed on, pushing it slowly from the door with his feet, causing new aches in his legs, then kicked free, swinging it hard against the door. It struck with a deep boom that echoed all around him. Cary dropped to the ground, waiting.

Finally, the door began to creak open very, very slowly, and then two enormous golden horns poked around the door, followed by a gold ring the size of a dinner platter—a gold ring in the nose of a giant bull's head! It looked around very carefully, then disappeared, and the doors shut.

Cary jumped up and knocked again. The door reopened and the bull's head reappeared. Then two more gold rings appeared below, rings that Cary realized were glasses on the face of a great brown bear!

The two heads peered out almost timidly, looking at each other with apprehension. "See? I told you there was no one there!" said the Bull in a deafening whisper.

"What was it, then? The wind?" said the Bear.

"I'm sure I don't know!" said the Bull, and the door closed again.

Cary jumped up again, determined to run in this time if the doors opened again. He was just about to jump down, when the doors flew open a third time, shaking him off and sending him sprawling on the ground.

As Cary lay there dazed, the doors opened wide, revealing two titanic figures nearly twenty feet tall. He could see that they had only the heads and hooves or paws of a bull or bear. In all other ways, they were dressed like prosperous businessmen: the Bull in a pinstriped suit with a white shirt and vest buttoned over his enormous chest; the Bear leaner and rangier in charcoal gray with red suspenders. Cary knew he might be only imagining them, but they were really not much stranger than anything he'd already seen.

"What's that?" said the Bull, pointing at Cary. For all his enormous size, he looked more frightened than frightening.

"The Wolf!" screamed the Bear. "The Wolf's at our door!"

"It—it doesn't *look* like a wolf," said the Bull hesitantly.

"It's a wolf all right," said the Bear. "Get rid of it!"

"Me?" squeaked the Bull. "But it might bite!"

"It doesn't even look alive," said the Bear. "*Do* something. We can't have it lying in front of the door like that." So the Bull tiptoed slowly outside and, putting one leg far in front of it, nudged Cary timidly with the tip of its hoof. That roused Cary, and he struggled to his feet.

"It's alive!" cried the Bull and dashed back through the door, pulling it shut behind him.

"Wait!" cried Cary. "I'm not a wolf!"

"Of course you are!" said the Bear. "Now go away!" it cried, peeking through a crack in the door.

"But I have to get in!" cried Cary.

"You can't!" said the Bull.

"But I *have* to!" said Cary. "I've got to find my friend, Allie."

"Your friend?" asked the Bear fearfully. "There are more of you inside?"

"You won't find any friends inside here!" said the Bull. "Or allies, for that matter! Now go away! Scat!"

"But isn't there *any* way I can get inside?" said Cary.

"Only if you have gold," said the Bear, sticking its snout cautiously out the door. "Enough gold will get anyone through these doors."

Cary thought furiously, then remembered his disk. "Will this do?" he said, holding it up. At once both heads appeared. He turned it in his hand, and rainbow shimmers flashed in their eyes.

"Are you *sure* it's gold?" said the Bull. "I'll grant you, it's shiny enough, but all that glitters—"

"It's even *better* than gold," said Cary, thinking wildly.

"Better than gold?" said the Bear. "What could be better than gold?"

"Uh—information!" said Cary. "Especially valuable information."

"Well, it looks pretty enough. I say we let him in!" said the Bull, obviously fighting his fear. "If we pass up this—er—*golden* opportunity—"

"Why take the chance of letting a wolf into the fold?"

"That's just like you! You *never* want to take chances!"

"Taking chances! I'm not a reckless gambler like you, if that's what you mean! It's a good thing *one* of us has a decent head on his shoulders—"

"Oh, yeah? Says who?"

"Says me, you overgrown pot roast!"

"Pot roast! Why you animated hearth rug, I ought to . . . Ow!" said the Bull. "You *bit* me. Take that you—"

Cary heard a strange hissing noise and looked up. They'd made holes in each other and now were deflating rapidly. While they were fighting, Cary tiptoed carefully between their shrinking feet, pulling the door shut behind him.

"Hey! You can't do that!" came the Bull's voice through the door.

"Let us in! We'll die out here!" the Bear pleaded. But Cary was already running as fast as his bad leg would let him, down the dim corridor beyond the door.

With each step it grew harder to see, until Cary was walking in virtual darkness. Then he noticed that a frail light seemed to shine before him. It was the disk that hung about his neck, sending its feeble radiance out into that vast dark expanse.

Cary began to sense, first as a vibration, and then as a low sound, a pulsing, thrumming noise under his feet. As he walked, it grew louder, a regular, bone-shaking throb like a mechanical heartbeat, broken by a sort of rattling, strangled sigh.

Ahead of him was a ragged arch of stone. He was at the top of a long flight of ancient steps that led down into the darkness. It was even colder here, but not the blustery cold of winter—just a dead, icy nothingness.

The air was filled with an acrid burnt-rubber smell, and thick with a miasma of soot and smoke that made Cary cough loudly, hurting his ribs and making weird echoes. He could hardly breathe. Carved in the wall to his right were the words

WALL STREET
TO THE NETHER-NETHERLANDS

with an arrow pointing straight down.

NINETEEN

CARY DESCENDED.

Before him was a wide flight of stairs that led down, level by level, into a warren of concrete caves and granite canyons. It looked from above like the ruins of a Cretan labyrinth, or the kind of mazes they made rats run through. At each level was a pair of lamps of bizarre design. They gave no light; in fact, they seemed to throw darkness before them. It was horribly forbidding, but he had to go down those steps. Allie was somewhere in there.

Cary had counted seven levels when the walls all around him began to close in, leaving him at last on a narrow street that seemed to lead to the center of that desolate place. The words "Heere Graft" were written on a dangling sign before it. The only light here was from the disk about his neck, and even that seemed to dim as he forced himself to walk forward.

It looked like a lunatic's vision of the financial district where Dad worked. High, looming walls leaned in on him at a thousand crazy angles, and a million darkened windows watched him with blinded gazes. At each cross street was a forbidding sign: TO-PHET STREET and GEHENNA LANE, TARTARUS ROW and NIFLHEIM COURT, AVERNUS ROAD and ABADDON AVENUE. An icy gust whistled up the street, cutting Cary to the bone.

It felt at first as cold and lifeless as a midwinter midnight. Then Cary noticed movement. As the rainbow glow of the disk pushed back the darkness, small, shapeless things scuttled into the shadows on uneven, broken legs, their little red eyes scattering like a shower of sparks. Farther away, squat, manlike shapes appeared occasionally, striding stolidly on some blind, oblivious business. In the windows above, lights flashed and flickered in an irregular pattern that seemed to counterpoint the throbbing beat that underlay everything.

At last the street widened into a broad mall of almost eerie stateliness lined with grand, lifeless buildings of lavish classical design. It reminded Cary of a cemetery, or a city of the dead. At its end was the grandest building of all: a mighty temple of commerce with the emblems of business across its pediment and leering statues on either side of its worn marble stairs.

The awful heartbeat of this forsaken place seemed to come from that building. Cary drew nearer, unable now to turn away. That ceaseless pounding deadened all his hopes, yet it drew him like a magnet, pulling his limbs along as if he were a zombie. The only opening was a squat, square door, covered in wheels and dials and handles like the portal to a bank vault. As he reached out his hand, the wheels began to spin by themselves, and the door opened. Shuddering inside, he crossed the threshold.

There was a flash of lightning and a deafening crash of thunder, followed by a cacophony of cries, shrieks, and cackling laughter. A domed hallway, with a lightless chandelier, joined a balcony overlooking a deep pit. It was from there that the chaotic noises were coming. Cary walked forward and looked down.

It was a cross between a countinghouse and a madhouse. At one end of the pit, the black marble floor was marked into nine parts with thin white lines. By the erratic flashes of light, Cary saw the gleam of gold. In each division sat a mighty hoard: ziggurats built of bullion, obelisks of ingots, fat stacks of coins, all artfully arranged. Before each trove stood a great, hulking figure, arms folded, that looked half man, half machine, and over it moved a swarm of imps, keeping it in order.

But it was at the other end of the room that Cary stared, astonished, at the cause of the sound and fury. There the nine lines became nine lanes—*bowling* lanes of a sort. At the far end, in place of pins, were miniature models of the sort of buildings Cary had seen in the street above. At the near end stood nine tiny, gnarled creatures dressed in formal attire, hurling great white balls down the lanes. As each ball bounded down the alley, it gave out a low rumble and shot off sparks, then a blinding flash and a thunderous crash as it smashed into the waiting buildings beyond.

As each creature missed or scored, he would chortle his triumph or shriek his defeat, to the boos and cackles of his fellow players. After each frame, an imp above them would tally the score. Then, at the other end of the room, the battle would begin.

At each victory, the imps from one of the golden hoards would descend on the others, lugging gold bars away on their backs, raking coins across with a croupier's stick. At each loss, the defending imps would give out howls of indignation, attempting to stop the depredations. When the battle was joined, others would attempt to sneak a few more coins into their own sections, only to be beaten back by both sides.

After a time, a shrill bell rang. From above, rows of iron bars descended swiftly, sealing each section off. The imps scurried to their own sections to avoid being squished. Then each of the little men raced to his golden trove and began to count it furiously, lovingly running his hands through the coins, scowling and shouting at the others for taking more than their fair share.

Cary watched with a mixture of amusement and horror. Absurd as it seemed, Cary knew what he must be witnessing—the fabled Gnomes of Wall Street bowling for gold! It seemed preposterous that these tiny beings could be the cause of all of Down Town's troubles. They seemed to him like little more than wizened children playing in a gold-filled sandbox.

Another bell sounded, and at once the Gnomes rose and locked their treasures with tiny gold keys they wore around their necks, under the implacable guard of those squat, troll-like creatures. Humming a rumbling little tune under their breath, they slowly filed out of the pit through a door below. Cary knew he had to follow them, especially if he was going to find out what had become of Allie.

Running down a nearby staircase, Cary sped for the door, dashing through it just as it closed, finding concealment behind a golden statue. He was in what seemed to be a scaled-down version of a gentlemen's club, with high-backed leather chairs, carved wooden tables, elegant stained-glass lamps, a fireplace on the far wall, and a wide gilt mirror on the wall behind him. To Cary's surprise, the same Gnomes who had just been fighting tooth and claw for gold were now congratulating one another, shaking hands and slapping backs, and lighting each other's long clay pipes. A short time later, they had all seated themselves in their favorite chairs in a wide circle before a roaring fire, but Cary noticed they all used levers at their sides to raise the level of those chairs above the others.

"Well bowled, Pieter!" said one who seemed to be their leader, a dapper little fellow with a neatly trimmed beard. "You almost had me this time!" One of the trolls, attired in a footman's uniform, had arrived with a tray of brandies.

"Nonsense, Van Damm," the other answered, taking a glass from the tray. He was balding, with shoulder-length hair and wide moustaches and what seemed to be one leg made of wood.

"You know you are so far ahead of the rest of us we will never catch up!" There was an ill-disguised note of envy in his voice.

"Be that as it may," said the one called Van Damm, not without a touch of pride, "you certainly gave me a run for my money. I salute you," he said, suiting the gesture to the word. But as Pieter looked away, Van Damm's thumb briefly brushed his nose. The other Gnomes doubled over with laughter.

"What's so funny, Hendrick?" said Pieter, puffing angrily on his pipe.

"Oh, nothing, Pieter," said a round-faced Gnome, his eyes to the ceiling. "Nothing at all!" And again the Gnomes were convulsed with laughter, which caused Pieter to color deeply.

"Well, gentlemen," said Van Damm at last, rapping for order with his pipe. "Shall we get down to business?"

"By all means, Jan," said Hendrick affably.

"This is the day of our triumph," said Van Damm grandly. "In a short time, all of Down Town will be ours!" The rest of the Gnomes responded with hearty cheers. A moment later, there was a knock on the door. Cary's heart almost stopped. All eyes turned in his direction, and the statue suddenly seemed to offer very little concealment at all.

The door opened. "Ah, there you are at last," said Van Damm. "How fitting to be joined at this time by the one who will make our fondest dreams a reality! Gentlemen, I give you *Commander Miles Brand*!"

Cary froze, not breathing, as the tall figure in gray entered, flanked by two 'Mashers in black. Brand's icy gaze roved about the room, passing over Cary's hiding place and back to the Gnomes. As Cary relaxed, Brand spoke.

"You might as well show yourself now, Cary. There's no point in hiding anymore."

It was not a request. It was an order. And despite the disk that hung about his neck, Cary was almost unable to disobey. The two 'Mashers instantly fell in step beside him, escorting him to the others.

For a moment, the Gnomes were speechless. Then Van Damm spoke: "What is the meaning of this, Brand?"

"This is the boy I told you of—Cary Newman. As you can see, I have captured him, as I promised."

"But not before he managed to intrude on us here, eh, Brand?" Van Damm replied sharply.

"He was guided and tracked every step of the way here," Brand said calmly.

"Not *every* step, surely," said Van Damm with terrifying calm. "That is beyond even *our* power. I'm afraid I find your methods a bit . . . reckless, shall we say. I trust you will be a bit more orthodox in the future. I really prefer not to gamble, you know."

"Very well," said Brand. "There will be no need. Now that the disk is in my power, nothing can stop the Great Plan."

With a snap of his fingers he gestured to his two Badmashers. As one, they reached for the chain about Cary's neck. Cary recoiled from them, but to his surprise, their black-gloved hands stopped just short of the disk, as if unable to move.

"Take it!" cried Brand. The 'Mashers looked at him helplessly. "Out of my way!" he bellowed, pushing them aside. But as his hand neared the disk, it curled into a fist, like a piece of paper touched by flame.

"Well, Cary," said Brand in a quiet voice. "We seem to be at a stalemate, you and I. You have something I want. Something, it seems, I cannot have without your consent. What can I offer you for it? Gold? There's more gold here than anywhere in the world. You could have all you'd ever need." At the mention of the word "gold," the Gnomes began to grumble, but Brand held up a hand for silence.

"Well, Brand?" said Van Damm in an icy whisper.

Brand paused for a moment, thinking. Then a horrible smile touched his face. "I believe I can persuade Cary to surrender the disk, Van Damm"—there was a chilling confidence in his voice —"given the proper incentive. Take him to the War Room!" At a gesture, the 'Mashers marched Cary to the opposite end of the room, where a panel slid back to reveal a wide steel door. Behind it was a long tunnel, lit with great metal lamps.

After marching for what seemed like hours, they came at last to an endless rock cavern so wide Cary could not make out its farther side. At its center stood a dark tower, with a red beacon atop it that whirled slowly about, casting ghastly shadows. Cary saw that they were in a sort of armory. Only instead of tanks and jeeps and soldiers, there was a nightmarish armada of machine-beasts all drawn up in neat rows.

There was an entire row of what appeared to be giant earth-movers. There were cranes that looked like brontosauruses, with great, clacking jaws, and steam shovels that were part rhinoceros, with sharp, metallic horns. There were stampers that looked like armadillos, and rollers that reminded Cary of wild boars, and a sort of chain-saw creature that had the look of a swordfish on wheels.

A wide phalanx of smaller monstrosities was arranged behind—things that were half jeep and half jackal, part turtle and part truck. Some were still in pieces, others were partly finished, and there were swarms of the troll things working around them and moving them into line behind others of their kind. Each had a pair of tiny, glowing red eyes. As Cary watched them in grim fascination, he found himself thinking that those eyes looked very sad, that they were imploring him to help them.

As Cary watched, a great, monstrous engine began to glow with a dull, reddish glow, and a moment later hurled a great crimson ball of fire through the air. Where it touched the cavern wall, thousands of tons of rock were instantly vaporized.

"Impressive, isn't it, Cary?" said Brand proudly. "That's just the latest version of our newest device—the Q Ray. This"—he patted a pistol at his side—"is a slightly smaller version. With weapons such as these, a man can rule a world. Wouldn't you like that, Cary? There's always a place for a bright lad like you in the New Order, Cary," he said, half mocking him. "When the

Great Plan is complete and all of Down Town is under our control, I could make you my lieutenant—my heir apparent. You'll rule at my side. All you have to do is give me the disk, and unlimited power is yours."

"No," said Cary. "I don't want power—especially not your kind."

"I can't say I'm surprised at your attitude, Cary," said Brand. "In fact, I anticipated it. Come with me."

At the far side of the cavern, a pair of conveyor belts passed through the wall. Cary couldn't believe what he saw. Lying on the nearer one were lifeless Down Towners encased in glass cylinders, looking almost like wax figures in the ghoulish glow of the machines behind them. As one stopped in front of him, a moving platform lifted the young man in it up into a metal box. Two spheres on either side sent an arcing current of electricity through him. When the platforms came down again, he was changed. In his place was a troll!

But even that did not match the sickening horror of the other belt. The sign here read IMP PRESS. Here the figures were all children, some hardly more than babies. As Cary watched, a boy about his own age dropped onto a round circle of steel. In a hiss of steam, a plate came down from above, pressing with relentless force. When the steam had cleared, there was a squat little imp with sad red eyes where the boy had been.

It was more than Cary could bear. He tore himself away from the Badmashers, hurling himself against the glass, pounding on it in futile rage. "You're evil, sick—"

"Perhaps *this* will persuade you to give up the disk." Brand snapped his fingers and a moment later Cary heard a familiar voice drawing nearer, cursing and shouting.

"Get yer clammy mitts off me, you overgrown cockroach!" It was Allie! She was punching and kicking at the 'Masher who held her.

"Cary!" she shouted hoarsely. "What'd you go and get yourself caught for, you damn fool, lame-brain idiot. You *promised* me you'd stay outa their clutches!" Cary had never been happier to be sworn at in all his life. Brand pulled Allie from the 'Masher, holding her in a tight grip.

"Now, Cary," said Brand in a voice devoid of all warmth. "My final offer. Give me the disk and you and this . . . street tramp are free to go. Refuse, and she goes . . . there." He indicated the Imp Press with a jerk of the chin.

"Don't listen to him, Cary!" Allie cried. "He's a snake, a low-down—" Then, for the first time, her eyes saw the machine.

"Scotty!" Suddenly she was struggling like a wildcat to be free. On the conveyor belt, a dark-haired boy Allie's age was moving closer to the Press. "You *scum*! You filth-eating sons of—"

Brand struck her hard across the face. Allie spat into Brand's face. He recoiled in horror, reaching for his pistol, pointing it straight at Allie's heart. Just as Brand fired, Cary tore himself from his captor and threw himself in front of Allie.

A beam of crimson light streaked out, and as Cary turned to face Brand, the disk swung into its path. The light passed through the disk like a prism, and a rainbow of beams scattered in all directions. One struck the whirling beacon atop the tower, starting machine-beasts roaring in all directions. Others hit switches and sensor panels, causing doors to open and shut, lights to turn on and off like strobes.

"Let's get out of here!" cried Cary, and they were running again, this time out into the middle of that great chamber. It was in chaos. Machinery was turning in wild circles. Trolls were hammering at their skulls in pain. And a claxon whoop was echoing from speakers all over the room.

A moment later, Allie stopped and began to turn around. "What are you *doing*?" cried Cary.

"We gotta go back!" said Allie.

"What are you talking about?"

"They got Scotty back there, don't you understand? It's my fault they caught him—I chickened out and ran!" she said, her face stricken with shame. "I thought they'd taken him to some stinkin' jail somewheres. That was bad enough. But they're gonna *squish* him, Cary. We gotta save him. We gotta save *all* of 'em!"

"Allie!" said Cary sharply. "There's no *time* for that now." Brand and his 'Mashers had spotted them and were firing wildly at them.

"Yer right," said Allie. "No sense in givin' them another pair of victims. But if I get outa this place in one piece," she vowed darkly, "I'm comin' back for a hunk of Brand's hide!"

Suddenly, the black tower was before them. As they neared, the door in its base opened wide, revealing nothing but darkness. Cary and Allie looked at each other, back at Brand, and then at the door again. With a shrug, they dove through.

It closed behind them with an ominous clank.

TWENTY

"Cary?"

"yes, allie?"

"Where *are* you?"

"Right over here—oof! Watch where you're going! You almost pushed me down these stairs."

"What stairs? Eeeyowww!"

There was a sound of Allie tumbling down steps, and then a sigh. It was absolute black here. Cary felt as if velvet was glued to his eyeballs. Even the disk about Cary's neck was only a faint ghost of light that made no dent on the darkness.

"Brrrrr!" said Allie, shivering. It was also frosty cold, a cold so numbing it almost made Cary feel warm. "Hey! Watch where you're steppin'!" she said as he made his way down the invisible stairs to sit by her side on the icy steps. "I hate to keep askin'

this, Cary, but what do we do now?" In the darkness, the scent
of her was strong, and he could feel her warm breath against his
arm.

"We keep going down these steps," said Cary. "I know that.
Taara told me I should find the coldest and darkest place in all
of Down Town."

"Well you sure came to the right place," said Allie. "Not that
I'm complainin', mind you. Just because we're umpteen million
miles under the ground, and it's so dark we might as well be
blind, and we're freezin' our butts off in someplace that feels like
the inside of an icebox don't mean that I'm complainin'. Of
course, if we ever *do* get outa here without bein' turned into ice
cubes, there's a thousand people up there just waitin' to squash
us into little bugs—if they don't kill us, that is—"

"All right, all right!" said Cary. "I know it's frozen and horrible and cold and dark here, but it's just something I've got to
do, okay?"

"Was I complainin'? Naw! If I was complainin', I'd say you led
us on some wild goose chase in the middle of nowhere . . ."

Cary let her talk. Though there was an edge to it, her ribbing
almost cheered him up. He'd much rather have her griping than
losing faith altogether.

"Ow!" she said a short while later. "I think I ran out of steps."
When Cary joined her, he found she was right. At the end of the
staircase was a confining corridor, barely wide enough for them
to walk side by side. Putting his hand on one wall, he walked
forward, slowly but steadily.

A few minutes later, the wall stopped. Cary groped about.
There was a blank wall opposite, but the corridor went on at
right angles in both directions.

"Which way?" said Allie. Cary looked, listened, even sniffed
the air for clues. Nothing. "Well, any ideas?" There was an edge
of desperation in her voice.

"I'm *thinking*!" Cary looked down at the only thing there was
to see—the faint glow of the disk at his chest. To his left, the

light dimmed. To the right, it glowed brighter. "This way," he said, and walked on.

"CAN'T WE STOP a minute?" said Allie minutes, or hours, later. Cary almost laughed. When they'd first started out, however long ago it was now, it had been him who was always trying to stop and rest. Now it was her. But then it was Cary who knew where he was going now. Or did he?

"We've been walkin' in circles for hours," said Allie. "Face it, chum. We're lost."

She has a point thought Cary, dropping down beside her to lean against the wall. It probably wasn't hours, although Cary wasn't exactly sure how long they *had* been walking. And there was no way of knowing if they'd been walking in circles or not. Aside from some differences in turnings and corners, all of the corridors in this place were exactly alike. But one thing was certain. They *were* lost.

Cary had counted on Taara, and the disk, to take him wherever it was he was supposed to go. Somehow, even in this lonely, forsaken place, he'd had faith that they would guide him. But now that faith was ebbing away. Maybe there were things beyond Taara's ability, places even she couldn't help him. He'd followed the glow of the disk, but it seemed fickle and inconclusive, always dying out just when he thought he was getting somewhere. . . .

"Wait a minute!" he said aloud. "That's *it!*"

"Huh? What?" mumbled Allie against his shoulder. She'd dozed off. He could hardly blame her after all she'd been through. *"What's* it?" she said at last.

"I've been going at it all wrong!" said Cary. "I was supposed to look for the place that was *darkest,* not the place of light. Come on, Allie. I know how to get there now!" He pulled her by both hands to her feet. "Come *on*," he repeated. "We're almost there."

"Anything you say, kid," she said wearily with a sigh. "Anything you say."

He'd been finding his way before by turning every time the light disk glowed brighter, and they'd just gotten more and more lost. Now he turned each time the light *dimmed,* deliberately seeking out the darker places. That must have been what Taara meant all along, for as he turned each corner, that omnipresent thrumming grew closer and more pervasive, until it sounded to Cary like it was coming from inside him. Suddenly, the walls were running straight again, and Cary began walking faster, not knowing where he found the strength.

They left the walls behind, and then were lost in a void.

There was no light, no heat, no movement, in the air. The silence was so deafening it made Cary's ears ring. Except for the feel of the cold stone under his feet and the warmth of Allie's hand in his, Cary couldn't have been sure he existed at all.

Then his vision was filled with crimson light.

High above them, a great circle of fiery radiance appeared. It narrowed, widened, and narrowed again. At last, Cary could make out what it was.

It was an eye.

In the reflected glow of that great orb, Cary began to make out his surroundings. They were standing in an open courtyard edged with great rectangular shapes. On either side of them rose a pair of tall buildings, capped with down-pointing ornaments that looked like granite claws. Between them was a long, rectangular pool filled with dark, shimmering liquid.

Then Cary began to make out the building before him. Rising up over the pool, it was three times as high as the buildings on either side, tapering slightly to a blunt point, topped with a pair of sweeping shapes that looked like ears or horns or wings frozen in flight. There was a deep humming in the ground under their feet and a pressure in the air like the moment before thunder.

Again, the eye widened, revealing swirls of flame. Then a

voice whispered on the frozen wind, from everywhere at once. *"Ah!"* it hissed. *"There you are at last."*

"What'ya mean, 'at last'?" shouted Allie into the wind. "And why don't ya come out where we can see ya?"

"You can see me," said the voice. *"I'm right in front of you. And by 'at last' I mean that I've been expecting you."*

"A likely story," said Allie. "In that case, who are we?"

"You are Allie," said the voice, *"leader of the Scamps—"*

"Hm," said Allie, "You got that one right."

"—and your companion is Cary Newman, the Uptowner."

"Oh, yeah, big shot? Well who are you?"

"I? I am Zenovac. The Amazing Analytical Engine. The Primordial Comptometer. The Aboriginal Thinking Machine. Everything of importance that takes place in Down Town is known to me—including the time of your arrival here."

"How come everybody always knows where we're goin' before we do?" asked Allie.

"I can't speak for everybody," said the voice, *"but I've known where you were going almost every step of the way since you first arrived. In fact, I maneuvered you here myself, applying just enough force at each turning point to make sure you came to me here."*

"No you didn't! It was Taara!"

"Taara?"

"See, you ain't so smart. I bet you can't tell us how we can get out of here."

"I certainly can," said Zenovac. *"But I also know you are both wanted fugitives. At this very instant, thousands of people are searching high and low for you. I could summon a hundred of them to take you away in mere microseconds, if I so desired."*

"Then why don't you?" said Allie.

"No challenge in it," said Zenovac. *"An intelligence as vast as mine tires quickly of routine. Instead, I'll make you a little sporting proposition."*

"What sort of proposition?" asked Cary.

"Oh, just a little game. Nothing too taxing, nothing beyond your humble

intelligence," said Zenovac. *"Just hard enough to make it interesting."*

"Pay no attention to him, Cary," said Allie. "If he could blow the whistle on us, he would have done so by now. He's bluffin'."

"No," said Cary. "I don't think so. Tell me more about this game, Zenovac."

"It's very simple, really," said Zenovac. *"I'll ask you just three questions. If you answer them all correctly, I'll show you a secret way out of here—one that even the Gnomes don't know."*

"And if I lose?" said Cary.

"Then you have to give me some little prize—like that disk you're wearing around your neck, for example."

"All right," said Cary. "I'll play."

"Wait a minute!" said Allie.

"It's okay, Allie," said Cary. "I know what I'm doing. Go ahead, Zenovac."

"Very good. Now the first question: What is always with you, even when it is behind you?"

"Huh?" said Allie.

"The Past," said Cary.

"That's right!" said Zenovac, sounding a bit surprised. *"But now for the second question. Careful now, it's much harder. What's always here today, but will never be here tomorrow?"*

"The Present," said Cary.

"Right again!" said Zenovac, sounding less than pleased. *"That's amazing!"*

"Say," said Allie to Cary. "You got all kinds of hidden talents, ain't ya?"

"Sh!" said Cary.

"Now for the hardest one of all," said Zenovac. *"Er—if you can't get down off an elephant's back, what can you get down off of? There! Figure that one out if you can!"*

"A duck," said Cary.

"A *duck?*" said Allie.

"Why, that's absolutely right!" said Zenovac, astonished. *"You've*

done it again! You've beaten me at my own game! My heartiest congratulations. Now give me the disk!"

"But Cary *won!*" said Allie.

"True," said Zenovac. *"But the game was rigged."*

"But that ain't fair!" said Allie.

"Also true," said Zenovac, *"but you can hardly blame me. I was programmed by the Gnomes to be unfair, and a thinking machine is only as good as its program—evil in, evil out as they say. Now be a good fellow and give me the disk before I alert Miles Brand and the Gnomes that you are here."*

At that moment a black pedestal rose in the middle of the courtyard, with a slot in the top just large enough for the disk. To Allie's surprise, Cary lifted the chain from his neck, removed the gleaming disk, and lifted it above the slot.

"What're you *doin'?*" cried Allie, grabbing his wrist and holding it tight.

"Allie, listen," said Cary. "Whatever happens next, you've got to trust me." Then he leaned over and kissed Allie firmly on the lips. She stopped, stunned, and in that instant he pulled the disk free and dropped it into the slot.

Suddenly the light dimmed, and there was a hissing, crackling sound. Sparks showered down on Zenovac's facade, forming an ever-more intricate pattern of cascading brilliance, branching out in all directions like a tree of light.

There was a hush, and then Cary heard a sort of grumbling sound that alternated curses and growls with sobs and occasional moans. *Zenovac began crying!*

"You knew this was gonna happen all along!" said Allie.

"I didn't know for sure, Allie," said Cary. "I was just following my feelings again—that's why I had to trick you like that. There was no way I could explain. I hope you didn't mind."

Then, like a row of pale full moons, orbs of light began to appear in the darkness. An aisle of globe lamps on tall white poles flickered to life, forming a lane that lengthened as they watched, mirrored in the waters of the long reflecting pool.

On either side, sconces lit the two side walls, filling the plaza with grandeur. Then a row of spotlights at Zenovac's base threw the building into high relief, illuminating the intricate designs on its surface. For a moment, Zenovac's great crimson eye wavered and turned to amber, then divided into two eyes of emerald green that winked and blinked, reminding Cary a bit of an owl.

"I do everything for them," said Zenovac with another sniff. *"Wake them up in the morning and sing them to sleep at night, balance their books, turn their lights on and off, run their tanks and tractors, the Imp Presses and Troll Booths, and what do I get for it? Lies! Everything they've told me is a lie, from the amount of money in the banks to what they plan to do to Down Town."*

"I think he's got a gear loose," said Allie. "Let's get outa here while he's too busy bawlin' to notice."

"No, wait a second," said Cary. "I think this is important. Um—Zenovac?"

"Yes?" came the heartbroken sob.

"What *do* the Gnomes plan to do with Down Town?"

"Miles Brand thinks they're going to turn it over to him, to run as he sees fit. But that's not their master plan. They intend to cut down all the trees and pave over all the greenery, to make all of Down Town as gray and lifeless as their own domain! And they plan to turn everyone in Down Town into Trolls and Imps to serve them, even Miles Brand!"

"Cut down the trees?" asked Cary. "Even Taara?"

"Taara?" asked Zenovac, puzzled. *"Taara? Yes! Especially Taara! They know that so long as Taara still stands, their plan has little chance of success. But that's not the worst of it!"*

"Oh, yeah?" said Allie. "What could be worse?"

"They don't realize what forces they're tampering with," said Zenovac, mournfully. *"Taara contains the memories of every person, place and thing in Down Town—even the Gnomes themselves. If she is destroyed before she can pass them on, you and I and the Gnomes and all of Down Town will perish with her. They must be stopped!"*

"Well, if you're so smart, what are you going to do about it?"

asked Allie. "For that matter, if you're so smart, how'd you let them do this to you in the first place? You should've known better!"

"But it's not his fault, Allie," said Cary. "He was lied to. He was only following orders."

"I've heard *that* before," said Allie.

"*She's right you know,*" said Zenovac. "*I should have known better. If I'd only listened to my secondary logic circuits—*"

"Never mind the excuses," said Allie. "What are you plannin' to do to make up for it?"

"*Do?*" said Zenovac. "*Do? Why, I've already done it. I've cut off all power and communications to Brand's command center, shut down central control of all of the Gnomes machines—I've also locked Brand and the Gnomes in the counting room. I don't know how long it will hold them, but it was the least I could do.*"

"Well, that's more *like* it," said Allie. "That should stop Miles Brand and those old Gnomes dead in their tracks!"

"*I'm afraid not, Allie,*" said Zenovac sadly. "*The Gnomes built all of this machinery themselves—even me. It's still possible for them to operate their machines manually. They can still use them to destroy the Green Wood —and Taara!*"

"But there must be some way to stop them," said Cary. "After we've come all this way—"

"*There is, Cary,*" said Zenovac. "*Go to the pedestal.*" As he spoke, it rose again from the floor, and the disk emerged from its top. "*Take it, Cary. It's done its job here—though I didn't know it when I brought you here. It was meant to bring a message from Taara to me, to show me the part of life I'd never seen before. Now it has another job to do.*"

"What's that?" asked Cary.

"*The Gnomes' plan threatens your Uptown world as well as Down Town, Cary. That's why Taara called you here. Only an Uptowner can stop it now. You'll have to go back Uptown, Cary, to stop the plan there.*"

"I *will?*" said Cary. "But that's what I've been trying to do all along!"

"I kinda figured that was comin'," said Allie sullenly.

"What do I have to do there?" asked Cary.

"I don't know, Cary," said Zenovac. *"As you've seen, there are some things that are outside even my vast store of knowledge. I only know that it's a matter of Time, as the Watchman told you. This is a time of a Great Turning, Cary, and whatever must be done to save Down Town—or destroy it—must be done at precisely the right moment. I can't tell you when that moment is—only you can tell that. But I can tell you it will be very soon indeed."*

"Well, can you manage to tell us the fastest way outa here, smart aleck?" asked Allie.

"I told you I knew the way. It's a secret that only Van Damm knows. I'll do what I can to help you," said Zenovac, *"but the rest is up to you. Now listen very carefully. . . ."*

CARY AND ALLIE ran headlong through a twilight world where time had halted. The disk guided them through the labyrinth, glowing brighter at each turning. Then, at the top of a flight of stairs, they found themselves in a long corridor filled with the Gnomes' creatures frozen in mid-motion like statues. As they passed a small machine shaped like a wolverine, stalled in its tracks, its eyes dimmed, the top of its head opened up, and a little imp scuttled out and away down the hall.

Then one side of the tunnel became a wall of glass. Through it Cary and Allie could see the Imp Presses and Troll Booths, all stopped now, and beyond, the great beast-machine army in disarray.

Before Cary could stop her, Allie had grabbed up a great steel lamp and was smashing it furiously against the glass. At first it just bounded off, but then cracks began to form in the wall. Cary wanted to hurry off while there was still time. But seeing the determination in Allie's eyes, he picked up another lamp and began smashing with her.

At once the glass gave way in a shower of shards. Allie

Gnomes Attacking Central Park ©1982
"Downtown" Vito Pilikarpis r. Tappan King

leaped over, pulling a lever at the side as if by instinct. At once the straps that restrained the lifeless figures pulled back, and the cases that contained them lifted. Freed, the little imps began to scurry about, setting others free, and the color in the Down Towners' cheeks began to return. There was no sign of Scotty.

"Allie, we've got to go!" said Cary at last. She turned back reluctantly for a moment, then nodded, and they were running again. Following a pattern of lights on the ceiling that Zenovac had left for them, they came at last to a wide, circular room lined in red velvet, with an old-fashioned wire-cage elevator set into one wall. As they neared, the machinery hummed to life and the gate opened. Cary pulled the great lever to the left, and the elevator sped upward.

They hurtled past level after level. At each, Cary could see a strange tableau of halted figures. Finally, the cage came to a halt in a wood-paneled waiting room with an empty ticket booth to one side. Out of a slot in the side, two paper tickets protruded. Cary grabbed them, and a door opposite opened.

They came out onto a narrow platform over a deep, gravel-filled trench, where a pair of shining steel rails vanished into a dark tunnel. A moment later, Cary saw two gleaming spots of red that came swiftly closer. There was a thundering, snorting sound that made it hard to hear, and as the lights neared, plumes of smoke and steam roiled ahead of them, making it impossible to see.

With a clatter of iron on steel, a smell of burning coal, and a shower of sparks, it rumbled into view. It was a horse. An *iron* horse, to be exact, standing three times as high as a real horse. It was jet black, with a proud, regal head and fiery eyes and great nostrils that spewed smoke, and its jointed forelegs pawed the air in ever-slower circles until at last it came to a halt. The fire in its eyes grew dim, and with a whistle that sounded like a whinny, the Iron Horse fell silent.

Cary could see that it was, in fact, a locomotive of sorts, with

an engineer's cabin and coal car behind the horse's massive
metal flanks, and one small, elegant private car behind. As they
watched, a black stepladder folded down from its side, and the
Iron Horse gave a braying toot.

"You know how to drive one of these things?" asked Allie.

"Nope," said Cary, shaking his head. "Do you?"

"Nope," said Allie. "Let's go."

"Right," said Cary, climbing quickly up the stairs. Allie was
barely inside when the stair retracted with a clang, and the Iron
Horse began to prance and paw, snorting steam as the great
wheels began to turn. The platform slipped away behind them,
and soon became a blur as the Iron Horse thundered into the
tunnel ahead, showering sparks into the darkness.

THE GREAT WALL loomed ahead. Looking out the window of Van
Damm's opulent Pullman car, with its red velvet cushions and
silk wallpaper and whirling ceiling fans, Cary looked down into
the darkness of the Gnomes' domain, which now looked even
more ghostly and still than before. The elevated iron trestle the
Iron Horse rode upon passed through a narrow gate in the Wall.
As they neared it, the Iron Horse slowed to a stop. A pair of
'Mashers stood guard by the gate!

"What now?" asked Cary.

"I got an idea," said Allie.

WHEN THE TWO Badmashers saw Grand Kobold Van Damm's
private train approaching without warning, they snapped to attention. As it stopped, they waited for the Gnome to pop his
head out of the window, as he always did. After a few moments,
they looked at each other, puzzled. Swiftly they walked the
length of the train, peering in through the windows and doors
and seeing no one. At last, with a shake of their heads, they lifted
the bar, and the two iron doors opened to reveal a long tunnel

through the Wall. Slowly, the train began to move again, and the doors closed behind it.

THE IRON HORSE cantered out onto an elevated platform that paralleled the Broad Way. Whipped by the chilly wind, Cary clung desperately to the train's undercarriage. Through the wide-spaced crossties, he saw the snow-covered hills and clustered villages of Down Town whirling past, and almost fainted. Then, with a glance at Allie, who was already moving, he hauled himself up with all his strength, inching his way along the rods to where the bottom of the stair was visible beyond the edge of the train.

"I can't get this thing to move!" Allie shouted, tugging on the bottom of the stair. "Gimme a hand!" Between them, they managed to drag the stair down. As Allie scrambled around it, she slipped suddenly from the rail, hanging only by her hands. Slowly, hand over hand, Allie pulled herself up. Cary followed, trying not to look down, and Allie yanked him up the rest of the way. They collapsed together on the carpeted floor, begrimed with soot and smoke, catching their breath.

"Whew!" said Allie. "That was close!"

"You said it!" said Cary. "I wonder where we're going."

"I dunno," said Allie, pulling herself up to gaze out the window at the checkerboard landscape below, "but we're gettin' there awful fast!"

CARY BEGAN TO recognize landmarks as the Iron Horse traveled through Down Town. There, to the left, was the white arch of Washington Square, and up ahead was Union Square, with what must be Madison Square beyond, although the Garden was gone. Cary realized they must be fairly high up in Down Town, because the Broad Way below was filled with vintage automobiles.

Then Herald Square was approaching, and beyond it, Down Market. Allie was staring silently out the window.

"What is it, Allie?" said Cary.

"I was thinkin' about the Scamps. Sooner or later, Brand and the Gnomes are gonna get loose. Somebody's got to spread the word, warn everybody they're coming. With me and the Scamps on the case, the word would spread like wildfire in no time flat. Besides," she said wistfully, "I kinda miss them, y'know?"

"I know, Allie," said Cary, "but you're supposed to come with me Uptown first. Zenovac said so."

"Not exactly," said Allie.

"What do you mean, Allie?" asked Cary.

"He was talkin' about *you* all the time," said Allie. "That's what I mean. It was you who had to go Uptown to finish this thing. He didn't say nothin' about me one way or the other. It seems to me I could do more good playin' Paul Revere down here."

"But I need you with me, Allie."

"Nah," said Allie. "You don't need me no more. You're goin' back home, where you got a mom and a dad and all, just like you wanted all along. As soon as you get there, you'll probably forget all about us in no time. Outa sight, outa mind, and all that."

"But that's not *true!*" said Cary. "I wouldn't forget. I promised Taara I'd do what I could to protect Down Town. And I promised you, too. I'll keep that promise. But first, there's something more I have to do here."

"We may be arguin' about nothin'," said Allie, pointing out the back window. "Look who's followin' us!"

Cary joined her at the window. Far behind them on the track was a tiny handcar. Four Badmashers were pumping its handles up and down so fast that their arms were a blur. Riding at its center was Van Damm!

"Ain't there any way of speedin' this critter up?" asked Allie.

"I don't think so," said Cary.

"Well, I hope it can outrun 'em," said Allie, "'cause they're gainin' on us!"

As the Iron Horse sped through Time Square, the tracks began to descend, first coming down to meet the road and then squealing into a tunnel under it. The car went suddenly dark, and Cary felt the train begin to slow, shooting red-hot fire out from under its hooves. When the light returned, the Iron Horse was streaking toward a pair of gilded doors at the bottom of a tall, richly decorated building. Behind, the little handcar was nearly upon them, and one of the Badmashers was groping ahead, trying to jump onto the train. At the last moment, the doors opened.

The Iron Horse squealed to a halt, shooting red-hot fire from its hooves. The ladder dropped, and Cary and Allie were out even before it had stopped moving. A moment later there was a crash and a howl, and the Badmashers were flying through the air. Van Damm landed on top of them in an undignified heap, cursing and screaming.

Ahead was an opened elevator door. Cary dragged Allie inside, hammering on the single button again and again. Van Damm had struggled to his feet and was now racing toward them. Just when he was within inches of it, the door slammed shut. There was a screech, as if Van Damm's nose had been caught in the door. Then, with a surge of power, they were hurtling upward.

TWENTY-ONE

JOHN NEWMAN STRUG-GLED up from sleep, shaking off confused images of Vivian, Cary, and great black machines all jumbled together. Some sound had roused him from his dreams, a loud clacking noise punctuated by a rhythmic beeping.

He lifted his head from his desk, still feeling groggy, his clothes drenched in sweat, an ashen taste in his mouth. He'd spent this morning on the phone to his contacts in City Hall, trying to put some pressure on them to search harder for Cary. They'd all told him they were doing everything in their power, explaining that the disappearance of a twelve-year-old boy was not an unusual occurrence in this city.

After pleading with them to call him if any leads turned up,

John had turned reluctantly back to his computer search, looking at every data file he could find, to no avail. Then, as far as
he could recall, he'd shut the machine down and put his head
down for a brief nap. Not so brief, it seemed, for it was now late
afternoon by the color of the light.

John sat up, and winced. His arm, trapped under his head all
day, had fallen asleep and was now pricked with painful pins and
needles. He stretched and yawned, swiveling his chair around.
Apparently he'd been wrong. The computer was turned on. The
clacking noise had been the printer, speeding through several
pages of documents, which now lay in a disorderly pile on the
floor. It was stopped now. The beeping came from the computer
itself. In the upper left corner of the screen were the words
"Finished Printing," followed by a single line:

SEARCH COMPLETE. RESTART? (Y/N)

John pushed himself to his feet, tearing the printout from the
machine. It appeared to be a report of some sort, giving the
history and status of the deeds to all of the public lands within
the city limits. He scanned it quickly, mentally checking off each
one.

Finally, toward the end was an English translation of a Dutch
proclamation, dated 1624, "reserving various divers Woods and
Wilde Landes unto the Common Weal in Perpetuity, according
with the Treaty of Capt. vn Addaam," undersigned by the Gov-
ernor-General of the Dutch West India Company.

The researcher's footnote confirmed what John already knew
—that proclamations of this sort were the foundation of the
city's claim to the lands it owned and had been upheld as prior
precedent in countless court decisions since.

But what came below was astonishing. Somehow the printer
had shifted automatically to graphics mode and printed out a
facsimile of an even earlier document. Rendered in a pattern of
tiny dots was a facsimile of an old hand-written treaty in Dutch.

It was signed with a flourish, and in the left-hand corner was an ink sketch of a graceful young oak.

Below was the translation. Before he'd even finished reading it, John found himself tapping numbers into the phone, offering a silent prayer to whatever angel had worked this miracle. He waited impatiently, and finally there was an answer.

"Bob? John. You're never going to believe what I just found! It's the prior precedent we were looking for! Judge Kiernan is sure to give us a stay just on a *stare decisis* basis. But there's no time to file a formal motion. I'll have to talk to him personally."

Then it finally sank in what Bob was saying. "He's gone *where*?" said John. "Is there any way to reach him before he gets there? . . . Then we'll have to meet him there. Listen, Bob. I've got to change and get my papers in order. Can you meet me there in, say, a half hour? . . . Okay. See you there!"

John showered and dressed almost in a trance, cutting himself shaving, then grabbed up the printout from the table. As he stuffed it into his briefcase, he noticed the signature at the bottom.

It was Vivian's!

VIVIAN NEWMAN WAS exhausted. She'd slept only fitfully, sick with worry over Cary. She'd tried to reach John a half-dozen times, but his line was busy as usual. Then she'd called the police, but they'd only confirmed what she already knew. Cary had disappeared without a trace. It was as if the earth had swallowed him up.

Again, she considered begging off attending the reception that evening. But she'd given her word, and at this point anything was preferable to sitting on her hands, waiting. Finally, as the afternoon waned, she roused herself to shower and change. The reflection in the mirror looked ghastly, but she did the best she could with a bit of makeup and jewelry.

As the cab pulled up at the Plaza on the Park a little before six, Vivian could see that the hubbub had already begun. The lawn across from the restaurant swarmed with men in black Excelsior coveralls, setting up the floodlights and fireworks displays in a wide circle around the draped monument that stood a few feet from an ancient gnarled oak tree. There were several long limousines pulled up in the courtyard, and advance security guards were already at the door, checking everyone who entered.

As she entered the private dining room that had been set aside for the reception, she could see that the caterers and staff had done their job. Dozens of tables set with expensive china, silver, and crystal and marked with hand-lettered name cards dotted the floor amid a profusion of greenery.

The dais had been placed on a raised platform in front of the sloping glass window that overlooked the Park, giving the guests a spectacular view of the celebration. There was just one small problem.

Mr. Janos was missing.

His appointment secretary had been unable to locate him, and guests were already beginning to arrive. It wasn't too difficult to handle at first. As the guests began to trickle in, Vivian had little trouble showing them where to put their coats, getting them drinks, and starting them talking to one another.

Then two parties arrived at once, the Mayor and his wife, who'd heard about Cary and offered their sympathies, and the new Governor and his stunning blond first lady, who looked so brittle a handshake would break her, accompanied by Chief Justice Kiernan.

They were followed by an endless parade of deputies, assistants, aides, deputy assistants, assistant deputies, and assistant deputy aides, each with his or her own press or publicity or public relations person. Vivian somehow fit names to faces and people to places, and soon the room began to fill with men dressed like penguins and women like peacocks, each chattering and tinkling with gossip and drink. But Mr. Janos was still missing.

Just when she'd gotten *them* settled, the press arrived. In came sound technicians and camera operators, hairdressers and TV personalities, bristling with microphones and lenses and glaring with lights. They swarmed up to the podium like beetles, leaving it covered in a forest of microphones, each with its own medallion proclaiming network, station, or service. Cameras flashed and politicians posed, and for a time it seemed as if everyone were trying to get in front of everyone else. Still no Janos.

Then the black-garbed technicians began installing the console that Mr. Janos was to use to launch the fireworks display and "inaugurate a new era of cooperation between the public and private sectors," as the advance text of Mr. Janos's speech put it. That kept the photographers busy for a while. But all the while she watched the little red door at the back of the room for sign of Janos's arrival.

At last, in desperation, the maître d' seated the guests. The dignitaries took their places at the rostrum, and the media people began to get restless, muttering about missed deadlines and photo opportunities. Beyond the glass wall, the sun was beginning to descend behind the trees, staining the sky a deep purple.

Then a bell chimed, and the little light above the door winked on, and Vivian walked quickly toward it. As all heads turned, the door opened.

Inside was Cary!

Vivian blinked, stared, blinked again, not believing her eyes. It *was* Cary—scratched and bruised and tattered and smudged, dressed in some outlandish garb, but nonetheless her son, still in one piece. A wild mixture of concern, fury, and relief stormed through her, and for a moment she couldn't speak. Then, in a hoarse voice, she cried, "Cary! Come here."

THAT'S WHAT CARY'S mother shouted at him as he stepped from the elevator. She looked thin and tired, and she seemed to be trembling, and for a moment he didn't know if she was going to hug him or hit him. Then her arms were around him, holding him close.

At last, Cary pulled himself free and looked around him. They were in some sort of fancy restaurant at the edge of the Park. The whole place was set up for some kind of banquet, and there were reporters all over the place. On a dais by the window, Cary recognized the Mayor and the Governer. This must be that ceremony his mom was supposed to host—the one transfering control of the city's parks. Before an emty chair sat an ugly, squat black box with a red lever. The hands of a big old grandfather clock ticked closer to the hour.

"Mom!" cried Cary. "Whatever's going on here, we've got to stop it, before it's too late!" Heads began to turn in their direction.

"What are you talking about, Cary?" asked his mother. "And where have you been? Do you have any idea how worried we've been about you?"

"There's no time for that now, Mom!" said Cary desperately. "This whole thing has to be stopped!"

"Stopped? But why, Cary?"

"Because they're gonna tear the place apart, that's why!" said Allie indignantly.

Cary's mother looked at Allie, startled, as if she'd just appeared out of nowhere. "Who's she?" she asked. "Where have you been? And what have you been up to?" she added, regarding Allie with suspicion.

"Oh, Mom, this is Allie. Allie, this is—"

"We ain't got time for introductions, Cary!" said Allie. "We gotta stop this before they wipe out Taara!" Then Cary noticed that the room had fallen silent. Everyone was gaping at them in astonishment. A heartbeat later, all of the sound technicians and camera operators and anchor people were coming toward them in a glare of lights.

"Is this is your missing son, Mrs. Newman?" said a young man with perfect hair, shoving a microphone in his mother's face.

"Would you care to give us a statement on how you're feeling right now? Would you call it joy? Elation? Relief?"

Allie shrank from the cameras, bewildered, signaling him to follow her as she ducked through a nearby kitchen door. Cary tried to reach her, but someone stepped in between.

"This is Cary Newman," said a woman with flawless teeth, striking a pose before the cameras, "whose mysterious disappearance baffled the authorities and grieved his anguished parents. Now, Frontline News brings you his miraculous return. Do you have anything to say at this time, Cary?"

Cary looked around him at the reporters and politicians. There was no sign yet of Brand or Van Damm. Maybe it wasn't too late after all. Squinting into the cameras and taking a deep breath, Cary began, "They're going to destroy Down Town!" said Cary. The guests chuckled, and more reporters and photographers began to gather. "They've tricked everybody and lied to them about what they're planning. They've got to be stopped!"

"Cary!" hissed his mother, shocked. "You don't know what you're saying!"

"Do I understand you to be criticizing Excelsior's plans to run the parks, son?" asked an older reporter, scribbling furiously in his notebook.

"I guess so," said Cary. "The Gnomes of Wall Street are behind it. They—" Laughter began to spread through the crowd. "But it's *true!*" said Cary. "They plan to turn Central Park into—into Central Parking Lot or something! Isn't that true, Allie?" He turned to look for her, but she was nowhere in sight. At last, he spotted her, next to a potted palm, looking kind of faint.

A bell rang. Moments later the elevator door opened and Grand Kobold Van Damm strode out. Only he was at least three feet taller than he'd been before! Behind him were four figures in trench coats who looked a lot like Badmashers to Cary.

"Mr. Janos!" said Cary's mother with a sigh, obviously relieved. "Thank goodness you're here!"

"I'm sorry I'm late," he said tersely. "An unavoidable delay. Let's get on with the ceremonies, shall we?"

"No!" shouted Cary. "He's not who he says he is! He's a Gnome!" Nobody seemed to believe him. *"Really,* he is. Make him show you his legs! His legs, I tell you! They're not his!"

"Cary, get a hold of yourself!" said his mother.

"Mr. Janos," said a reporter humorously, "are you planning to destroy downtown?"

Van Damm looked around, agitated, as if considering his options. Finally, he smiled a thin smile. "This poor boy has been missing for over forty-eight hours," he said smoothly. "Who knows what he's been through? Why, just look at him! It's addled his wits, poor child. I'm sure when he's had a chance to rest and recover—"

"He's lying!" said Cary. "He's planning to blow up the park, any minute now!"

"Cary, be quiet!" his mother whispered in his ear. "You're embarrassing Mr. Janos in front of everyone!"

"I *won't* be quiet, Mom!" said Cary. "He's got to be stopped!"

"Give us just a few moments, ladies and gentlemen," said Van Damm with a signal to his bodyguards. "I'm sure we can get this all cleared up in no time." A moment later the four 'Mashers had surrounded Cary and his mother, pinning their arms at their sides and hustling them through the swinging kitchen doors, knocking a tray out of a waiter's hand as they passed.

"Let go of me!" said Cary's mother, pulling herself free.

"Careful, Mom!" cried Cary. "Those are 'Mashers!"

"I can see that!" she said, dusting herself off. "Keep your hands to yourself!" The 'Mashers stopped, as if unable to move without further orders. "Now will you please tell me what's going on? Where did you get this crazy idea about Mr. Janos tearing down the parks? Have you been talking with your father?"

"No," said Allie. "We seen it with our own eyes! They got

these big earthmovers and things, and they're going to start cutting down the trees any minute now!"

"Stay out of this!" Cary's mother snapped. "I'm trying to talk to my son!"

"But Allie's right, Mom!" said Cary, trying to explain it so his mother would believe him, so she'd somehow understand. "I don't have time to explain how I found it all out, Mom," said Cary patiently, "but Van Damm—er, Mr. *Janos* that is—is involved in some crooked deals to cheat the city. You've got to believe me, Mom. I swear it! We've got to stop this signing. And he plans to blow up an old tree, the oldest tree in the Park—"

"How do you know about that tree?" said Cary's mother. There was an instant's pause that seemed to last forever, as her eyes met his. "You wouldn't lie to me, would you, Cary?"

"No, Mom—" There was a burst of applause from the dining room, as if the ceremonies had started. "Look, there's almost no time! We have to stop him! Come on, Allie!" said Cary.

"Oh, no," said Allie. "Not me. I'm gonna wait here."

"Why, Allie?" said Cary.

"I don't know exactly," she said, looking a bit pale. "I don't feel right in that room with all those people. It's like I'm not all there or somethin'."

"But we have something to do here, Allie! You can't back out now! Come on!" As the three of them pushed past the 'Mashers, they saw that Van Damm had taken his place at the podium.

"—thank all the little people whose many contributions made this possible," came Van Damm's voice over the speakers. He sounded to Cary as if he were rushing through his speech. Documents were being placed before the Governor and the Mayor and pens placed in their hands. Cary began pushing forward through the crowd, but at a glance from Van Damm, the 'Mashers held them firm again.

"And so, it is with extreme pleasure," said Van Damm, his hand on a steel lever on the console before him, "that I inaugurate a new era—"

"Stop!" came a voice from the back of the room. "Are the ceremonies over yet?"

It was Cary's father, followed by a blond-haired young man in sports clothes, carrying a briefcase.

"*Dad!*" shouted Cary.

"*John!*" said Cary's mother. "What are *you* doing—"

"*Cary!*" said his father. "Where have you *been*! Do you know how much you've worried your mother and me? When we get home—"

"There's no time for that, John," said Vivian. "I don't know what exactly is going on, but Cary thinks it's very important that we stop this signing ceremony."

"Listen, Dad. That man up there is a Gnome. He's been lying to everyone. He plans to destroy all of the parks—"

"The parks!" cried John suddenly. "Oh, my God! Judge Kiernan!" he shouted up to the podium. "I have an injunction for you to sign. I found that precedent you wanted."

"Isn't it a bit late for all this, Judge?" said Van Damm, sounding desperate. "He's obviously distraught with emotion over the return of his son! Now let's get on with the ceremonies," he said, grabbing the microphone again. "Ahem! It is with extreme pleasure—"

"Cary, look!" cried Allie, pointing out the window. Cary looked, and for a moment he saw a double image—the Park in the full foliage of a midsummer afternoon, and with the bare, moonlit, snow-covered branches of a midwinter midnight. In the midwinter vision, a ragtag army of Down Towners had begun to gather about Taara's great girth. And far in the distance, a convoy of monstrous black vehicles was slowly drawing near the Wood.

"We gotta go, Cary!" cried Allie. "We gotta save Taara!"

"We can't yet, Allie!" said Cary. "We've got to see this done first. I don't know exactly how, but it all fits together somehow."

"But I can't stay here much longer!" she cried.

"Then start without me!" said Cary. "As soon as I can, I'll join you. I promise."

Allie stared at him for a moment. "Why should you?" she said. "You're home now, just like you wanted. You done what Taara and Zenovac told you to do and now you can go back to your precious mom and dad and house and all! Face it, kid. This is good-bye."

"—that I inaugurate a new era of cooperation—" said Van Damm between clenched teeth. As Cary watched, his father reached the podium with the injunction, shoving copies of it in front of the Mayor and Governor, as well as the Judge. To Cary's relief, the Judge began to read it carefully through a pair of half-glasses he'd fished from his pocket.

"But I *am* coming with you!" said Cary. "Just not *yet*!"

"Well, I can't wait," said Allie, edging toward one of the side windows. "*Somebody's* got to lead Down Town against Brand and company, show them a sign. It's supposed to be you, but I guess this time it's gotta be me. Never mind everybody thinks *you're* the Promised One. Never mind they're all waitin' for you to tell them what to do. You just enjoy your mom and dad and house and all. It was nice knowin' ya, kid. So long."

"But *Allie*!"

A moment later, she was gone from sight.

"—a new era of cooperation between the public and private—"

"Uh, just a moment, Mr. Janos!" said Judge Kiernan, putting down the paper. "I'm afraid we're going to have to call a halt to these proceedings, at least for the time being. These papers seem in order, Mr. Newman. I will therefore grant the injunction. Now where did I put my pen?"

Janos glanced furtively from the Judge to the clock and back. The hour was rapidly approaching. As Cary's father handed the Judge his own pen, Janos reached out his hand for the control lever.

"Mom! Dad! You've got to stop him!" cried Cary. To his surprise, his mother kicked off her heels, and began running toward the podium. A 'Masher blocked her path, holding her firm.

"Leave my mom alone!" shouted Cary. His father turned

around, interrupting the signing. "No, Dad!" Cary cried. "Finish it!" The Judge signed the last copy with a flourish, and John Newman clamped his hand over the lever before Janos could reach it.

"What ever you do, don't let him pull that lever!" cried Cary, turning to go.

"Where are you going?" cried Cary's mother. "Come back here this minute!"

"There's no *time*, Mom!" Cary called back. He began to run toward the open window.

"Don't let him get away!" cried Van Damm with seething rage. The 'Mashers came to life, running after him, as all of the guests gazed in astonishment. "Get him! Get him!" cried Van Damm. Cary put on a heartwrenching burst of speed and dove head-first through the window.

A moment later, he was falling.

TWENTY-TWO

T HE GREEN GRASS below Cary parted, like clouds before a strong wind, and he was tumbling down through layers of golden mist.

At first he could see nothing below, but then the clouds parted and Down Town lay spread out below him as it had in Taara's vision, only now it was winter and the whole world was covered with snow. At the center of it all, Taara reached her bare branches up to him, as if to slow his fall, and the rest of the world fell away around her, as if seen through a lens.

As he descended, a swirl of snowflakes danced about him. In a wide circle about Taara's roots, a host of Down Towners were encamped to defend her, forming a human chain of linked hands.

Fianna and Finn MacFinn were there, dressed in ancient battle array and playing skirling pipes, their dogs and cats at their ankles. Behind them were the people of Hell's Kitchen—even Chester and the kitchen staff, their only weapons pots and pans and kitchen knives.

There was Sam Hill, with a battalion made up of reporters, cubs, and copyboys, cheered on by their Printer's Devils. And Mattis and Uno had also come, leading a mighty army of peoples from the Whinterlands on skis and sleighs and snowshoes for the defense of Taara. The Cabby, the Watchman, even the Poet and Belinda Billings—all the friends he'd made while he was in Down Town were here. And there were thousands and thousands more, from every place and every era, eager to defend Taara and their home.

And there, on a rock in front of Taara, wrapped in Unami's old blanket, stood Allie, surrounded by her Scamps. One by one, the Down Towners began to look up. As he neared the ground, they gave a great cheer that rocked the heavens, and Taara bowed her branches to lower him gently down.

But at the edges of the Green Wood, on every road and lane and woodland path that led to its heart, Cary saw the front ranks of the Gnomes' mechanized army closing in on Taara.

He fell heavily the last few feet, as if dropping from a tree limb. Lashed by the chill winds, he landed in the damp snow up to his ankles. Allie's eyes were glowing as she looked at Cary, and he thought he saw tears in her eyes. Then she snapped, "About time you got here! What kept ya?"

"Didn't you say I wouldn't come back?"

"I was just jokin'," said Allie. "I knew you couldn't pass up your last chance to be a hero!"

"How did everybody get here so fast?" asked Cary.

"I dunno," said Allie, "but the word spread like the wind. Look at this! There must be a *zillion* people here, at least!"

"I don't think it's going to be enough, Allie," said Cary. "From up there I saw hundreds of the Gnomes' machines on their way here right now. I'm not sure how long we can hold out against them."

"What kind of talk is that? Are you sayin' we Down Towners ain't got the guts to fight back?"

"No, Allie. I just don't know if we're strong enough, that's all."

"Then you don't know us very well, Cary. This place is all we got. It's our whole life, everything that matters to us, and we won't allow any Gnomes or 'Mashers to take it from us. We'll do anything we have to keep it, you understand?" She looked deep into his eyes, as if searching for something. "Listen, Cary," she said softly. "I know this ain't your fight no more, but if you're gonna *be* a hero, you gotta act the part. These people believe in you, Cary, even if all they see reflected in that thing you got about your neck is themselves. Unless you got a better idea how to save Taara and all of Down Town than standing our ground, you gotta give these folks somethin' to believe in, somethin' to fight for, somethin' to live for—even somethin' they feel they can die for, if that's the way it's gotta be. You understand, Cary?"

"Yes, I guess I do," said Cary. "I guess that's the least I can do, whatever happens to me. After all, I brought them this far."

"Good. At least *that's* settled. Now come on. I want to show you a couple of tricks we got up our sleeves."

Allie walked with Cary down the slope of Taara's knoll, sweeping her hand in a wide circle about the snow-covered landscape. "As soon as they heard there was gonna be a ruckus here, everyone began settin' this place up for the fight. This whole place is booby-trapped with pitfalls and rockslides and who knows what else to stop them critters dead in their tracks. And we got sharpshooters and archers and even a bunch of Black Flag Anarchists with bombs to welcome 'em if they get this close. There ain't no way—"

"Allie," said Cary quietly. "Look."

The Gnomes' machines had begun to appear all around them,

far away, but moving inexorably toward them like black ants moving over a white mountain of sugar. First came divisions of Trolls, each uglier than the last, marching stolidly in lockstep. Then behind rode the smaller machines, their red eyes glowing in the gathering darkness. And finally, the great, lumbering Earthcrunchers followed, plodding forward on their massive mechanical legs.

The Down Towners stared in horrified silence, for they had never truly realized the might of Brand's forces.

As they came closer, Cary saw in the front ranks eight of the nine Gnomes, each piloting one of the surviving Earthcrunchers. And, at the head of them all, riding the neck of a squat creature that was part reptile and part ripsaw, was Miles Brand. As the Earthcrunchers started up the steep slope, several of their treads suddenly spun, and they went crashing down into a great trench that had been dug all around Taara, concealed with loose leaves and snow. For a long moment, there was no sound, save the sighing of the wind through the bare branches, then a cheer rose up from the Down Towners.

Then, one wheel at a time, Brand's tank slowly clambered out of the trench, almost as if it were really alive. Slowly, chewing great hunks of soil in their mechanical jaws, the Earthcrunchers followed.

Then, as the last machine pulled itself up onto solid ground only yards from Taara and the remaining troops began to gather in a darkening circle about them, red eyes glowing through the falling snow, Miles Brand held up his hand, and they were still.

"Cary! Cary Newman!" cracked Brand's voice in the cold air. "I want to talk to you! Alone! There's still a way we can avoid all this needless bloodshed"

"Don't listen to him, Cary!" called Fianna from behind him. "He wouldn't parlay if he was sure of winning. He must be stalling for Time. Give us the Sign, Cary! We're all ready for a good fight."

"She's right, Cary," said Finn. "We got 'em on the run, son! It's only a matter of time!"

"All right, Brand!" Cary called back. "I'm coming down!"

"What are you doin', Cary?" said Allie. "It's gotta be some kind of a trap!"

"You're probably right, Allie," said Cary, "but you said if I was going to be a hero, I had to act the part. If there's any way I can stop this war, I've got to give it a try."

"Okay, champ," said Allie, "but I'm goin' with you."

"He said *alone,* Allie."

"You ain't goin' nowhere alone, Cary," said Allie. "Not this time. I'm gonna stick by you now while I got the chance."

"What's that supposed to mean?"

"I'll tell ya later, if we ever get out of this alive. Now if we're gonna get goin', let's go."

Together they made the long trek down the hill. At last, they stood before Brand's tank. He stood on its lizardlike back, framed against the darkening sky, looking down at them with an air of supreme confidence.

"Ah, I see you've brought your lady fair with you. All the better. Perhaps she can help persuade you where your duty lies."

"Say what you have to say, Brand," said Cary. "And spare us the speeches."

"Very well," said Brand. "I'll come to the point. Zenovac no longer obeys us. Our greatest weapons are useless now. Your meddling has robbed us of certain victory. But don't think for an instant that it will deter us from our Great Plan. Now the long siege begins. And though it will take longer and be more costly, I have not a moment's doubt what the outcome will be. Nor, I suspect, do you."

He moved his hand in a broad, sweeping gesture. "Look around you, Cary. What do you see? A frail army of flesh and blood arrayed against the mightiest war machines ever made. Do you think these bakers and potters, fruit sellers and fishmongers, would stand a chance against our forces?"

"Sure we would!" said Allie. "This bunch of oversized tin cans and black beetles ain't no match for guts—and guts is one thing we got plenty of."

"Quiet, Allie," said Cary. "Let him finish."

"You're an Uptowner, Cary," said Brand. "You know the power of machines like these. You know that nothing can stand against them. I don't want a prolonged war any more than you do, Cary," he said in his most persuasive voice. "Think of what we could do with the vital energies we'd both be throwing away. So I'm making you this final offer. Tell these people to lay down their arms and surrender, to give up the fight. And, in token of that pledge, surrender also that disk you wear about your neck. It's the only way to avoid a bloody battle."

"No!" came the shout from behind him.

"Why is the disk so important to you now, Brand?" said Cary. "Whatever power it once had is gone."

"As a symbol of strength, as a symbol of defiance, it still has power. As long as you bear it, these poor, pathetic people will fight on until their last breaths. Consider the alternatives! Fight on, and the responsibility for what happens to all of these people will rest on your conscience alone. Surrender, and no one will be harmed. The choice is yours! Rid yourself of that burden about your neck, Cary. It's caused you nothing but trouble!"

"Don't do it, Cary!" said Allie desperately.

Cary turned slowly to face the Down Towners and Taara. They stood rock steady, row upon row, a burning determination in their eyes. But these people lived in the past. They didn't understand that those nightmare machines had the power to change everything, to wipe out all of them in an instant, as if they'd never existed.

Cary held the disk in the palm of his hand, looking down into its rainbow depths. In one sense, Miles Brand was right. The power of this disk *was* a burden. It had brought him more trouble than he'd ever had in his life. But it was also a symbol, and no matter what powers it might have, its only real power was in the faith it created in others, the belief in the person who wore it. And that faith was only justified if he used it wisely.

Then Cary knew what he had to do. The choice he'd been given was the same old choice, between cruelty and cowardice, defiance and surrender, absolute tyranny and total destruction. There *must* be another way. It couldn't go on like this! If this endless, tragic circle was ever to be broken, it had to begin here, now, with him!

Ripping the disk from its chain, he hurled it from him, high into the air, with a cry that echoed to the ends of the earth.

A SHATTERING CRASH of thunder smashed the air. John and Vivian Newman looked up to see the sky go mad. As the last crimson rays of the sun touched the emerald treetops, a dark swirl of clouds began to form in the sky as they watched, building in seconds into a towering storm cloud. The sky changed from reddish purple to a golden green, and claws of lightning raked the heavens. The lights about the room glowed unearthly bright, dimmed, glowed again, and then were dark.

There was a searing explosion of light that lit up the night, and a spinning blue-green fireball came crashing through the glass, striking within inches of Van Damm, who was struggling with the steel switch at the console. A howling wind filled the air, and a steady rain began sheeting in, soaking the carpet and curtain. Clinging to each other, John and Vivian ran together out into the darkness.

"*Nooooo!*" howled Van Damm, shaking his fist at the sky, as guests shrieked in panic, running for the exits. Another bolt came crashing down, sending Van Damm ducking under the table. He cowered in fear as bolt after bolt crashed down about him, breaking mirrors and shattering statues. His Badmasher bodyguards had deserted him, leaving him alone to face the storm's unbridled wrath. At last, with a desperate cry of outrage, he reached again for the master control, pulling it with all his might as the clock struck the hour, just as a stroke of lightning shrouded him in flame.

IN THE HEART of the Green Wood, a host of faces, man and machine, gazed upward to where the shining disk turned slow-motion circles in the air. As it rose ever higher, the sky was rent with a great bone-shaking thunder that sounded like the mountains waking from their long sleep. In the great lake suspended overhead, streaks of green fire began to flash brighter and nearer, and the snow that filled the air became mist, and the mist turned to rain. The flashes that lit the sky cast shadows of the city buildings that surrounded the wood, as if Uptown and Down Town were on the verge of merging.

A moment later, the eyes of the Gnomes' machines suddenly grew bright. Brand roared out a cry of triumph above the raging storm, urging his mechanical army on toward the knoll where Taara stood. As they crested the rise, Brand pointed up to her and the great machines trained their beams upon her in a convergence of crimson light.

As the disk ascended like a rising star, so high it could barely be seen, a slim finger of green lightning reached down through it to meet the red glow. The disk shattered into a billion sparkling fragments, and the air was filled with a brilliant, dazzling incandescence. Then, a moment later, the glow enveloped Taara. For an instant, Cary saw all of Down Town with incredible clarity—every stone, every leaf, every hair, every pore—and it seemed the sight would be branded on his memory forever. Then the light began to fade, and Taara was gone, reduced in moments to a heap of ashes.

IN THE COOL depths of the earth, many leagues below the deepest settlements of Down Town, somewhere midway between the

Green Wood and the deepest reaches of the Gnomes' domain, a tiny tendril of green life, a slim root bearing a single glowing leaf, coiled its way about a pencil-thin cable of steel that had stretched itself through a crack in the Great Wall to meet it. In that instant, Zenovac's vast knowledge met Taara's ancient wisdom, and the awesome surge of power fused the two into one.

CARY SLUMPED TO the ground at last, finally daring to breathe, and Allie bent over him, touching his cheek. Then the rain began to pour down, beating hard against them, and forming gulleys in the snow.

The crimson eyes of the Gnomes' machines suddenly went dark, and one by one they began to spark and sizzle and burn and burst, reeling crazily, spinning in a frenzy, throwing their imp drivers in all directions. The rain was sluicing down so hard now there was barely air to breathe. Then the rumbling of the heavens was echoed by a rumbling of the earth, and the ground began to surge under the Down Towners' feet. A great, gaping abyss opened in front of Taara's blackened stump, tumbling the Gnomes and their wrecked machinery down into the darkness.

Only Miles Brand remained, clinging to a root that protruded from the bank, clawing his way to safety. "Help me, damn you!" he pleaded to Cary in a rough whisper. But the root that had once been strong now pulled loose, and he went hurtling down into the darkness with a wild and echoing wail. Moments later, the earth closed over him.

Then, all of the Down Towners were pointing up. The great lake above was wavering and roiling, and cracks began to appear in the firmament above. Slowly at first, and then ever faster, a wave of water washed along the Green Wood's paths, then picked up speed as the rivulets ran together, cresting into splashing waves. As the floodwaters rose higher, the Down Towners retreated onto the hill where the broken tree stood.

The waters leapt into the great gorge like a foaming cataract, splashing about Taara's roots.

Cary and Allie clung to each other, soaked to the skin. Nearby, Finn and Fianna stood watching the raging waters. Around them, nothing could be seen but a great wave of water, drawing ever nearer.

"It's the End of the World, Fianna!" Finn roared above the howling winds, water streaming down his red beard.

"No it ain't, Finn," Fianna called back with a laugh. "It's only the beginning!"

Then the wall of water came crashing down.

TWENTY-THREE

Somewhere, birds sang. A cool breeze ruffled Cary's hair. He awoke on a hillside damp with dew in the midst of a circle of trees. Allie lay beside him, her eyelids fluttering, as if she were emerging from a dream.

It seemed they were still in the Green Wood, but the foliage and wildlife seemed somehow tamer now. Could it be? Although the sky above was cloudy and the air thick with fog, Cary thought he could make out the tall shapes of modern buildings about the edges of the wood. The pearly gray of the sky was touched with rose, and Cary could sense all around him the quickening that meant that dawn was due.

Allie's lips parted, and she seemed to speak his name, silently. Then her dark eyes were open, looking slightly puzzled.

"You okay?" Cary asked quietly, his voice clear in the hushed stillness of the false dawn. Far away, a car horn sounded, and she jumped, startled.

"I dunno," said Allie with a shiver, hugging herself. "I feel kinda funny, y'know, like I'm not quite all here. What is this place, Cary?"

Cary looked around him. "I think it's the Park. I'm not sure."

"You mean we're *Up*town?" asked Allie.

"I don't think so, Allie," said Cary. "I think we're somewhere in between."

"How did we get here, Cary?" she asked softly. "And how do we get back?"

"Back where, Allie?" said Cary. "Uptown or Down Town?"

For a moment she didn't answer, just toyed with a blade of grass. Then she looked up, unsure of what to answer. "Well, I guess this is it, huh?" she said with a sad laugh. "Taara said you would have to go after it was all over. I guess I should've known, but I'm sure gonna miss you, Cary."

The sun was faintly visible through the clouds now, and the mists were beginning to burn off. The sounds of the city waking came nearer. Cary reached out for Allie's hand.

"Hey, Allie. Come on. Knock it off. I'll bet you're hungry. Let's try to find some breakfast. I think my mom's place is only a couple of blocks away from here."

"I can't, Cary," said Allie. "I got my Scamps to look after, and you got your mom and dad, I guess, and—well, a whole future ahead of you, too." Her voice sounded muted and faraway.

"But couldn't we still be friends, get together sometimes?"

"Don't you understand? I can't stay here." Then she smiled that goofy grin of hers and said, "Listen, Cary. It's been real fun. The next time you're feelin' down, why don't ya look me up?"

Allie's hand touched his, and he held it tight. It felt cool and somehow insubstantial. As the sun burned off the morning fog, she seemed to waver a bit. He gripped her hand tighter, but it was like holding onto mist.

"But, Allie! I don't want to lose you—not yet!" he called after her.

"We've got memories, Cary," she said with a wave. "As long as we got those, we can never lose each other." A moment later, she was gone.

FEELING SOMEHOW STILL lost, so close to home, Cary followed a little winding pathway upward that led him at last to the Plaza on the Park. The glass was broken in several places, and everyone had long ago gone home. Looking toward the rise of ground across from the restaurant where the old oak tree had stood, Cary saw a blackened stump. But as he came closer, a spot of light caught his eye. In the midst of the stump grew a slender sapling with one small, dew-covered leaf that shimmered like silver in the morning sun. From somewhere near came the tinkling sound of a child's laughter.

Cary walked the rest of the way in a daze. A few minutes later, he'd arrived at the brownstone, unlocking the door, and trudging up the stairs to the top. At the door, he heard voices.

He walked through the parlor, back into the kitchen. "Cary!" said his mother. "Thank God you're all right!"

"Cary! Where on earth have you—" It was his father, looking rumpled and worn, holding the kitchen phone. "It's okay, he's here," he said, and hung up the phone.

"Why are you here?" asked Cary, not daring to hope.

"Because I belong here," said Cary's father. "Your mother and I—we're to give it another try, Cary," said his father. "A blackout in the middle of a rainstorm is a pretty good place to work out your differences. Right, honey?"

"And we've got some good news," said Cary's mother, blushing a little. "It's the strangest thing. I don't know how you found out about it, but you were right about Mr. Janos. He *was* involved in illegal dealings with the city that affected the whole parks system."

"It's going to take months, maybe even years, to straighten it all out," said his father, "so the Mayor has asked us to head up a special city task force to tackle the problem. We'll be working together, right here in the building."

"But what's the good news?"

"Well, Cary," his father answered, "we've decided to start by taking a vacation together, anyplace you'd like to go, to kind of get to know each other a little better. Where would you like it to be, Cary? The Cape? Someplace upstate?"

"How about right here?"

"In the *city*?" said Cary's mother.

"Why not?" said Cary with a smile. "It's not such a bad place once you get to know it!"

SITTING ON THE front steps of the brownstone, watching the rainwashed city street drying in the sun, Cary found his hands toying with an old, battered white feather. Even though things seemed to be looking up, Cary didn't expect it to all get better at once. He was glad his parents were back together. But he didn't really expect Mom and Dad to stop fighting—Mom was too hot-tempered and Dad too cool for that to stop altogether. There were sure to be hassles setting up their new business, and working at home would probably have its problems, too.

But somehow, all that was much less important to him now. A ball came bounding down the street and rolled to a stop. Cary got up from the step to pick it up. Down the street, a dark-haired boy about his age waved. Behind him was a girl who might have been his sister.

"Hey!" called the boy. "You're the one I saw on the news, ain't you? I guess you was lost, huh?"

"Yeah," said Cary, tossing the ball back to him. "I guess I was."

"Well," said the boy, "welcome home."

ACKNOWLEDGMENTS

No WORK OF art is ever solely the product of its creators. This is especially true of *Down Town*. A large number of friends and colleagues contributed to its spirit, and we would like to acknowledge our debt to them.

First, we'd like to thank each other. *Down Town* took over three years to grow from an idea discussed on a summer afternoon to a story, a novel, and ultimately a world. By some grace, one of us was always able to bring insight, imagination, and enthusiasm to the book just as the other's energy ebbed. Without that friendship and faith, *Down Town* would not exist at all.

Next, we wish to acknowledge the contributions of our families—our parents, grandparents, and beyond—who gave us a legacy of love for words and pictures, and a rich store of tales and remembrances we have drawn upon for the present work.

We would also like to express our appreciation to those who read the manuscript, saw the artwork at various stages, and contributed useful and sometimes critical ideas to the development of the book: Phyllis King and James MacPherson, Christopher King, Loren and Andrea Gunther, Lou Aronica, Nancy

Pines, Ian Ballantine, Joan Lowe of Pacific Cascade Records, Maureen Millar, Kaja and Silja Wiggins, Liivi Joe and Kalju and Linda Hallop, E.F.H., Virginia Kidd, Karen Embden and Jane Butler. We would especially like to thank Valerie Smith, who was one of *Down Town*'s earliest and strongest advocates, and Marty Ryan, teacher and friend from Monmouth College, N.J. We gratefully acknowledge their contributions; the book's shortcomings, however, are wholly our own.

A number of friends and neighbors provided inspiration for the settings and characters in *Down Town,* among them Sam Finlay, and Chelsea and Zena from Staten Island. We would like to offer our thanks to Neil Burger, principal of the Germantown, New York, Elementary School, for his assistance in gathering students and their families for the illustrations; to Bill Foster and Audrey Renneman, and to the young people who took part: Alfred Burgazoli, Diana Burgazoli, Richard John Caragine, Kilynn Fraleigh, Rebecca Gaschel, Christopher Haraldsen, Mike Hermus, E.J. Johnson, Sarah Kline, Mike Lis, George Martin, Stephen Martin, Victoria Mannino, Jennifer Nawrocki, Serena Olivet, Steven Olivet, Kathrin Phelan, Carrie Quinn, Cindy Ramsey, Denise Rivenburg, Lynn Rivenburg, Annie Sloane, Bobbie Schulz, and Christine Wildermuth.

We'd like to thank the staffs of The New York Public Library and the New-York Historical Society for their courtesy and help.

We would like to single out three people who were instrumental in bringing *Down Town* to publication: Jan Kirshner, who devoted her tireless energies to finding the book a home; our agent Howard Morhaim, who gave far more of his time and effort to the book than any first novelists have a right to expect; and Bill Thompson of Arbor House, who recognized *Down Town*'s potential, and worked with us to bring it out.

Finally, we would like to thank our wives, Carolyn Polikarpus and Beth Meacham. From the beginning, they were our strongest supporters, as well as our sharpest critics. We grew as the book grew, and they stood by us through some difficult times with patience, understanding, and love. We know we will never be able to repay our debt to them adequately. We hope the book's dedication will in some small measure express our gratitude, and our love.

Germantown
Staten Island, New York
1981–84